LITTLE BLACK GIRL LOST 5:

The Diary of Josephine Baptiste—Lauren's Story

LITTLE BLACK GIRL LOST 5:

The Diary of Josephine Baptiste—Lauren's Story

KEITH LEE JOHNSON

www.urbanbooks.net

Urban Books, LLC
1199 Straight Path
West Babylon, NY 11704

Little Black Girl Lost 5: The Diary of Josephine Baptiste—Lauren's Story copyright © 2010 Keith Lee Johnson

ISBN-13: 978-1-60162-260-0
ISBN-10: 1-60162-260-0

First Printing February 2010
Printed in the United States of America

10 9 8 7 6 5 4 3 2 1

This is a work of fiction. Any references or similarities to actual events, real people, living, or dead, or to real locales are intended to give the novel a sense of reality. Any similarity in other names, characters, places, and incidents is entirely coincidental.

Distributed by Kensington Publishing Corp.
Submit Wholesale Orders to:
Kensington Publishing Corp.
C/O Penguin Group (USA) Inc.
Attention: Order Processing
405 Murray Hill Parkway
East Rutherford, NJ 07073-2316
Phone: 1-800-526-0275
Fax: 1-800-227-9604

*Dedicated to my uncle, James "Too Sweet" Hooker Jr.,
currently residing in Las Vegas, Nevada.*

Bloodlines/Cast of Characters

The Mustafa Family
  Ibo Atikah Mustafa—Seventh daughter of first wife
  Jamilah Mustafa—Ibo's mother
  Faisal Mustafa—Ibo's father

The Jibril Family
  Amir Bashir Jibril—The prince—Seventh son of the fifth wife
  Asenath Jibril—Amir's mother
  Adesola Jibril—Amir's brother—Heir to the throne

The Rutgers Family
  Joseph Rutgers—Captain of the Windward
  Jonah Rutgers—Younger brother of Joseph
  Tracy Combs Rutgers—Wife of Joseph—Jonah's consort

The Torvell Family
  François Torvell—Plantation owner on the Isle of Santo Domingo
  Helen Torvell—Wife of François
  Herman Torvell—Slave of François—Butler and manager
  Marcia Torvell—Wife of Herman—Cook and friend of Helen

The Tresvant Family
  Alexander Tresvant—Damien Bouvier's first slave
  Jennifer Tresvant—Alexander's wife
  Walker Tresvant—Master of Château Tresvant
  Marie-Elise Tresvant—Walker's wife—Beaumont's sister
  Dorothy Tresvant—Walker's half sister—White slave
  Kayla Tresvant—Damien's daughter by Jennifer
  Christopher Tresvant—Walker's granduncle
  Simeon Tresvant—Walker's granduncle

Jude Tresvant—Overseer—Slave—Has a thing for Dorothy
Kimba Tresvant—Slave—Dorothy's love interest

The Bouvier Family
Damien Bouvier—Owner of Alexander Tresvant Bouvier
Beaumont Bouvier—Master of Bouvier Hill and Bouvier Sugar
Cadence Bouvier—Beaumont's Wife
Beaumont Bouvier Jr.—product of Cadence and Tristan
Damien Bouvier—product of Cadence and Tristan
Xavier Bouvier—product of Cadence and Tristan
Josette Bouvier—product of Cadence and Tristan
Tristan Bouvier—Beaumont's brother
Christine Bouvier—Tristan's wife
Aubrey Bouvier—Slave—Butler—Bookkeeper
Joshua Bouvier—Slave—Blacksmith
Lauren Renee Bouvier—Ibo Atikah Mustafa

The Beauregard Family
Sebastian Beauregard—Patriarch
Mason Beauregard—Former fiancé of Marie-Elise Tresvant

The Delacroix Family
Emile Delacroix—Father of Cadence
Guinevere Delacroix—Cadence Bouvier's friend and confidant
Javier Delacroix—Guinevere's only son
Lacey Delacroix—Guinevere's oldest daughter
Madeline Delacroix—Guinevere's daughter
Yvette Delacroix—Guinevere's daughter
Chantal Delacroix—Guinevere's youngest daughter

The Baptiste Family
Rokk Baptiste—Student of Prince Amir
Antoinette Gabrielle Jacqueline Baptiste—Daughter of Rokk
Josephine Baptiste—Daughter of Antoinette

The Nimburus
    Pearl Nimburu—Madam Nadine
    Solo Nimburu—Pearl's son

Miscellaneous Cast
    Lieutenant Troy Avery—French garrison soldier
    Julian Bailey—Beaumont Bouvier's attorney
    Pierre St. John—Mortician—Owner of Pierre's Funeral Parlor

The Diary of Josephine Baptiste:

Lauren's Story

Recollection

Hi, y'all. I'm back again to share more about the Wise family tree. At the end of *Little Black Girl Lost 3: Ill Gotten Gains,* I told you all that Josephine's diary read like an engrossing novel. Was I lying? I'm told that some of you, the fans of Johnnie Wise, didn't understand that book one of *The Diary of Josephine Baptiste* was just the beginning and that there was more to come. Well, here we are again, set to begin book five in the *Little Black Girl Lost* series, book two of the *Diary*—a series within a series, if you will. Since so many of you read the series out of sequence, I think a review is in order, don't you?

In *Little Black Girl Lost 4: The Diary of Josephine Baptiste,* my great-great-grandmother, Ibo Atikah Mustafa, was set to marry the heir apparent to the throne of Nigeria. The author has gotten many e-mails wanting to know how her name is pronounced and why the novel isn't about Josephine. For the record, her name is pronounced "Ebo." Josephine isn't in the book yet because the diary is a historical record of the Mustafa family tree and how the Wise family came to be.

While Ibo Atikah Mustafa is the New World matriarch, Josephine is the curator.

The best place to start, I think, would be with the first person to arrive on the shores of the New World. To do otherwise would not do justice to each woman in the diary since the life of a human being is a story. It's called history and in this case, herstory, see?

Anyway, back to Ibo's arranged marriage. Faisal, her father, had promised her hand in marriage to Adesola. However, Ibo loved another—Amir Bashir Jibril, Adesola's younger brother from another mother. Full of defiance—their sense of right and wrong dulled by lust—Ibo and Amir stole away together the night before her marriage. Just when they thought they were safe, Dutch slave traders stumbled upon them. After a fierce battle and the death of ten slave traders, Ibo and Amir were captured and taken aboard the *Windward,* which then set sail for the Americas.

Shortly after becoming the chattel of Captain Rutgers, who had often traded with Ibo's father, a slave trader himself, the breaking of the slaves began. One slave, a male, was lashed so severely with a bullwhip that he died on the deck and was summarily tossed to the sharks. When that didn't break Amir, who was viewed by the other slaves as their savior, yet another slave, a female, was beaten and tossed to the sharks alive. Amir was unmoved by this act of barbarity too. After this, Captain Rutgers shot a man and tossed him overboard to the sharks, quickly followed by his daughter, who couldn't have been more than six years old. Father and daughter watched each other being eaten alive.

While even this didn't break Amir, it devastated Ibo. When she broke and cooperated, so did Amir. After this, the debauchery aboard the *Windward* kicked into high gear and continued every night until they reached New Orleans. But along the way, Ibo saved Captain Rutgers's life. Rutgers had raped a slave and was brazen enough to fall asleep with a loaded pistol within arm's reach.

The slave girl put the gun right under his nose and was about to blow it off when Ibo grabbed her arm. The weapon discharged. The sound awoke Rutgers and he chased the girl up on deck. Knowing they were going to kill her anyway, the girl, running at full speed, tackled Mr. Whitaker, a deckhand, and they both plummeted into the murky depths of the Atlantic Ocean in the blackest night and were never found.

While Captain Rutgers felt indebted to Ibo, he didn't feel so indebted that he would return her freedom. Instead, he promised to sell Amir to François and Helen Torvell, friends who lived on the Isle of Santo Domingo, modern day Haiti. The Torvells were Christians who would not only treat Amir well, but give him the opportunity to buy his freedom. This gave Ibo hope of a better tomorrow, the chance to reunite with a man she worshiped.

He also educated Ibo, who was already a gifted but unpolished linguist, using Shakespeare as his primary method of instruction. He taught her to read and write on the voyage, and her keen intellectual capacity ignited and then exploded. Her essays on the works of Shakespeare both fascinated and intimidated the Dutch captain. While she could speak English and five other languages, her ability to speak and enunciate English hastened and astonished the *Windward* crew.

Rutgers kept his word once they reached the island and sold Amir to the Torvells, but a group of organized runaway slaves, called the Maroons, attacked the Torvell mansion that very night. A great slaughter began at the mansion and spread throughout the island. François and his house slaves, Herman and Marcia Torvell, were butchered like cattle. Poor Helen was repeatedly raped by a line of black men that was probably reminiscent of a Universal Studios Theme Park line. I exaggerate a bit, but I think you get the point. Captain Rutgers and Ibo fought for their lives and barely escaped the angry mob. Amir and other Torvell slaves were freed and joined the uprising. Amir, being a captain of the king's army, trained the Maroons, and they became an even more lethal and cunning fighting force.

Upon reaching the shores of America (New Orleans, to be exact), Ibo was sold to Beaumont Bouvier, another friend of Captain Rutgers. Beaumont was a sugar plantation owner and the unquestioned master of Bouvier Manor and Bouvier Sugar. He was also a homosexual, as were the seven house slaves—all men. Beaumont urged Ibo to change her name to fit in with the rest of his servants. She cooperated as a way of staying alive and remaining unmolested in hopes of one day taking revenge against those who had enslaved her. A few hours after being purchased, Ibo Atikah Mustafa became Lauren Renee Bouvier.

The next day, Beaumont Bouvier and Louis, his lusty young male servant and lover, were found in Beaumont's bedroom dead, gruesomely bludgeoned to death. The killer had cut off their penises, stuck them into each other's mouths, and arranged their remains in a sixty-nine position.

Cadence, Beaumont's wife, was carrying on two adulterous relationships. The first was with Tristan, her husband's brother, and had been going on for years. Several children were produced from this union. Beaumont knew of the relationship and even knew that none of the children Cadence birthed were his. Nevertheless, he kept quiet about the affair, which helped conceal their clandestine relationship because it afforded him protection from the law. Homosexuality and adultery were against the law at that time in America. What I found particularly strange was that the secret was no secret at all because everyone who lived in Bouvier Manor knew of it. The other adulterous affair was with Bouvier Hill's resident blacksmith, a slave named Joshua.

Prior to Lauren learning of Cadence and Joshua's relationship, she had planned on recruiting Joshua, who was quite taken with her beauty. He was tall, powerfully built, and ornery enough to lead a rebellion against the master of the plantation—or so she thought. After Aubrey, the head butler and supposed friend who had given Lauren her name, implicated her in the murders of Beaumont and Louis, she heard Joshua sneak into the house, climb the stairs, and enter Cadence's bedroom. She watched them claw and tear off each other's clothing before closing the door. But the closed door could not contain their unrestrained howling.

Afterward she listened to them confess to the murders and their undying love for each other. During their lengthy post-sexual conversation, neither murderer showed any remorse for what they had done. They seemed to be quite pleased with themselves for having gotten rid of the thorns in their sides— those thorns being Beaumont, Louis, Aubrey, and the other five menservants. Aubrey and the other men had been executed after a quick investigation by Lieutenant Avery, who had been left in charge of the local garrison. Now all they had to do was wait to see what Beaumont had left Cadence in his will.

Much to their chagrin, Beaumont's will wasn't exactly the way Cadence, Tristan, and Joshua thought. He had not only freed the house slaves, but had also left them a significant portion of the Bouvier fortune, as well as providing for their educations, homes, and start-up money for their own businesses. However, there were a few stipulations. They had to keep the Bouvier name and they could not leave New Orleans. With all the housemen dead, having been shot via firing squad, their entire share fell to my great-great-grandmother, Lauren Renee Bouvier, making her wealthy beyond her wildest dreams.

Lauren, who had promised to find the love of her life, Amir Bashir Jibril, sent for him on the Isle of Santo Domingo, as she could never leave New Orleans and take her fortune with her. After months of waiting, the ship she had been waiting for had finally returned. Amir had been found. He was alive and well. Shortly after they embraced each other and expressed their undying love, a stranger walked up to Amir and blew his brains out of his head and all over Lauren.

And now . . . *Little Black Girl Lost 5: The Diary of Josephine Baptiste—Lauren's Story!*

Act 1

The Game of Death

During slavery there were several Negroes in the South, especially Louisiana and South Carolina, who would be accounted millionaires today. Most of them were slaveholders. These rich Negroes were treated in nearly every respect like white people. They could marry white wives—at least many of them did; they could buy white men and women—they did in Maryland and Louisiana until 1818, and in all probability, Florida, too; and even in the stage-coaches they did not ride Jim-Crow.

Joel Augustus Rogers

Sex and Race Volume II, p. 242 & 243. 1942.

Chapter 1

"I forgive you, Jonah."

Lauren Renee Bouvier could not contain the cauldron of joy that bubbled within when she saw Amir Jibril Bashir running down the gangplank. She had been talking with Captain Rutgers when she saw him. But when she heard Amir call her name, it was as if a great magician uttered the famous word, "abracadabra," and Rutgers disappeared. The sound of Amir's voice seemed to make the entire world stand still, like the citizens on the dock became papier-mâché cutout people who had no life in them. The dock was usually a noisy, bustling place of perpetual movement, wagons coming and going, men shouting instructions, crates being unloaded, gulls screeching, waves crashing against the ships. Now there was silent serenity as the two lovers raced toward one another, their hearts pumping at a feverish pace as the anticipation of embracing mounted.

Full of excitement, Amir shouted, "Ibo!"

They fell into each other's arms and held on tightly, almost melding into one flesh. The sheer joy of seeing one another after having been apart for so long was a resurrection of sorts because they had given up all hope of ever being together again. They pulled away, but held hands, looking into each other's eyes. Both of them realized that their love was still there, still strong, and had somehow grown in spite of lost hope.

"I am told that you are a wealthy American now," Amir said in Yoruba, their native tongue. "Is this true?"

"It is," she replied in the same language, smiling broadly. "Come," she continued, "I have so much to tell you."

"As do I," he said. "I want to hear it all."

"Do you still want to marry me?" she asked. "I am still a maiden—your maiden, if you still want me."

"I do want you, Ibo. Virgin or not." He kissed her. "I love you so."

"I love you too," she said and kissed him back.

"I've learned so much. I now understand my mother and why she was willing to sacrifice her life for us. She found peace, and so have I. In exchange for peace, I have forgiven Captain Rutgers. I am forever free now. Have you found peace, my love? Please tell me you have."

Before she could answer, a man she had often seen at the docks whenever she was there walked up to them. He smiled pleasantly and in English said, "Excuse me, good sir," bowing as if Amir were Louis XVI, who would be executed by guillotine January 21, 1793, less than a year from now. "Did you just arrive from the Isle of Santo Domingo?"

Lauren was about to answer when Amir said, "I've learned to speak English." He looked at the man and said, "I was on the island, sir, yes."

"That's what I thought," the man said. "And this is for you."

He pulled out an ivory-handled flintlock pistol. The barrel was sparkling silver. The smile he wore was still visible when he pulled the trigger and *bang*, blew Amir's brains clean out of his head.

Lauren had seen it, but she could not believe it. Amir

stood perfectly still for a few precious seconds as his eyes lost their light. Then, as if by slow motion, the rest of him realized they were dead and floated to the ground, making no effort to brace the fall.

"Noooo!" Lauren screamed.

The man leaned over Amir's dead body and screamed, "That was for François and Helen Torvell! Helen was my sister! And you savages raped and killed her!"

Pow! Another shot rang out.

Captain Joseph Rutgers had killed the man with the same gun that a female slave had held under his nose on the voyage to the Americas. "And that was for killing an innocent man." Then he fell to his knees and wept bitterly. "This was my last contract. I was finished after this." He didn't seem to be talking to anyone in particular. He didn't seem to know he was speaking. The words just found their way out of his open mouth.

Jonah, his estranged brother who had seen it all, walked over to Rutgers and stood next to him. Many years had passed since Jonah had bedded Tracy Combs, Joseph's former wife. Many years had passed since he'd begged his brother for forgiveness, only to be met with a silent, disdainful stare. He never said a word. He just looked down at his brother.

As his life of rebellion against his God flashed before his eyes, as he thought about all the slaves he had transported across the Atlantic, as he pondered just how far he had fallen away from his Christian beliefs, Joseph sensed someone was staring at him. He turned to see who it was. When he saw his brother's compassion, Joseph wrapped his arms around his legs and said, "I forgive you, Jonah."

Chapter 2

How can there ever be any peace in a place such as this?

It had all happened incredibly fast; so fast in fact that no one could have prevented it because no one could have seen it coming. Just seconds ago, Ibo Atikah Mustafa, who had become Lauren Renee Bouvier, had been reunited with the love of her young life. Although she thought she would never see him again, she had often dreamed of marrying the man she had left all for. She had told herself that if Amir was ever found, if they were ever reunited, she was going to convince him to put away his sword. She was going to convince him to put the past behind him, accept their fate and stay in America, marry, and live out their lives as Americans. But all of that was over now. There would be no happily ever after. That fairy tale had come to an abrupt end when a single ball of lead left an assassin's pistol and burrowed its way into her beloved's head.

Lauren noticed that the citizens who had previously been papier-mâché cutout people were now suddenly alive and moving, running to the scene of the gruesome crime, albeit in slow motion. She looked down at Amir's lifeless body. His blood poured out of his head, covering the dock, staining it crimson. Dizzied by what she had seen, her knees wobbled and threatened to give way to her weight, which suddenly became an enormous burden. She wanted to give in to her emotions. She wanted to acquiesce and drop to her knees and weep. There was no shame in it, but she couldn't, because the flame of anger had been rekindled and now it was unquenchable.

She looked at the man who had killed Amir. His blood was pouring out of his head too. Smoke was rising from the pistol he still clung to. She looked at Captain Rutgers. He was still holding on to Jonah's legs, sobbing uncontrollably. She continued staring at him as all of what had happened to her flashed in her mind. One after another, colorful, vivid images of past events came to mind, complete with sound and realism; all of them were filled with sex and violence, cries for mercy and moans of ecstasy, blood and gore, death and destruction. And at the center of each image was Captain Rutgers. All that she had seen, all that she had been through could be traced to him, she knew. But at that very instant, something that Amir had said entered her mind.

He had said he found peace and had forgiven Captain Rutgers. Then she remembered that he had asked her if she had found peace. If Amir had lived five more seconds, she would have told him that if she hadn't found him, there would be no peace, but having found him alive, she was willing to give peace a chance; she was willing to put aside her burgeoning thirst for revenge.

Now all of that was gone with the wind, never to surface again. *Peace? What is that? What does it look like? How can there ever be any peace in a place such as this?* As far as she was concerned, New Orleans had a simple code: kill or be killed. That's when it occurred to her that she had to live and have children, or her story would never be known, never be told.

If that happened, it would be as if she and Amir never existed. And she could never let that happen.

They did live.

They did love—a lifetime's worth.

But it was only for a few unforgettable days.

Chapter 3

"Everything's going to be all right, Lauren."

Lauren continued staring at Captain Rutgers. She wanted him to feel her daunting gaze, just as he no doubt felt his brother's gaze when he had fallen to his knees. Her focus was so taut, her anger so intense that it forced his head to swivel to the right so he would know with certainty that her heart was severely injured by what happened to Amir. She watched his once steely ocean blue eyes soften and become even more watery. She wanted him to know that she blamed him exclusively for what had happened to Amir.

As their eyes locked, the flashing images returned and moved from one scene to another. First she saw herself in his quarters on the *Windward*. Then everything that happened on the Isle of Santo Domingo materialized. They were running out of the Torvell's mansion and had barely escaped the Maroons. After that, she saw herself in the slave market in New Orleans, standing on the auction block, looking at the men who were watching her as they placed their bids. The sound of the whip that Jude Tresvant handled with precision as he skillfully carved up Kimba's back exploded in her ears.

All of a sudden she saw Captain Rutgers and Beaumont Bouvier standing in the market just before he made his first bid. Then the images switched to the night she had saved his life, then to him teaching her how to read and write, then back to Amir being murdered—all in a matter of seconds.

When Rutgers saw the hatred in her eyes, he said, "Lauren, please, you must believe me. I never meant for any of this to happen. Bringing Amir to New Orleans had been a welcomed relief because it eased my conscience. It had been speaking to me for quite some time now. Eventually it started shouting so loudly that not even my favorite blend of brandy could quell its demand for peace and quiet."

Lauren continued her unabated stare.

"Lauren, please hear me out. When Beaumont Bouvier was murdered, it helped me decide to leave the slave trade and begin life anew. His death helped me realize just how short life really was. Beaumont was a good friend, and while I'm saddened by his demise, I'm glad you gained considerably from his death. You deserve it after all that has happened to you."

Although Lauren was unmoved by his comments, she continued listening to them.

"I thought it was appropriate that my ship, the *Windward,* be the ship to retrieve Amir because it was the one that both enslaved and delivered him to the island. I was happy to bring him to New Orleans so that you two could fulfill your dreams of being together. I had gotten the silly notion that with your newfound wealth, you two could make a nice life for yourselves here. I was planning to change my life too. I was going to find a good woman and settle down. I had spoken to Amir at length about that very thing on the voyage. I knew I had to atone for what I had done to you both. Now that Amir is dead, I fear that I will be eaten alive by my conscience. I now know that it's not enough to leave the slave trade. I know I have to take an active role in bringing about its destruction. And I promise you I'll help finance those who are brave enough to bring it to an end."

When Lauren saw his watery eyes staring into hers, she knew he was asking, if not begging, for the same forgiveness that Amir had granted. As much as she wanted to give what Amir had graciously given, something inside her would not make that allowance. Something inside her refused to forgive what had happened. After all, with Amir dead, none of it made any sense. What was it all for? She had sacrificed all to be with him and that had been taken away not once, but twice. Now she was ready to do some taking of her own.

Still looking into Captain Rutgers's eyes, she believed he was feeling a sense of overwhelming guilt, and she could use that against him in the immediate future. Someone had to pay for everything that had happened, and Rutgers was going to help whether he knew it or not, whether he wanted to or not. She would solicit his help by first being in need of it. She began the importuning by giving in to her emotions. Tears formed and slid down her cheeks. She allowed the mourning process to continue, and before she knew it she felt weak in the knees, and fell to the dock. She knew no man could resist her charms, and they certainly couldn't resist them in her time of distress and need to be taken care of.

Rutgers stopped crying when Lauren nearly fainted. He let go of his brother, rose to his feet, and helped Lauren to hers. He picked her up, just as she knew he would, and took her to her carriage. As they rode back to Bouvier Hill, he stroked her hair, and said, "Everything's going to be all right, Lauren." His touch was so gentle that it completely relaxed her. He watched her closely as she slowly drifted, lingering between the conscious and unconscious worlds. Soon she was sound asleep in his arms.

Upon returning to Bouvier Manor, Rutgers carried Lauren to her third-floor bedroom and put her to bed. Before he left, he explained in detail what happened on the dock to Cadence.

Chapter 4

Cadence

Cadence's maiden name was Delacroix. Beaumont had courted her for several months, and when she turned eighteen, they married. For the first five years of their marriage, she was childless. Besides personal hygiene and grooming, she had next to nothing to do. She didn't even have to cook or clean the premises, as they had plenty of servants who handled those duties. Her only job was to remain beautiful for as long as she could and to be a conduit for Bouvier children.

Birthing children was a highly unlikely endeavor for the couple, given the infrequency of their conjugal relations. For the first two years of their marriage, not only was she childless, but she was practically alone. First she asked, then she begged Beaumont to teach her the sugar business, or at least give her a job she could sink her teeth into to break the monotony of being the equivalent of a kept woman. After two years of begging, he finally built her a dress shop in the French Quarter, which was located at the corner of Royal and Conti.

Two years later Cadence thought she had turned what was supposed to be a hobby into a bustling moneymaker, pulling in over two hundred dollars a month. She saw tremendous potential for growth and wanted to expand; given the yearly Quadroon Ball, debutantes' balls, weddings, and, of course, Mardi Gras, the idea had much merit. She was convinced she had proven herself and wanted to show Beaumont that her slender shoulders could handle more. She hoped that a managerial position would become available at Bouvier Sugar. Her enthusiasm, however, was met with a harsh scolding she did not expect, and would not soon forget.

Beaumont had told her that successfully running a dress shop was one thing, but being at the helm of a thriving plantation was quite another. He'd told her that she couldn't handle a "real" enterprise, particularly the behemoth that Bouvier Sugar had become. He went on to tell her that she owed whatever success she had to him, because he had persuaded his business acquaintances to have their wives, daughters, and other female family members buy their dresses at Cadence's shop to ensure that she would have something to do other than haranguing him about what he considered real business. For those reasons, she began to resent him and eventually hate him; all of which led to her tryst with Tristan, her husband's brother.

After Beaumont's death, Cadence soon learned that being the head of Bouvier Sugar, Bouvier Manor, and Bouvier Hill was a daunting undertaking. Being a preeminent feminist, she had originally thought that if a man could do it, so could she—only better. She adhered to this school of thought long before British feminist Mary Wollstonecraft wrote her consciousness-raising response, *A Vindication of the Rights of Men*, to Edmund Burke's 1790 piece, *Reflections on the Revolution in France*, which argued for and attempted to justify an unequal

society founded on the passivity of women. Feminist philoso-
phy notwithstanding, Cadence had no idea how much work
there was to be done on a plantation that had over two hundred slaves.

Later, however, she realized that being at the helm of a
large enterprise was not about gender; it was about leader-
ship, organization, and management skills. Before becoming the sovereign of Bouvier Hill, she wore the crown of
arrogance, which led her to believe she could do it all; and
not only that, she could do it all well and do it all by herself.
She had somehow forgotten that her predecessor delegated
much of his authority to Aubrey and other men who had
proven themselves skilled leaders. She needed help, but it
took her six difficult months to realize it.

During her initial six months at the helm, she had been
too proud to ask or seek advice from anyone, for fear it
would appear that Beaumont had been right all along when
he had said, "You are an insufferable idiot when it comes to
running a business." Never mind that there was no basis and
no evidence whatsoever for the accusation. Beaumont had
Aubrey and others to help him run the day-to-day opera-
tions. Beaumont made the major decisions, but he trusted
Aubrey and those who Aubrey counted as trustworthy to
handle the minor issues.

Now everyone was coming to her for every little decision;
jobs they seemingly had done without supervision, or so she
thought, and it had her on the verge of pulling her hair out.
With the exception of her blacksmith lover, Joshua, no one
made a move without her say-so. They were all too afraid to
say anything; too afraid to do anything; too afraid to even
suggest anything since she'd had Aubrey killed, the man
who knew absolutely everything there was to know about
Bouvier Hill. She had Aubrey shot down like a dog without
hesitation, never having contemplated how much the plan-

tation would miss his meticulous attention to detail when it came to inventory, and every other facet of the Bouvier Plantation. When he was alive, the slaves never ran out of anything; never even came close. Aubrey was that good at what he did.

Chapter 5

The Lauren Situation

It had been six months since Beaumont, Louis, and the men who ran Bouvier Manor were murdered, yet Cadence still had not selected full-time house servants. Much of her reasoning had to do with the freedom she now had to increase Joshua's regular nightly visits. She had temporarily replaced all the men with women who were handling the vacated jobs, but so far, no one was allowed to live in the house except Lauren, who, thanks to Beaumont's generosity, was no longer Bouvier Manor's personal property. Although she was not of French and African decent, Lauren was now considered a member of a distinguished group of free Negroes called *gens de couleur*, meaning she could come and go as she pleased, which in many ways incensed Cadence, who was inebriated with her newly acquired power.

If Cadence had her way, she wouldn't allow Lauren to live in the house either, because she sensed the young woman had become haughty and had the nerve to start thinking she was as good as a white woman. Lauren was obviously smelling herself like dogs she had seen. It had gotten to the point where she was looking Cadence in the eyes, like she was Walker Tresvant or a nigger of his ilk. She didn't like Walker, but she could at least tolerate him because he was one of the wealthiest men in New Orleans, black or white. Besides, Walker had been educated at the Sorbonne and had an air of quiet elegance about him. He was self-assured with millions of dollars the Tresvant family had earned, and could not be bullied by other powerful men or women.

Lauren, on the other hand, hadn't earned anything, yet she roamed the house at will like she owned the place; she ate Bouvier food, used the Bouvier slaves to drive her to and from New Orleans to The Bouvier House of Fine Dresses & Accoutrements, the shop she now owned. Whatever money she had was initially Bouvier money. She did whatever she wanted like she was back on her father's farm in Africa with no one to answer to, not even her mother and father, which infuriated Cadence.

But when Lauren realized Cadence's attitude changed after the reading of the will, and began to sense that Cadence wanted her out of Bouvier Manor, she pretended she didn't notice. She played the dumb nigger role to the hilt, so as to keep Cadence from suspecting that she would one day answer for her crimes against Beaumont, Aubrey, Louis, and the rest of the housemen she coldly had shot to death for crimes they did not commit. She felt she owed Beaumont at least that much because he had done right by her from the very beginning, unlike nearly everyone else she had met in the New World.

Listening to Julian Bailey read the letter Beaumont had written six months earlier had nearly driven Cadence mad with jealousy. She wondered what was so special about Lauren Renee. How did she worm her way into her late husband's heart in a single day? It was a feat she hadn't been able to accomplish during two decades of marriage. Upon returning to the mansion, she practically ran up the stairs and continued past her room and entered Beaumont's bedroom. She turned the place upside down looking for Aubrey's books, which Beaumont kept in his room.

Having found them in the closet under a piece of wood flooring, she examined them closely. She flipped through page after page, looking for something, anything that would tell her about the newly emancipated rich little black girl she formerly owned. Viewing Aubrey's books and seeing what Beaumont had paid for Lauren almost pushed her over the edge. That's when she gave serious consideration to killing her too.

Chapter 6

Vexed

According to Aubrey's meticulously maintained books, Beaumont had paid an astounding five thousand dollars for Lauren. If Beaumont were not a homosexual, she may have understood to some degree why he would pay that kind of money for such a young, well-put-together beauty like Lauren, but she wasn't going to be a bed wench, and at the time, he could not have known what her value would be to Bouvier Hill. She slammed the ledger shut. Her suspicions had been confirmed. Lauren was a pampered, good-for-nothing nigger wench who was taking advantage of her; she was a bona-fide freeloader, who was siphoning off any and everything she could get her greedy little hands on. If it were possible, rising heat would have been seen above Cadence's head.

What angered her even more was that Lauren never offered a dime to pay for anything, nor did she offer to help clean the mansion—not that Cadence did any manual labor herself. She justified her lack of effort to clean, dust, and polish by being the reigning queen of the mansion. Lauren had no such title, nor did she have the longevity, but acted as if she did—that was Cadence's point of view anyway. Everyone on the plantation had duties to perform except the expensive nigger who lived on the third floor of the mansion free of charge. As far as Cadence was concerned, Lauren should have given her back the five thousand Beaumont paid for her out of the eighty thousand she inherited.

Cadence thought this would be a more than fair deal. She had only owned Lauren for three days. During those three days, she didn't get one iota of work out of her. Not one single day! It just didn't seem fair to Cadence that she had to put up with Beaumont's homosexuality for twenty-two years, put up with his insults, and then finally kill him to inherit the thirty percent she believed she had earned. She felt as if she had been a slave for two decades, and Lauren had only been one for a paltry seventy-two hours. Yet she got one third the sum Cadence received? Never mind that Lauren had inherited 10 percent because Cadence and Joshua had cooked up an elaborate scheme to get the Bouvier fortune in the first place. The fact that the scheme backfired in her face was blamed on Lauren too.

Cadence didn't want anyone in the mansion that she didn't have full control over, but there was nothing she could do about it since Beaumont had made it quite clear in his will that his house servants could continue to live in the house as long as they wanted, or until a home of their own, which his estate would pay for, was built. For six months she had made not-so-subtle hints to Lauren about property that was available near the Mississippi, or how a particular piece of land was near the dress shop Lauren had also inherited.

The more hints Cadence made, the more determined Lauren was to stay in Bouvier Manor to be her resident thorn in the side, smiling in her face, pretending to be the fool her former mistress thought she was. Cadence had considered adding Lauren's name to her long list of murder victims, and would have, but the last thing she wanted was for

Marie-Elise, Beaumont's sister, to benefit. According to the will, Marie-Elise would inherit the remaining 10 percent of the Bouvier fortune, which meant Walker Tresvant would have 70 percent control instead of the 60 percent he and Marie-Elise now enjoyed.

Besides all of that, Cadence's children, all of them sired by Tristan, her brother-in-law, had returned from visiting relatives in Tallahassee, Florida, ten days after Beaumont's death. She had given birth to three boys and one girl. Their names were Beaumont Jr., sixteen; Damien, fourteen; Xavier, twelve; and Josette, ten. They had all fallen head over heels in love with Lauren; particularly Beaumont Jr. and Josette. This, too, vexed Cadence. It seemed as though everything they said had something to do with Lauren.

Whenever Lauren walked into the room or was in the vicinity of Cadence and her children, they would leave the woman who bore them without excusing themselves and sprint to Lauren, clinging to her the way children clung to Jesus Christ. Again, she wanted to get rid of Lauren, but didn't, because her children had recently lost the man they all believed was their father. She thought that if Lauren was killed too, the children, especially Beaumont Jr. and Josette, would never recover. As much as Cadence didn't want to admit it, Lauren's presence had eased much of the pain of losing their supposed father, and she couldn't take that away from them.

Today, however, everything was about to change. Cadence was going to get the help she had needed to run Bouvier Manor. She had contacted her family and acquired the services of Guinevere Delacroix, a Negress, who was her long-time friend and confidant. Guinevere and Cadence had been best friends and had grown up together, playing with dolls together even though Guinevere was a slave at the time. She would allow her to choose her own staff, but she would be the only servant allowed to live in the house. More important than anything else, she expected Guinevere to steal the hearts and minds of her children and deliver them intact to her. She trusted Guinevere, who was fully aware of the circumstances surrounding her marriage to Beaumont and her current tryst with Joshua.

Chapter 7

Unconscionable Recklessness

Lauren opened her eyes and realized that she was in her third-floor bedroom in Bouvier Manor. She felt her stomach rumble, reminding her that she hadn't eaten. The death of the love of her life came to mind immediately. She could see it all again as if it were in a perpetual cycle of images. Hard as she tried to control them, she was at their mercy. It was like she was there again, on the docks, seeing the stranger about to commit murder. But was it really murder, she wondered. Couldn't a white man kill a black man for any reason without fear of legal retribution? That was what she had experienced so far in the New World. She had no reason to believe anything else.

Tears filled her eyes again and slid down her checks. *Amir. Dear, sweet Amir.* She loved him so. All that she was and all that she would be was tied to him. Now that he was gone, she felt like a part of who she was died with him. It seemed as if all that was good, lovely, and likable about her was no more. She closed her eyes again, and thought of him as he was, ten feet tall, more handsome than any man who ever lived, manly, yet gentle. That's how she chose to remember him anyway.

She wasn't sure how long she'd slept, but it was dark now. She cleared her throat and stood up. As she walked over to the window, she wiped the tears and sleep from her eyes. Then she looked out the window and saw a full moon staring back at her. What had begun as a small vibration in her stomach became a roaring lion. Hunger registered again. She wondered what Guinevere, whom she had met the day before, had cooked and if there was anything left.

She went to the door and listened before opening it, wanting to know if anyone was up. She wasn't in the mood for visiting. If Cadence's children knew she was awake, they would want her attention. She just wanted something to eat and to lie back down. She opened the door and stuck her head out. The oil lamps in the hallway were lit, which meant that someone was probably up. She looked to the left and seeing no one, she looked to the right. Even though no one was in the hall, she thought about returning to her bed, but the demands of her empty stomach vetoed the idea.

As quietly as she could, she left her room and closed the door gently, hoping no one would hear her movements. She made her way down the empty hallway. As she crept past Aubrey's room, she heard what sounded like a man and a woman making love. She stopped at the door and listened for a few seconds. She rolled her eyes while disgust twisted pretty into unpretty. It was Cadence and Joshua. They couldn't control themselves and it angered her. It was bad enough that they had committed multiple murders, but to have sex in Aubrey's room after murdering him was too much. And to do it with her children one floor beneath them was unconscionable.

She listened to them for a few more seconds, shaking her head all the while, becoming more and more unpretty as she listened. Cadence was enraptured by whatever naughty things Joshua was doing to her. Although Lauren couldn't understand what he was saying, it sounded like Joshua was giving Cadence orders of some sort. To whatever he was saying to her, Cadence's response was musical in tone. Lauren thought Cadence had missed her calling. She was definitely a singer—a soprano. Perhaps the opera house she had heard people in the city talking about building would have been the appropriate venue for the concert she was listening to.

She finally moved on to the top of the stairs and descended, still angry with them, still shaking her head, thinking about Cadence and Joshua's recklessness. What they were doing took a lot of nerve. So did cold, calculated murder. Or perhaps they just didn't care anymore. Maybe that's what being the architect of a multiple murder plot did to a person. Once a person killed a human being, let alone eight of them, perhaps nothing bothered the person anymore. Only the murderers knew for sure if they had any conscience left. Either way, she loathed them for what they had done and what they were now doing.

Chapter 8

Lust: The Joshua Situation

Cadence was twenty-three years old when she began her adulterous affair with Tristan, but her second tryst began a little over a year ago. While the dress shop kept her busy Monday through Saturday, Sundays were reserved for worship and equestrian endeavors. She was thirty-nine and rapidly approaching forty. The eyes of New Orleans's wealthy, elite gentlemen followed her when she was in the city, as she was still beautiful and quite shapely for a woman who bore four children. Though many men had approached her and attempted to win her heart, they had all failed.

Sixteen years of bedding Tristan had lost much of its luster. The sex was still okay, but it was far from what it used to be—spontaneous and decadent. She probably would have ended the relationship altogether, but she still had needs that he met and although it was no longer the Fourth of July when they copulated, it did relieve a measure of tension. After sixteen years, it was no longer a secret, although everyone, including her deceased husband, had pretended it was. Now her amorous interests had shifted to another man.

They had shifted to the man who took care of her stable of horses; a man she owned—Joshua Bouvier.

Whenever Cadence went to the stables, she would inevitably see Joshua, who was only twenty-four years old. He worked at one end of the stables, while she groomed her horses at the other. She often felt his eyes gazing upon her shapely figure when he thought she was unaware of it. She often gazed at him too when his back was turned. She would watch his trapezius and tricep muscles flex as he pounded iron on his anvil, forcing it to obey his will. From time to time they would look at each other, lock eyes, but he would look away, which was expected of him, being her subservient slave. As time passed, Cadence found that it was becoming increasingly difficult, if not impossible, to ignore his working-man, manly exterior, a visual that neither Beaumont nor Tristan offered.

Joshua's body developed into that of a god earlier on when he was a pubescent teenager. A combination of great genetics and hard work in the stables turned him into an Olympian. He was nearly six feet six inches tall and covered with muscle. He was bald with coffee-colored skin. His square chin looked as if it were made of granite. Rippling lean muscle covered his stomach. Chopping wood turned his back into a well-defined work of art.

He wore the traditional blacksmith attire: hard-soled shoes, leather apron, sleeveless shirt, and trousers that spilled over his shoes to prevent falling burning debris from entering them. Not only was his body difficult to ignore, his piercing brown eyes forced her to look at him because Cadence could sense his lewd scrutiny. He often watched, riveted by what registered in his mind, staring at her mindlessly, in a way that a slave should never stare at his mistress; frequently getting lost in his deadly desire to bed her every time she bent over to pick something up.

At first it made her feel uncomfortable having a big, dark-

skinned black man like him leering at her, like nothing
would please him more than ripping off every stitch of clothing she had on and then forcing himself inside her. While
she would never admit it, she loved it when he looked at her
like she was the most beautiful creature known to man. This
was the dichotomy of her psychological makeup. It was both
her nightmare and her fantasy. She probably wasn't the only
Eighteenth-century white woman who struggled with this
conflicting desire.

As time passed, she realized that he would never ever
force himself on her, even though that was exactly what he
wanted to do recklessly, but without actually raping her. She
assumed that whatever sexual tension he had developed for
her he transferred to one of the slave girls, as he was the
reigning plantation stud. He had his pick of over one hundred women, ages ranging from sixteen to sixty. Even the
older, toothless females wanted him to visit their quarters on
cold nights.

She found herself thinking about him daily, yet she never
said anything to him. One night, she had an erotic dream
that she could not force out of her mind when she woke up
the following morning. All day long, images of their bodies
entwined, doing sinful, unmentionable things to each other,
dominated her every thought. For months she tried to ignore the dream, but when she saw him, the images magically
reappeared. Again she tried to ignore the images, but the
more she tried, the more they crept into her mind and into
her dreams, becoming more and more erotic with each subsequent reverie.

Chapter 9

Executing Amir's Strategy

Most people would have been devastated if they had lost someone as close as Amir and Lauren were. She was all alone now, thousands of miles away from Dahomey, with no one to depend on but herself. She had to figure out a way to survive. She had seen so much death in her young life that she couldn't properly grieve for the prince. She didn't even know what happened to his remains after being whisked away by her former captor.

She wondered if the American savages left him on the docks for the birds and other animals to feed on. When she considered these things, her anger intensified and threatened to send her into a rage that probably would have meant her death. She took a couple of deep breaths to calm down and regain control, which was essential if she was to figure out how to repay them for the lives they had stolen.

Continuing down the stairs, she began to formulate her plan to settle all accounts. Everybody was going to pay. She thought about Captain Rutgers, whom she wanted to destroy as well, but he had given her a measure of justice by killing the man who took Amir's life. When she thought about it, she wondered if the justice he provided was enough. Did he still owe her a debt for capturing them in the first place? If he hadn't bothered them, if he wasn't so determined to have her and to sell her to the highest bidder, she thought she might be frolicking on a beach of Sierra Leone like Amir had promised she would. She might even be with child, Amir's child. If she were pregnant, she wondered if it would be a boy or a girl, and if Amir would have built his first ship by now.

At first she thought she needed to push those thoughts out of her mind, believing they would make her weak. Then she realized she needed to think of these things often because they would strengthen her resolve to do to others as they had done to her and Amir.

Downstairs now, light from the kitchen could be seen in the dark hallway. Something smelled wonderful. She could hear movement, a fork scraping a plate. Someone was eating, she assumed. She stopped for a moment and considered returning to her room, but the vibration in her stomach gave her strict orders to journey on; her stomach sent a message to her mind, telling her to eat and get strong; telling her to develop the warrior's spirit.

At that instant she remembered when she was aboard the *Windward,* Amir had told her to get Captain Rutgers to relax and when he least expected it, they would come out of the shadows and kill them all. It was an excellent strategy then, and she thought it would still be an excellent strategy now. The execution of his plan would begin in a few seconds, in the kitchen with whomever was in there.

While she was very hungry, she didn't want a lot of attention, particularly from the people who had enslaved her; people she considered her enemies. It didn't matter that she had only been a slave for three days. It only mattered that people, black and white, enslaved others and that it was perpetual. The strange thing about it was that she didn't put her father, who was a slaver himself, into the same category. She never even thought about what he had done and what he was still, in all likelihood, doing in her absence.

The thing that eluded her most was her own complicity in the tragedy she was starring in. It still hadn't occurred to her that if she had not left her fiancé at the altar while she and Amir stole away in the middle of the night, she wouldn't be in New Orleans. Never did she consider the great sacrifice Amir's mother made to ensure their plan of escape was a successful one. Nor did she consider Amir's mother an accomplice to what befell them, being the adult who had the most wisdom. Lauren didn't blame Amir's mother because she agreed with the decision to flee and now they were all paying a heavy toll for that choice.

Having reached the kitchen, she decided to take a quick peek and see who was there before going in. She crept to the doorway, put her back against the wall, and tried to relax. She took a deep breath and blew it out gently. Then she peered around the opening. There was only one person in the kitchen. It was the woman she had meet earlier that day—Guinevere Delacroix.

Chapter 10

Sins of the Father

Guinevere Delacroix was a very light-skinned thirty-nine-year-old Creole, an octoroon, having only one-eighth of black blood surging through her veins. She could pass for white. She was born in 1753, sixteen years before the advent of plaçage, an extralegal arrangement where white French and Spanish men entered into what would be considered today as common-law marriages with beautiful women who were a mixture of, or any combination of, African, Native American, and European descent. Although she had never been married, she was the mother of five children; one boy and four girls. Her first sexual encounter was with her father, who found her extremely alluring.

He had watched Guinevere grow from a toddler into a striking, well-developed twelve-year-old girl. It seemed as if she had blossomed overnight. By the time she turned thirteen, he began to see her as a female who needed to be plundered. Not long after those depraved thoughts coursed through his mind, he began to covet the innocent maiden. Unable to resist his escalating desire to ravage the child he himself had sired, ravage her he did, the night of her fourteenth birthday. And while he was ashamed of himself for doing so, he enjoyed the experience so much that he ravaged her again, promising her that if she didn't fight him, if she let him do it again, he wouldn't hurt her and it would be the very last time.

However, the second experience with his daughter was more pleasurable than the first. Nevertheless, he put his hand over his heart and swore to his God that he would never do it again. He knew and clearly understood that what he had done was perversion of the first order, and he did his best to keep his word. He did everything he could to avoid being alone with her. It worked for a while.

He was quite pleased with himself for having the discipline to stop. In fact, he started having conjugal relations with his wife again, but sex with her yielded no "real" satisfaction. One night, after a round of decidedly monotonous intimacy with his wife, his body began to crave Guinevere's. He fought the battle, the urge to take his daughter again, but lost. Although he knew better and tried to do better, the following night he recklessly entered his daughter a third time.

Afterward, he made no promises to stop. He had no intention of stopping at that point because he no longer had the will to. This particular violation was so erotic that he lost whatever discipline he had developed. Sex with his daughter had become a habit he no longer wanted to break. He refused to deny himself the sweet rapture no other woman gave him. What made the third time so alluring was that his daughter showed clear signs of enjoying what he did to her.

While she would never admit it, she didn't want him to stop either. And so he ravaged his daughter nearly every night for months—even during her menstrual cycle. Eventually she began to show signs of being with child. Nearly everyone on the plantation knew of his salacious activity with Guinevere, but they all pretended they didn't. Her mother knew too, and did nothing about it.

Chapter 11

A Little Competition Might Start a Fire

Guinevere Delacroix became a mother for the first time at age fifteen. The delivery was a difficult one. She had given birth to a boy. She named him Javier. He was twenty-four now and studying medicine in France. When he thought her birth canal was healed, her father returned to her and entered her again, night after night, until she was pregnant again. This time it was a girl. She named her Lacey, now twenty-three. She, too, was educated in France and became a placée of the placage system at eighteen. She lived in what's called the Faubourg Tremé. She had three children of her own with a wealthy Spaniard, who also had a legitimate white family at his sugar plantation a few miles outside New Orleans.

A month-and-a-half after giving birth to their daughter, her father returned and impregnated her three more times—all girls, Madeleine, twenty-two, Yvette, twenty, and Chantal, eighteen—all educated in France—all became placées with wealthy French and Spanish men who offered a hefty dowry, bought them homes, and provided them with servants and a sacred promise to pay for the educations of however many children were birthed as a result of their union. Having placed all her girls with wealthy white men, she had acquired more than enough to purchase her freedom from the Delacroix family, and did, but had decided to stay with them.

Living on her own never appealed to her. The Delacroix plantation was the only home she knew. It was comfortable and she had plenty of "freedom" to do as she pleased. Even while she was their slave, she was never treated like one. She was treated nearly like a member of the family. While the off-spring of most slaves were the property of the owner, she was afforded the freedom to place her girls in the plaçage system and to keep all the proceeds from it, which was one of the reasons she loved them.

She never felt the sting of the lash on her delicate back, and never worked outside the house. She was a house ser-vant through and through and even thought much like her owners. Whatever they believed was right, she believed was right. With her quiver of children grown and on their own, Guinevere Delacroix accepted the invitation to be the head of Bouvier Manor, and couldn't wait to reunite with her long-time friend, Cadence Bouvier.

Peeking in a second time, Lauren saw Guinevere sitting at the kitchen table heartily eating a slice of what smelled like freshly baked crème brûlée. Her back was facing the door-way. Guinevere was still quite good-looking, meaty in the right places, about five feet eight inches tall. Her hair was black, but Lauren couldn't tell how long it was, as it was wrapped in a multicolored tignon (tiyon), which Creole women were required to wear in public by a 1785 law.

The law was enacted because Creole women were so dev-astatingly beautiful that they were envied by lots of white women because they could not compete with them. Some women complained that French and Spanish men accosted them, wanting to get to know them carnally, thinking they were Creole. This was so prevalent that Governor Esteban

Rodriguez Miró had to put a stop to it and maintain class distinctions—hence the tignon laws.

Lauren had seen hundreds, if not thousands, of beautiful Creole women wearing bejeweled tignons, whose manner of dress was pleasingly flamboyant. She had seen the attention they were getting from the French and Spanish men in the city. She too was made to wear the tignon and drew the same wanton looks from the same men. When she considered these things, it occurred to her that she may have found the key to bringing down Cadence and Joshua. She thought she could create a rift between Cadence and Guinevere where Joshua was concerned. Cadence was good-looking too, but Guinevere, being of mixed blood, was better looking.

Joshua had been the plantation stud before he started bedding Cadence, but for the last six months, she was his only lover. Lauren thought he had to be ready for something new. Most men, including her father, Faisal, had a penchant for more and more women. She didn't think American men, slaves or free, were any different, especially if the women were as gorgeous as the Creoles of New Orleans. Besides, Joshua had seriously flirted with her the day they had met, and he was bedding Cadence at the time. She thought that if he would make a play for her, with a little encouragement, he would certainly make a play for Guinevere. She made up her mind on the spot. Bouvier Manor needed a little competition. She would see to it.

Chapter 12

"Is there no God in Africa?"

Lauren stood in the doorway for a few more seconds, trying to think of the best way to approach her enemy's lifelong friend, who was no doubt selected to be the house spy. She had to win her over first, or at least try to, before executing her plan to dethrone the reigning queen of Bouvier Hill. Whether she won Guinevere over or not, Lauren understood all too well that she could never trust any house slaves. Because of Joshua's treachery, she wasn't sure she could trust any field slaves either. That left the free blacks of New Orleans and Captain Rutgers. She didn't like any of her choices for potential allies, so she decided she wouldn't trust any of them—not yet anyway. They would all be pawns in an elaborate game of death.

"Will you stand there all night, child?" Guinevere said without turning around. "Or would you like something to eat? You must be hungry by now."

Surprised that she knew she was standing there, Lauren remained quiet, unsure of what to say. She knew anything she said, or did for that matter, would be told to the Master of Bouvier Manor and would certainly be used against her.

Again without turning around, Guinevere pulled out a chair. The floor screeched as it slid. "Come, sit, eat, talk to Guinevere. Tell me all that's in your heart."

Tentatively, Lauren walked into the kitchen and sat in the chair that had been pulled out for her. *All that's in my heart? Please, you couldn't handle all that's in my heart. I'm planning to destroy you and your murderous friend—Joshua, too. And anybody else that gets in my way. I might even burn this place to the ground before I'm finished.*

She locked eyes with Guinevere, knowing full well they were her greatest and most reliable assets. With the exception of her father and Amir, no one had been able to turn away from her magnetic gaze before she released them.

She could tell by the dead silence saturating the kitchen that Guinevere was mesmerized. She forced herself to smile at the serpent sitting across the table from her. It was the kind of smile that said, *"I'm your friend."* It was the kind of smile that also said, *"I'm a very dangerous woman. You have no idea who you're dealing with, do you?"*

Lauren released her by looking away for a quick moment. Then she said, "I thought I was being quiet, Mademoiselle Delacroix."

"Quiet as a mouse, you were," Guinevere said. "But even in a big house such as this . . . when it is consumed with quiet . . . the quietest mouse can be heard."

"I suppose that's true, Mademoiselle Delacroix, but I didn't know you were in here. And I certainly did not want to disturb you."

"But you knew someone was in here, yes?" Guinevere said, offering a smile of her own, one that was cunning, one like Lauren's that offered a counterfeit friendship. "I think it was *you* who did not want to be disturbed, yes?"

"Oh, I wouldn't say that, Mademoiselle Delacroix," Lauren said, lying. "I think company is exactly what I need right now."

Using her fork, Guinevere put some more of the delicious crème brûlée in her mouth before saying, "Come
now, child . . . if that's true, why didn't you want your footsteps to be heard?"

Lauren smiled, but offered no explanation. *The old girl has
a sharp mind. Maybe I better not underestimate her. Maybe I better
be very careful or I might end up like Aubrey and the rest of the
housemen.*

After filling her mouth with more of the crème brûlée,
Guinevere walked over to the ten-plate stove. Using a thick
cloth, she picked up a plate of food and brought it to Lauren. She set it before her along with a fork and said, "I thought
you would be getting up soon, so I kept a plate warm just in
case. There's more if you want it."

Having lived in New Orleans for six months, Lauren had
developed a palate for crawfish, red beans and rice, gumbo
in all its classic forms, andouille sausage, and her personal
favorite, jambalaya. She also developed a bit of a sweet tooth,
enjoying many of the desserts she'd eaten. Some of her fa-
vorites were cherries jubilee, Creole pudding, Macadamia
nut brownies, pecan pie, and a host of others; the kind of
goodies that threatened to expand a woman's hips. The
plate Guinevere set before Lauren was a dish called shrimp
Creole.

Her mouth watered when she saw the food. The idea of
having crème brûlée as a dessert danced in her mind, too.
She picked up her fork and dug in. Just as she was about to
put the food into her mouth, she felt Guinevere's bewilder-
ing stare. She stopped short of putting the food in her
mouth and looked into Guinevere's face, which was twisted
into an angry scowl.

"What's wrong, Mademoiselle Delacroix?"

"Is there no God in Africa? Or is it full of ignorant niggers
with no idea of who created them and why?"

Chapter 13

"Will you teach me?"

Besides the personal affront to the people responsible for her existence, the thing that struck Lauren was the word "niggers." It astounded her that the people who looked like her and had come from the same continent used the same demoralizing word that their slave masters uttered when addressing each other. She remembered that when she heard Joshua use the word he had said, "Niggas." Guinevere sounded like the sailors aboard the *Windward* when they used the word.

The heat of her fury was starting to simmer, but she knew she had to quell it and quell it quickly. She had to play the dumb role to keep her new nemesis off balance. She had to let the spy who loved her captor more than her own life believe what she thought of her own people; that they were ignorant and had no belief in the God of heaven. That way, her enemy would let her guard down and perhaps say things to help Lauren's cause.

With as much sincerity as she could muster, she said, "God? What do you mean, God, Mademoiselle Delacroix?"

Guinevere frowned and said, "Child . . . you've never heard of the God who created the heavens and the earth."

It was all Lauren could do to keep from laughing in her face. Of course she had heard of the God who created the heavens and the earth. Her mother had taught her about spiritual things when she was just a little girl. Amir's mother, Asenath, had reinforced those things whenever she visited with her. Besides that, she had read the Bible cover to cover over the last six months. However, given all that she had experienced, God was the last being on her mind. She looked at Guinevere and said, "You mean somebody created the earth. It wasn't always here?"

Guinevere shook her head, pitying Lauren, who was obviously a heathen. She thought all Africans were. Never mind that the white people born on the continent are Africans too. With rancor she said, "And I suppose you've never heard of God's Son, Jesus Christ, either, huh?"

Laughing on the inside, she said, "Who?"

Frowning, Guinevere said, "How long have you been here, child?"

She locked eyes with her, "Six months, Mademoiselle Delacroix, but I have not eaten all day and I'm starving. May I please eat some of your delicious-smelling food?"

Guinevere laughed and said, "I'm so sorry, child. I plum forgot about that. You can eat right after you say your grace."

Lauren knew what she meant, but said, "My what?"

"Your grace. It's a short prayer we say over our food to thank God for providing."

"You mean the God that created the earth made this food for me, too?" Lauren said, playing the dumb role to the hilt.

"No, girl." Guinevere laughed heartily. "I made the food, but let's just say God created all the ingredients and I mixed it all together."

Lauren frowned and looked around. "So where is he?"

"He? God is not a man. God is a woman. The good book says so."

Suddenly all of this was no longer funny to Lauren. Suddenly it was all so serious. Guinevere was the worst kind of idiot. Her idiocy was complete and she had no idea how bad a shape her mental condition was. Aubrey's intelligence made him godlike in comparison. At that pivotal moment, she remembered a Bible verse that read, "if the blind leads the blind, both will fall into a ditch."

"The good book?" Lauren questioned.

"The Bible," Guinevere said. "It tells us how everything got started on earth."

"I don't mean to be pushy, Mademoiselle Delacroix, but I'm starving. May I please eat?"

Guinevere laughed heartily again. "I'm sorry. When I think about the good Lord, I forget what I'm supposed to be doing. Let's say our grace." She bowed her head. "God is great. God is good. Let us thank him for our food. By his grace we must be fed; thank you, Lord, for our daily bread. Amen."

Lauren couldn't resist saying, "But, Mademoiselle Delacroix, we're eating shrimp Creole." She looked around the kitchen. "Where's the bread?"

Shaking her head, Guinevere laughed hard and from her belly. "It doesn't have to be bread, child. It's whatever you're eating."

"Okay, well, why didn't you say, 'Thank you, Lord, for our shrimp Creole?'"

Still shaking her head, Guinevere said, "Just eat your food, child. You've got a lot to learn and you're not going to learn it all in one night. They tell me I'm thirty-nine, and I didn't learn all I know in one night."

When she heard her say that, Lauren realized a marvelous opportunity had just opened up. Guinevere thought she was dumber than a pile of bricks, when in truth it was the other way around. She thought Guinevere wouldn't suspect she was being played if she only talked about a subject she herself had brought up—her age, for instance. She swallowed her food before saying, "You're thirty-nine? You don't look it." She knew most women were quite vain about their appearances. She certainly was. She thought an attractive woman like Guinevere had to be too.

She smiled, acknowledging the compliment. "Yes. I don't feel like I'm thirty-nine though."

"So someone told you that's how old you are?"

"Yes. Mrs. Delacroix told me yesterday before I left. She's the smartest woman who ever lived. Knows all about the Bible and everything."

"Mmm, this is so good, Mademoiselle Delacroix," Lauren said, finishing the last mouthful of her food. "May I have some more while you tell me more about the Bible and the Delacroix family and just absolutely everything you know? I want to be smart like you. Will you teach me?"

Guinevere offered a wide grin, picked up Lauren's empty plate, and walked back over to the stove where two large pots sat. She removed the first lid, picked up an iron spoon, and dipped out more of the white rice. Then she lifted the other lid and dipped out two helpings of the shrimp Creole, put it on the plate, and brought it back to the table. Testing her, she said, "So what do you want to know about first? The Delacroix family or the Bible?"

Chapter 14

"She just told me what it said and that was good enough for me."

Lauren thought very carefully before she opened her mouth. Her first thought was to say she wanted to know about the Delacroix family, but everything in her led her in a different direction. She thought it better not to mention the Delacroix family, not yet anyway. While Guinevere was stupid, she still had to be careful just in case she was playing a very good game of chess, being the house spy. Lauren knew Cadence's choice of a live-in servant was calculated; Guinevere had been chosen for a very specific reason, she surmised. If she started asking questions about the Delacroix family, Guinevere would certainly tell Cadence.

For her plan to have any chance at success, Cadence couldn't be suspicious of anything—nothing at all. "I think I want to know about the Bible. You seem to know so much about it. Have you read it?"

Without hesitation, but with an air of pride, Guinevere said, "No. I can't read."

Lauren was astounded when she detected a measure of pride in Guinevere with respect to her inability to pick up a book and read it for herself. She translated Guinevere's words to: "I'm smart enough to know my place. I'll never be an uppity nigger like Walker Tresvant." Lauren wanted to say something about it, but knew better. It broke her heart a little to recognize the level of ignorance perpetrated upon people who resembled her in New Orleans and on the Isle of Santo Domingo. They seemed to love ignorance, while simultaneously relishing out-and-out lies about themselves and where they came from. The most egregious lie the unpaid laborers had purchased from their pasty captors was that those who were clothed in white skin were godlike compared to those who were clothed in black skin. It angered her.

She took a deep but unnoticeable breath to conceal her indignation and then said, "Really?" Offering a penetrating stare, she said, "So . . . Mrs. Delacroix told you God is a woman? And that *she* created everything?"

"Yes. But she told me never to tell Master Delacroix. He would get mad if I did. That's why when we say our grace, we say him and not her, see? We have to keep the menfolk happy."

Pretending to be confused, Lauren asked, "Why would he get mad?"

"Well, I don't really know, to tell you the truth, but Mrs. Delacroix says it's because men don't like to be reminded that God created woman in her image and that man was made from the rib of a woman. That's why."

Oh my God! It's the other way around! No wonder they don't want their slaves to read. That way they can tell them anything and they'll believe it. Trying to look innocent and sincere, Lauren said, "I don't understand, Mademoiselle Delacroix."

"What don't you understand, child?"

"Well . . . if . . . excuse me . . . since God is a woman, how is it that the men run everything? Even in Dahomey, the men are in charge. The king is a man. The heir to the throne is a man. My father could have as many wives as he could afford, but my mother could only have one husband. It's all so confusing. Why would this God of yours, being a woman, allow this to happen to us women? It seems to me that we would do a much better job than the men if we were in charge."

Guinevere laughed. "I asked the same question and Mrs. Delacroix told me that God put woman in a place called the Garden of Eden and told her not to eat any apples from the apple tree. If she did, she would die. Mrs. Delacroix explained that dying was the same as losing control, you know, losing all her power over the man. Anyway, God told Eve that it wasn't good for her to be alone, so God made her fall asleep and when she woke up, a man was there. The man ate the apple and forced the woman to eat it because he was bigger and stronger than her."

Lauren's mouth fell open. She had read the story and there was no mention of an apple. She resisted the urge to ask why God made the man stronger than the woman since the man came from the woman, but that would have been too easy. The question may have destroyed the foundation of Guinevere's belief system and may have forced her to stop talking and actually think deeply about what she had been told. She wanted to keep Guinevere talking, keep her feeling good about the knowledge she thought she had, and then lead her down a path that she wanted her to go in.

In keeping with the conversation, Lauren said, "Okay, so tell me how things got turned upside down. How is it that women are on the bottom now when the first woman was in charge?"

Scratching her head, Guinevere said, "You know, Lauren, the thing sure is puzzling. I asked the same questions and Mrs. Delacroix told me that God got so mad at the woman for eating the apple that she put the man in charge to teach her and all women a lesson. So now we have to pretend to let the men think they're smarter than us when really, we know more than them."

"That makes sense," Lauren said, nodding, trying to keep Guinevere talking and not thinking. "So who is this Jesus person? You said something about him being the Son of God."

"Yes. Jesus is God's son, and a woman gave birth to him to take away the sin of the first man." Lauren was about to ask another question, but Guinevere interrupted. "I know what you're going to ask. You want to know why Jesus wasn't a woman, right?"

"Uh, right . . . right," Lauren went along, letting her run her dignified, but unlearned mouth.

"Well, the man that God gave the woman let himself get tricked by a snake. Since it was a man who messed everything up, a man had to fix things."

Lauren quieted her intellectual spirit, which was dying to ask more questions she knew Guinevere could not answer satisfactorily. The first question that came to mind was, Well, did this Jesus fix things? That question might have ended the conversation because men were still in charge and things were still not right. If they were, how was it that she, being a woman, was a slave? Yet her white mistress, being a woman, was not? It made no sense and she needed the conversation to continue. So she nodded her head like she agreed with everything she had heard. An idea to change the subject to the Delacroix family suddenly emerged. "Can Mrs. Delacroix read?"

"Yes. I told you she's the smartest woman that ever lived. You simply must meet her. She can probably answer your questions better than me."

"That sounds like a wonderful idea, Guinevere. Maybe she

can read us the story someday. Mrs. Delacroix read the Bible to you, right?"

"Well . . . she never actually read it to me, no," Guinevere replied, frowning, wondering why the question was posed. Then she added, "She just told me what it said and that was good enough for me."

Chapter 15

"Someone is coming."

Lauren wanted to tell Guinevere she could read and that she would be more than happy to read the story to her, to expose Mrs. Delacroix as an out-and-out liar, but that would defeat her real purpose, which was to find out if Cadence knew the creation story. If Cadence told Guinevere the same lie, she could use the truth to separate them. Lauren believed once trust was broken in their friendship, it would be very difficult to restore it. She believed Guinevere would reexamine everything Cadence ever told her from the time they were children. She believed that when Guinevere learned the truth, she would then examine her friendship with Cadence. Then she would know what Lauren knew.

Guinevere would know that the people she had held in high esteem could not be trusted. She would know that if they lied to her about one aspect of her life, they could have lied about other aspects of her life. Her eyes would open and she would see that the two women she had trusted most were in reality her mortal enemies. Upon realizing this it would become clear that both mother and daughter had worked in concert to use her to have the best that life had offered, while Guinevere and others like her weren't given anything worth having.

She would then see that the Delacroix family was the worst kind of enemy because they were pretending to be her friends. Once Guinevere saw this very real truth, she would experience real freedom. It would then be possible for her to discard the illusion they sold her. She could then embrace what her God had freely given the moment she was conceived—the right to choose her own destiny.

Lauren had already decided to ask Captain Rutgers to read the story to Guinevere so the revelation of being lied to would become self-evident. "Well, it's an interesting story. I bet it would be nice to hear it read, you know?"

Guinevere's eyes lit up. "Yes, it would be nice to hear the story read."

Lauren's heart pumped fast and hard. Guinevere was falling right into the trap she had skillfully set. She decided to ask a question without asking a question. "The next time you're at the Delacroix plantation maybe you should ask her to read it to you. I'm sure she won't mind."

Having no idea Lauren was siphoning personal information, Guinevere said, "I did ask her, and she said I didn't need to have it read to me. I should just take her word for it." She diverted her eyes to the floor and seemed to relive the rejection she had felt. She looked at Lauren again. "To be honest, her refusal was disappointing. I really wanted to hear the story, you know? The Bible is such a big book, and Mrs. Delacroix has told me so little of it."

Lauren fought hard to keep a smile from bursting forth. Guinevere didn't know it, but she was about to become the first pawn moved in a strategic game of death. Full of confidence now that her prey had taken the bait, she wanted to extract more information by making the obvious suggestion. With insincere concern, she said, "Well, maybe your friend could read it to you."

Deflated, Guinevere looked at the floor again. Her voice was low and full of emotion when she said, "You mean, Cadence?"

When Lauren saw the disappointment in Guinevere's eyes, she believed her strategy had an excellent chance for success. She realized then that Guinevere had already asked her friend and her friend had refused the request. Relishing the moment, she said, "Yes, why not? It's the least a friend could do, right?"

Guinevere's face twisted into a scowl of confusion. "I thought so too. So I asked her one day and she said the same thing."

Lauren now knew she had struck the mother lode. She took a deep breath, trying to control the exhilaration. She knew it would be difficult, but she had to be patient and let Guinevere volunteer the rest. She knew to only ask questions that were expected during the normal course of conversation. "What do you mean? She told you the same story?"

"Yes, but she also told me I didn't need it read to me. That disappointed me too, because we've been friends since we were children. I asked her six, maybe seven times to read it to me. I stopped asking when she yelled at me. She said I better stop pestering her about reading the Garden of Eden story or she would tell Big Papa—" She paused for a second. "Uh, Master Delacroix, to have me sold to another plantation."

It took an enormous amount of strength to keep her ability to read a secret. She felt sorry for her, but like a military commander, she remembered her objectives. Besides, after meeting Joshua, she wanted to trust him too. Later she found out that even though he was a field slave, he couldn't be trusted either. Wanting it to appear as though the idea had just occurred to her, she said, "Hmm, well, I have a friend in town. He might be willing to read it to you. Would you like that?"

A cautious frown emerged. "Who is it?"

"Monsieur Bouvier's friend, Captain Rutgers."

"You mean the white man who brought you home yesterday?"

"Yes. Him. He owes me favors. I'm sure he'll do it if I ask him. I'll probably see him in the morning. Would you like me to ask him?"

Guinevere hesitated.

Lauren's heart pumped harder. She had to fight the urge to pull her along, which might make her wonder why she was so interested. Guinevere was the house spy, she told herself. Guinevere had to decide on her own to accept the invitation. "I'll tell you what; think about it and let me know. I'm going to go to bed now. I have a lot to do tomorrow. I have to find out what happened to the man I was going to marry. He was killed yesterday. Did anyone tell you?"

"No, no one told me, but I overheard your friend telling Cadence what happened on the dock." She thought for a moment. "Do you think I could go into town with you tomorrow and meet with this man?"

Guinevere didn't realize it, but she had just shown a major crack in her armor of solidarity with Cadence. By asking if she could go into town to hear the Bible read to her, she was really saying she didn't want Cadence to know what she was doing. Lauren then realized that if she was willing to hide that from Cadence, she might hide something else from her as well. Her plan of attack was working marvelously already; better than she dreamed it would. But to be sure her theory was sound, she said, "Oh, you don't have to come with me tomorrow. I'll ask him to come out here and read it to you."

Guinevere looked toward the door and listened intensely; so intensely that Lauren turned around to see if someone was standing there. She couldn't hear anything, but maybe Guinevere could. Guinevere leaned in and whispered, "Someone is coming."

Chapter 16

"Hi, Lauren."

Lauren frowned, cocked her head in the direction of the doorway, and listened for footsteps. In a hushed tone she said, "I don't hear anything."

Guinevere leaned in a little closer, still looking at the door for who would enter the kitchen, and whispered, "This is just between you and me. I don't want your friend to come here. If Cadence found out, she might get upset. If it's okay with you, I'll go into town with you tomorrow."

Lauren knew she had her now. It wouldn't take much to separate them. She clearly understood that there was no substitute for truth. Truth was unrivaled; it had no competitor. She knew that the fundamental nature of truth exposed the thoughts and intents of the heart, and for that reason, it always removed the mask liars had to wear and exposed them for who they really were. The fact that Guinevere was on the verge of telling everything she knew confirmed this. Nevertheless, she knew she still had to be cautious and patient. "Well," she began, purposely hesitating. "I don't know, Mademoiselle Delacroix. I don't want to cause any problems around here."

Still whispering, Guinevere said, "Please, Lauren. I love that story. I don't see what's so wrong with me hearing it read. I just want to hear the story one time before I die."

Lauren exhaled hard, still paying strict attention to Guinevere's expressions, still calculating every response, carefully treading the friendship terrain. Then she whispered, "Mademoiselle Delacroix, I don't want to get in the middle of anything between you and your friends. I'm only living here because of the goodness of Monsieur Bouvier's final request. I'll be getting my own place soon according to his will. But if Mrs. Bouvier finds out I had Captain Rutgers read the story to you and your friendship sours, both of you will blame me. I don't need that in my life right now. I have too much going on."

Desperate now, Guinevere said, "You said your friend owed you a favor. What if I owed you one too? Would you take me with you then?"

Lauren fought off a budding smile. That was exactly what she wanted to hear. She didn't have a specific favor in mind, but she learned from her mentor, Captain Rutgers, that it was better to have debtors than to be in debt. Nevertheless, she had to maintain a level of reluctance to make the con authentic. "Hmm. Maybe," she said, pretending to weigh her options as she looked at the floor. Then she raised her head and locked eyes with Guinevere. Before speaking, she narrowed her eyes. "Mrs. Bouvier will want to know why you're coming to my shop. What will you tell her?"

Excited now, feeling like she was about to get what she wanted, she smiled and whispered, "I'll remind her that I've never been to New Orleans and that I'd like to spend some of my money on a new dress or something."

"Wait a minute," Lauren said without thinking, feeling sorry for her enemy. "You're thirty-nine years old and you've never been to New Orleans? Tell me you're not serious."

Still whispering, Guinevere said, "I've never been. I've had no reason to go until now. Everything I've ever needed has always been brought to plantation Delacroix. I'm a free woman now. I think I should see the city before the good Lord takes me home, don't you?"

"I don't know," Lauren said, playing her like a fiddle. "I've been working in New Orleans for six months now. It's a lively place, no doubt, but I don't know that you're going to see anything there that you haven't seen here. But I suppose you could see my dress shop and some of the French Quarter." She carefully studied Guinevere as she spoke, watching her sparkling blue eyes come alive as she made New Orleans sound like a place she ought to see. "And I suppose you could go over to Rampart Street in the Tremé area and see Place de Negres. I'm sure you've heard what the slaves do on Sundays; how they go over there to sing and dance and play music, right?" Guinevere was grinning now. Her smile was wide and grand; invitingly so. "And then I suppose you could stop at one of the many eateries and have a bite to eat or maybe something to drink. Or perhaps you could see all the shops the thriving people of color own. But other than that, there's not much there."

In a dry, sleepy voice, ten-year-old Josette Bouvier said, "Hi, Lauren."

Chapter 17

"I have to check on something."

Lauren turned around and looked at the blue-eyed little blond girl. Josette was standing in the doorway of the kitchen, wearing a flowing cotton pullover gown that stretched down to her creamy ankles. Looking at her, Lauren got the feeling the child thought she might be interrupting something and was fearful of entering the kitchen. It was like she needed an invitation to enter a room that she had more right to be in than she did.

"Hi, sweetie," Lauren said and smiled, opening her arms wide, beckoning her favorite of the Bouvier children to accept the embrace she was offering. "What's the matter? Couldn't sleep?"

Josette practically ran over to Lauren and threw her arms around her. She kissed her on the right cheek. She pulled back so she could look into Lauren's eyes. She could tell Lauren was trying to hide what she was feeling. She said, "I'm so sorry about what happened to your friend, Prince Amir. I was so looking forward to meeting him."

The genuine love Lauren felt oozing from the innocent little white girl instantly burrowed its way through the hard shell protecting her heart and touched her emotional nerve center. For a fleeting moment, she remembered what it was like to be surrounded by corruption, yet being unsullied by it. She took a deep breath and said in her heart, *Oh, God, if I could just go back! Oh, how I wish I could return to Dahomey and change my mind! If I could just do it all over again! I swear I would do things differently!*

Lauren wrapped her arms around Josette and nearly squeezed the life out of the child. While she had much love for the child, by holding on to her, she was attempting to embrace what used to be. Knowing she never could, knowing she could never change what she did, what happened to Amir, and the things she had seen, she began to weep. A little at first. A sob. A sniff. And then the anguish of remembering him—Amir, her sweet Amir, came rushing to the surface like a sudden violent oceanic storm. It was the kind of anguish that could be felt by the other two females in the kitchen. Instinctively, they knew what she was feeling. She wailed uncontrollably. She cried so hard that she began to shake. And when Guinevere saw it, she wept too. So did Josette.

Guinevere had almost forgotten about Amir's murder. She had almost forgotten her assignment as well, which was to spy on Lauren, to make her life at Bouvier Manor a living hell, and to retrieve the hearts and minds of Cadence's children. But watching the touching scene play out with Josette, and remembering that Lauren had promised to do for her what her childhood friend would not do, made her rethink the matter. The things that Lauren had said made her consider her condition for the very first time. And she began to wonder who her friends really were.

Guinevere had freely given the Delacroix family half a lifetime of loyal service. As she wept, she tried to think of what she had gotten in return. As tears streamed down her face, she thought hard, but couldn't think of a single thing they had actually done for her above and beyond feeding and clothing her. When she thought about it, she realized that she had never eaten a meal before they had eaten.

She had been conditioned to think their scraps were a delicacy. She had never owned a new dress or a new pair of shoes. Anything that Cadence had worn and no longer wanted made her feel as if she were getting something fit for a queen. Those former ideas were now being challenged. They were being challenged by the conversation with Lauren, which had already begun to influence her in ways she couldn't begin to comprehend. But she liked the way she was feeling and she wanted to go on feeling that way.

The soft voice of Josette cut through the thick haze of emotional anguish they were all feeling when she said, "You shouldn't be alone, Lauren. Is it okay if I sleep with you tonight?"

Even though Lauren was still hurting, even though tears were still pouring out of her eyes, she found a way to smile through it all. *This ten-year-old child has more sense and has shown more concern for me than people four times as old as she. Don't these people know what I'm going through? Don't they know what I'm feeling? Of course they do. They just don't care! It's hard to imagine that Cadence was once like this child. What happened to her?*

She brushed Josette's hair away from her eyes and kissed her forehead. "Sure, honey. You can sleep with me tonight. Come on. Let's get to bed. I've got a busy day tomorrow."

"Uh, Josette . . ." Guinevere interrupted, remembering that Joshua and Cadence were still in Aubrey's bedroom heavily engaged in carnal activity. "Uh, wouldn't you like to have a slice of crème brûlée before you go back to bed? It might help you sleep."

Josette smiled. She loved crème brûlée.

"Lauren, do you mind getting her a slice? I have to check on something. I'll be right back."

Lauren knew what Guinevere was going to do. She couldn't let Josette find out that the lady of the house, her mother, was no lady—far from that lofty idea, in fact. She hoped the day would soon come when Guinevere realized that Cadence and her family weren't who she thought they were. As she watched her leave the kitchen, she wondered what Guinevere would willingly do once she awakened from the deep coma she was in.

"Sure, Mademoiselle Delacroix, I'll give Josette a slice," Lauren said, wiping her eyes. "I'd like a slice of crème brûlée too. I think it will make me feel a whole lot better than I do right now."

Chapter 18

Preparing for Battle

Early the next morning when Lauren woke up, she was surprised to see that Josette was already gone. She had slept soundly. It may have been the tears she shed for Amir. For a quick moment she thought about home. Jamilah, her mother, would often threaten to spank her for being selfish and doing other things children did without thought. Although Jamilah rarely delivered the punishment she promised, when she did, it was well deserved because it had been earned. After having been severely spanked, she always slept soundly. That's how she felt now. She took a deep breath. She felt refreshed. While she cleaned up and planned her day, she thought of Josette.

She was glad that Josette had come into the kitchen the previous night. She was glad the child had shown real love, real emotion, real concern; it allowed her to accept what she had been feeling since the day she and Amir were taken. She knew she had to limit her moments of what many would consider weakness, but as her mother had explained after her grandfather died, there was a time and a season for everything under the sun. And to mourn the dearly departed was not only appropriate, but it was good for the mourner as well. Her mother explained that the God above had given all mankind tear ducts for this very reason. She further explained that to fight the flood of emotions that one felt when someone close to them passes from this life to the next, not only dishonors the dead, but it denies those who are still alive the opportunity to fully experience all that life has to offer. But that was last night.

She had not only embraced Josette for loving her from the heart, the previous night, she had embraced her own anguish; the anguish that she felt on the deck of the *Windward* when Amir stood tall and proud. She had never been more proud of any man and she would always remember the strength it took to look death in the eyes, and remain unmoved by it. She remembered how Amir had transferred his strength to her with a single glance. He never said a word. His eyes alone were the conduit of strength and pride. Now it was time to be that strong again.

Not only would she draw upon Amir's strength, but she would draw upon her own. For reasons unknown to her, she had forgotten that she'd had the strength to kill too. Captain Rutgers and his crew had stumbled upon Lauren and Amir while they were sleeping. She warned Amir, but he was tired. He hadn't slept in three days. When Lauren realized it was either kill or become a slave, she decided to fight for her freedom.

Using Amir's sword, she had cut a man's throat and watched his blood pump out the side of his neck while he desperately tried to stop the bleeding. It was a horrific sight, and perhaps that was why she pushed the thought of doing it so deeply into her subconscious that it didn't surface again until now. She remembered being shocked by the man's death and the fact that she was his executioner. She could see it all playing out now in her mind's eye, but she was no longer repulsed by it. In fact, she wanted to remember what she had done. That way, if she ever felt her life was in danger, she could do it again. She understood that soldiers didn't just kill one man on the battlefield; they killed as many as stood before them.

Amir had told her that before the battle began, the soldiers would first get into formation. The officers called the soldiers to attention. Then the commander would remind the soldiers of battles they had already won. He would remind them in intricate detail of how they had already slaughtered their enemies by taking off their heads at the shoulders, plunging spears into their hearts, or ripping out their bowels.

These pep talks would always energize the troops; so much so that they always cheered and rushed into battle without fear of what their enemies were going to do to them, but rather, what they would do to their enemies. This idea would be her mantra, her rallying cry, but it would be safely tucked away in the recesses of her mind, where no one could see it, feel it, or touch it.

It was time for that kind of strength, that kind of energy. And so she would remember not only the man she had killed, but the many men Amir had killed. She would also remember the people she had never seen before and never knew their names, who were slaughtered at sea and aboard the *Windward*. They too would become a constant fixture in her mind, along with Beaumont, Louis, Aubrey, and the rest of the housemen. All of these would harden her heart and strengthen her resolve to do what she thought must be done. The season for tears had come and gone. A new season was dawning. The season of strategic manipulation, calculated offensives, and shrewd survival was on the horizon.

Chapter 19

"Now . . . I know you meant no harm, but, it just ain't proper."

Before Lauren could fully implement her plan, the prince had to be taken care of. She longed to see him again, yet she didn't want to see him in his current state—dead with a gaping hole in his head. She wanted to see him alive and well, but the finality of death would forever prevent that desire from becoming a reality. Saint Louis Cemetery would be Amir's final resting place. During the previous six months, when she was freed according to Beaumont's will, she explored the city and had accidentally stumbled upon the cemetery while strolling along Conti Street north of the French Quarter in the Faubourg Tremé.

She had gone into the cemetery for reasons she didn't fully understand herself. But with nothing better to do, in she went, strolling along, reading the names on tombs dating as far back as the 1760s. Never did she dream in those six months of waiting to see if Amir was alive and could be retrieved from the Isle of Santo Domingo, that she would leave his remains in what is now known as the "City of the Dead."

Captain Rutgers had allowed her to keep all of her personal belongs. He had even given her a trunk to transport them in. Having finished cleaning up, she put on another of the frocks that Amir's mother made especially for her. The only black dress she had was far more elegant than what she needed to attend a funeral. She still felt the need to dress for him, to look good for him, as if his spirit would be there, watching, considering her final acts of love for the man she would love forever.

She had developed a growing fascination with perfumes; so much so that she immediately began importing fragrances from London, Paris, and Germany. Her favorite perfumes were those of the Creed House, established in London thirty-two years earlier in 1760. She was now selling perfumes to New Orleanian women along with dresses and other accoutrements.

She went over to the mirror, picked up an emerald-shaped bottle and pulled off the cap. Immediately she smelled a mixture of jasmine and roses. She dabbed a little behind her ears, on her throat, and at the top of her chest. Satisfied with her appearance, she put on her multicolored tignon as the law required. She beheld her image staring back at her. Being conceited from the time she noticed that men couldn't keep their eyes off her, she smiled at what she saw in the mirror, knowing she was quite good-looking. Now that she was ready, she hoped Guinevere would be ready to leave too.

When she opened her bedroom door, she smelled quite another aroma; one that changed her mind. Now she hoped Guinevere wasn't ready to leave. Someone had cooked what smelled like a scrumptious meal, and she wanted some of it. Hurriedly, she rushed down the hall, pausing at Aubrey's room, listening for the lovers to see if they had any decency left. Hearing no sounds of intimacy, she continued down the stairs at a quick pace, wanting to feed on whatever it was that drew her to the kitchen. She assumed Guinevere was still in there. She decided to test her hearing and crept up to the door opening. She peeked in much like she had done the previous night. She noticed that Guinevere wasn't wearing her tignon. Her hair was black and luxurious, stretching down past her shoulders.

"Come on in, Lauren," Guinevere said. "I heard you long before you started tiptoeing down the hall."

Lauren was impressed, but didn't let on. She walked into the kitchen and offered a friendly smile, saying, "I'm starved. Is there anything left?"

"Plenty, Lauren," Guinevere said. "I was so excited about going into New Orleans, I could barely sleep. I got up before the rooster crowed and started cooking breakfast. To show you how grateful I am, I made you something extra nice because you promised to take me to town today. I made you grilled ham steak, scrambled eggs, baked apples covered in cinnamon, grits, and my famous biscuits!" Like a child who had been promised something she was looking forward to, but not quite sure the person who promised was going to deliver, she said, "You're still going to take me with you, right?"

"Take you where?" Cadence said, smiling, walking like she was on a cloud as she entered the kitchen.

Unable to contain her bubbling joy, Guinevere's smile lit up the room. She said, "Lauren's taking me to New Orleans today!"

Cadence's face twisted and her smile evaporated when she said, "Why . . . whatever for?"

Guinevere set Lauren's meal on the table and said, "Make sure you say your grace before you dig in." She turned to Cadence, smiled again, and said, "I thought I might get m'self a new dress."

Cadence's face twisted even more. "Like I said . . . whatever for? Ever since we were children, haven't I always given you my dresses? Some of them I had only worn few times. What's the matter? They no longer appeal to you?"

Although she didn't appear to be, Lauren was paying

strict attention to every word, every movement in the "play" that was being performed. She was listening for any weaknesses Cadence had that she could exploit. In just a few sentences, she had already learned that Cadence did not want Guinevere going into New Orleans. She would use that to agitate her, get her to say something she hadn't planned on saying, and exploit that too.

To start the game of death, Lauren opened the volley with what would appear to be an innocent question on the surface, but it was wickedly designed to annoy Cadence. She looked at Guinevere and said, "Mademoiselle Delacroix, where are my favorite children, Josette and Beaumont Jr.?"

Cadence's face drained of blood. She glared at Lauren, who was looking at her plate while she ate, like she wanted to kill her for calling Josette and Beaumont Jr. *her* children. Even though she knew Lauren didn't mean she actually bore the children, that didn't matter. Then she looked at Guinevere, expecting her to correct Lauren. She would have done it herself, but she didn't want Lauren to be in a position to tell the children that she couldn't do this or that with them anymore because their mother didn't approve. She wanted her flunky to do it instead. That's why Guinevere was there—to do her dirty work. That way she could appear to be nonchalant about Lauren's growing relationship with her children.

Even though Lauren was looking at her plate while she ate, she could sense Cadence's anger. She could feel the hatred filling Cadence like it was being poured into her from a large barrel. She kept her cool and smiled within, knowing the first salvo had gotten to her and that there would be many more to come before they even left the house. Now she could feel a different pair of eyes staring at her—Guinevere's. But it wasn't a threatening stare. It was one that didn't want to get in the middle of something that would ruin her chances of going into New Orleans and hearing her favorite

Bible passage read. Lauren was relishing it all and had to fight the urge to smile. The game was afoot, but she was the only one who knew it.

"Well, Lauren," Guinevere said, treading lightly, immediately recognizing that she was in a figurative minefield, "all the children are at school. I fed them earlier this morning."

Still looking at her food, fully cognizant that Cadence wanted to choke the life out of her, Lauren said, "And what about Beaumont Jr.? I know he's not in school." She smiled broadly and continued, "Isn't this the week my boy heads off to Harvard?"

"Yes, it is," Guinevere said, faking a laugh in hopes of staving off Cadence's anger, who looked as if she was about to lose all control. "But it isn't proper to call Mrs. Bouvier's children *your* children. Now . . . I know you meant no harm, but it just isn't proper."

Lauren finally looked up from her plate, just in time to see Cadence's face quickly untwist and become a priceless, but counterfeit smile. "I'm so sorry, Mrs. Bouvier. I assure you I meant no harm at all. It's just that we all just love each other so. And while it's not the same kind of love you all have for each other, it's still precious. Especially now that Amir's been murdered. I'm sure you understand, Mrs. Bouvier, since your loving husband was murdered too." She paused for a second, pretending to be thinking about something that just came to mind. "Well, I guess Amir's death is altogether different from Monsieur Bouvier's and Louis's murders. I know who killed Amir. Captain Rutgers dispensed justice right away. But we still don't know who killed Monsieur Bouvier and Louis."

Chapter 20

"Well . . . what do you think, Mrs. Bouvier?"

Lauren watched Cadence to see if her words had at least pricked her conscience a little. She knew Cadence was ruthless because she and Joshua had not only planned Beaumont's and Louis's deaths, but blamed the murder on Beaumont's best friend, Aubrey, and then had him summarily executed for a crime she knew he did not commit. If it were possible, they added insult to injury when they had sex in the house the next night.

For all Lauren knew, they had been having sex in Beaumont's house all along. The previous night, they'd had sex in Aubrey's room, which made her believe they were so cold, so brazen, that they probably had sex in Beaumont's bed too. And if they hadn't already done it, they were probably going to have sex in all the housemen's bedrooms. But Cadence showed no signs of remorse, which made it easier to continue the joust.

No longer smiling, Cadence said, "Why . . . we most certainly do know who killed my dear husband. It was the housemen, don't you remember? You were here when they all confessed to the crime. Why . . . that's why I had them all executed, dear."

Knowing her life was on the line, Lauren delicately replied, "Aubrey said he didn't do it, Mrs. Bouvier. What if he didn't? What if the other men only said they had killed Monsieur Bouvier because they were trying to protect Aubrey?"

Serious now, Cadence said, "They knew the penalty was death, Lauren. Why would they confess to a crime they didn't commit, knowing they would be executed?"

Lauren quieted herself, pretending to give serious consideration to Cadence's boldfaced lies, and then said, "I admit it is quite the riddle as to why, no doubt about that, Mrs. Bouvier. But at least one of the men did say he didn't do it. He could have been telling the truth."

Guinevere knew about Cadence's affair with Joshua, but she had no idea that her friend had orchestrated her husband's death. She had always admired Cadence's ability to articulate as clearly as any educated white man. Throughout much of her life, she wanted to be Cadence. She wanted to look like her, and have her skin, even though she could pass for white already. She wanted to wear her clothes, and live in her house, yet she wasn't jealous of her, at least that's what she thought.

But now, as she observed the two women, and listened to their verbal exchanges, her respect for Lauren, which began the previous night, was growing with each of her responses. She could tell the young maiden was intelligent and had good reasoning skills. She noticed that while Lauren spoke to the Master of Bouvier Hill with deference, she seemed to be fearless with her sense of logic, fair play, and above all, justice. But what made Guinevere beam with a certain measure of pride she didn't know she had was that Lauren was a nigger too—a stunningly beautiful nigger with her own money and her own business.

In full costume and mask now, Cadence continued the

masquerade, "Why . . . whatever are you suggesting, Lauren? That someone else killed my husband and our servants?"

I not suggesting it, I'm flat out saying you and Joshua killed them. You! Not, Aubrey, you lying, murdering strumpet! "I'm not suggesting anything, Mrs. Bouvier," Lauren said calmly, showing no signs of her agitation or her desire to see Cadence shot in the face by a brigade of French soldiers as she had done. "I was only saying that we know for sure who killed my Amir. I was there and I saw the man who did it. But there may be a question as to who killed your husband, because there were no witnesses. That's all."

Feeling Cadence's anger starting to reach a boiling point, Guinevere decided to play peacemaker and said, "Well, it's good that someone paid for both crimes. It was a shame for both men to meet their end the way they did. God knows all and sees all, and in the resurrection, all will be revealed. No need to fret about it now. Nothing will bring our loved ones back—nothing at all—except for Jesus Christ himself." She looked into Cadence's eyes. "You remember telling me how Jesus raised . . . now let's see, what was his name again? I forgot. But he raised somebody from the dead, didn't he?"

"Lazarus," Cadence said, almost mumbling.

"Yeah, that's right, Lazarus," Guinevere repeated, smiling. "He was dead four days. I love that story too."

Lauren noticed that Cadence's eyes fell to the floor when Guinevere mentioned God knowing all and seeing all. She would see if there was a way to use that against her too. She finished off the ham steak, scrambled eggs, and biscuits. She picked up the plate, put it under her nose, and inhaled the cinnamon apples. She looked at Cadence again. She seemed to be still thinking about God and him knowing what she had done and how there would be a reckoning for it. Sensing her weakness, she said, "I bet your husband never misses a meal, huh, Mademoiselle Delacroix?" She kept her eyes on Cadence to see her reaction.

Unaware of what was really going on in the kitchen, Guinevere offered a flattering short laugh, and said, "Why thank you, Lauren, but I don't have a husband."

Still watching Cadence in her time of reflection, Lauren said, "Really? Is your husband dead too? Somebody killed him too?"

"I've never been married, Lauren."

Now Cadence snapped out of whatever fog she was in and was paying unwavering attention. Lauren sensed her stare again. She loved it all, knowing that now was the time to serve up another seemingly innocent volley and watch both their reactions. She smiled innocently as if she'd had a grand epiphany. "Mademoiselle Delacroix, you know what? I bet you and Joshua would make a wonderful couple. I mean, you're so pretty and shapely and he's a good-looking man."

Both women were looking at each other, stunned that Lauren would make such a suggestion. "Not as good-looking as my Amir, but he runs a close second or third in my opinion. To tell you the truth, when Aubrey was showing me around Bouvier Hill my first day here, Joshua told me I could come to his cabin any time." Cadence didn't realize it, but she was beside herself with anger, her face was red; so Lauren poured it on, knowing neither woman could acknowledge the truth they didn't think she knew. "I knew what he meant. To be honest, I hadn't seen Amir in a long while and didn't know if he was alive or not. I told myself no, but taking him up on his offer was on my mind for a while."

Guinevere was as frightened as Cadence was angry.

Smiling now, Lauren said, "Well . . . what do you think, Mrs. Bouvier? Don't you think Joshua and Mademoiselle Delacroix would make a great couple?"

Chapter 21

More Well-Placed Daggers

Cadence offered a fake smile that seemed uncomfortable and made her look as if her undergarments were cutting into her skin when she said, "Of course not, Lauren. The idea of Guinevere and Joshua is quite comical to be totally honest with you." She faked a short laugh. "Guinevere is old enough to be the boy's mother. She's nearly twice his age. Besides, she already has five children of her own. A buck like Joshua would want to have a few pickaninnies with the woman he marries, I'm sure."

Lauren looked at Guinevere to see what she was feeling, given that her friend pretty much called her an old maid. Guinevere wasn't laughing and seemed just as uncomfortable with how the conversation had turned into a romance between her and Joshua. She also looked as if she felt insulted by Cadence's offhanded assessment of her physical attributes. Of the three women in the kitchen, Lauren was the only one completely at ease. She was very pleased with herself for being able to illicit the reactions she wanted; the reactions she had set up. She was in full control and she knew now was the time to end the conversation. She would stir the pot some more later.

Lauren looked at Cadence and said, "Well, I suppose you're right, Mrs. Bouvier." Then she locked eyes with Guinevere and said, "If Joshua's too young, I bet there are plenty of men in New Orleans who would love to have a beautiful woman like you cooking their meals for them." An idea popped in her head along with another opportunity to twist the dagger already in Cadence's heart before leaving Bouvier Manor. She was relishing the notion of leaving Cadence with an idea that would continue to swirl in her mind for the next few days, if not longer. "You know what . . . I think I'll need some help at the shop on a regular basis. If you worked for me, you'd be in town every day. It goes without saying that I wouldn't expect you to work for nothing. I'd pay you a nice wage and you would have plenty of chances to meet eligible men who would appreciate a woman like you; men that wouldn't think you're too *old* and *decrepit.* And . . . if you want, you might think about saving up enough money to open your own eatery! What do you think about that, Mademoiselle Delacroix?"

Guinevere looked at Cadence as if she were still her slave in need of permission to enter the status of the quasi-free Negroes, who worked on weekends to earn money to purchase their freedom. Lauren could tell that Guinevere was still smarting from Cadence's comment about her being old enough to be Joshua's mother when she was regularly bedding the "boy" herself. She could further tell that she was considering the offer of working in town and earning money of her own.

Even though Lauren's offer sounded good, Guinevere still felt a certain amount of loyalty to Cadence. They had grown up together and had been friends since they were children. Being a free woman could not erase nearly four decades of memories—many of them good, as slavery for her was not a life of daily fear and dread. It was one of pseudo privilege and pseudo social status, all of which appeared to be freely bestowed. But in reality both privilege and status exacted a high price. It produced a form of pride in Guinevere while simultaneously producing a form of jealousy in those slaves who were witnesses of the disparity of treatment.

"Thanks for the compliments and thanks for the offer, but I already have a job right here at Bouvier Manor," Guinevere said, to put Cadence at ease. She wouldn't say anything in front of her longtime friend, but the idea of working in New Orleans and perhaps even opening her own eatery really appealed to her because she still had a stipend of money from the dowries she was paid for her four daughters.

Chapter 22

"Come on, let's head to town."

Lauren could tell Guinevere was doing her best to keep Cadence from losing her composure. She knew that just talking about paying Guinevere was producing a level of anger in Cadence that she was working hard to mask. Realizing another opportunity to stick yet another dagger into Cadence's heart had presented itself, Lauren said, "With you and Mrs. Bouvier being friends and all, I'm sure she would love the idea of you making even more money than what she's currently paying you, right, Mrs. Bouvier?"

That was the last straw as far as Cadence was concerned. She was about to tell the young upstart off, but when Guinevere saw it, she quickly said, "Uh, Lauren . . . uh, well . . . I'm not being paid anything. It's my pleasure to help a friend who needs me. That's what friends are for, right, Cadence?"

"Right, Guinevere," Cadence replied, trying not to show her smoldering fury. "Friends *always* do *favors* for each other. Sometimes the *favors* are small. Sometimes they're big *favors*. But they are *favors* nevertheless and friends *never* asked to be paid for them."

Cadence had no idea that she had been totally and completely manipulated into boxing herself in. She had no idea how unfair she must have sounded to her so-called friend, talking about friends doing favors and never asking to be paid, yet, she wouldn't do a little thing like read the true account of the Garden of Eden story to Guinevere, her life-long friend. Lauren knew that at some point, Guinevere would put it all together on her own. Guinevere would one day realize that *she* was the only friend in the friendship and that *she* was the one doing all the favors. She would further realize that people of color in New Orleans were paid for doing so-called favors, yet she had received nothing in the form of wages from Cadence or the Delacroix family for nearly four decades of "favors."

Lauren looked at Guinevere and said, "Well, I think it's a really great thing that you two are such great friends and that you do favors, great and small, for each other." After that comment, Guinevere's head tilted forward toward the floor, giving the impression that she realized she had gotten no favors from Cadence or the Delacroix family. Having seen the beginnings of the dismantling of their "friendship," Lauren sighed and said, "Well . . . I'm ready to go if you're ready, Mademoiselle Delacroix."

Guinevere's gregarious smile burst forth. Grinning glee-fully, partly because the conversation was over and partly because she was going into New Orleans for the first time, she said, "I'm ready too, Lauren! Let's go!"

Cadence tried to sound pleasant when she asked, "What time do you think you'll be back, Guinevere? The children will be hungry when they get home from school and there's a lot of work to be done around here."

Guinevere said, "I'm not sure what time I'll be back. This is my first time going into New Orleans! And I'm so excited I might not come back until nightfall! If I'm not back when your children get home from school, could you do me a favor and feed them?"

Stunned by the sudden reversal, Cadence stood there stone-faced, looking at Guinevere like she must have been out of her mind asking her to feed her own children.

Lauren couldn't help answering for Cadence, saying, "Sure she will, Mademoiselle Delacroix. She just said friends do each other favors. I'm sure you can depend on her to feed her children. Come on, let's head to town. I have so much to do and you have so much to see."

Act 2

Illumination

Chapter 23

A Decades-Old Rivalry

Cadence glared unceasingly at Guinevere and Lauren as they left Bouvier Manor through the kitchen door. Her eyes followed them down the path to the stables where Lauren kept her carriage, her wagon, and the team of horses she purchased months ago when she took over Bouvier House of Fine Dresses & Accoutrements. As she continued watching, she remembered the day when Lauren insisted on learning how to handle the horses and wagon herself, using the argument that she would be responsible for collecting her own shipments at the dock. Cadence admired her then, but she admired her more now because she, for all intents and purposes, was still very much a foreigner; yet she had taken over her business and not only had she not lost a customer, her new fashions brought in more.

Lauren had requested Joshua, but Cadence gave the assignment of teaching her how to handle a team of horses to Dupre Bouvier, her former driver. She also told him to drive Lauren to the dress shop each morning as he had done for her. Giving Dupre a different mistress to drive to and from errands made it easy to slide Joshua into the position he formerly occupied. In addition to being Cadence's lover, Joshua was her new personal chauffeur.

However, Cadence made it clear to Lauren that she would eventually have to either buy her own slaves, or hire someone to drive the carriage for her, but she could not use Bouvier slaves free of charge indefinitely. However, that did not mean Cadence wanted Dupre to become her chauffeur again. Joshua was handling his extra duty and other more personal duties just fine.

Still standing in the kitchen doorway, Cadence pushed open the screen door and went out on the veranda so she could continue watching the two women as they made their way over to the stables. She needed to see Joshua's reaction to Guinevere. While she would never ever admit it, she had always been jealous of her lifelong friend, which was one of several reasons she refused to read the true account of the Garden of Eden story.

She was jealous because everyone, including her father, loved Guinevere and lavished her with affection when they were growing up. Cadence might have understood or at least been more accepting of it if she had been one of her siblings, but Guinevere was a common slave. When she realized that Guinevere admired her, she played it for all it was worth, giving her shoes and dresses she no longer wanted. She loved the way Guinevere eagerly accepted whatever she was given like a dog that hadn't eaten in a few days.

Even though Cadence was an exceptional beauty, it really bothered her that Guinevere was better looking than she was and everyone, including her parents, always made it a point of conversation. "Guinevere is such a pretty girl. Look at her skin. Isn't she beautiful? I bet her children are going to be gorgeous too." She got so sick of hearing that sycophantic tripe. It made no sense. She was their slave, not the governor. And from her parents no less. It nearly drove her insane. That's why when Lauren pointed out how beautiful Guinevere was it reminded her of how everyone fawned over her. And when Lauren mentioned that Guinevere and Joshua would make a good couple, it felt like someone had unexpectedly punched her in the stomach.

Chapter 24

The Flame of Jealousy

Joshua was hers and hers alone, Cadence was thinking as she continued watching Lauren and Guinevere as they neared the stables. She wasn't about to share him with her childhood friend. He was supposed to be her sexual tool to use at her disposal, but after months of bedding him, or rather, him bedding her, she had willingly surrendered her power over him. Now he was the master and she was his slave. She willingly did whatever menial task he required, sexual and otherwise. She knew that he, like most men, had a desire to bed other females. One woman was never enough. She feared that her unspoken and unacknowledged rivalry with Guinevere would begin anew for his affections. What had started out as base infatuation was now love's opiate. It had quickly become a sick kind of love. The kind of love that made people lose themselves and begin to worship those who were unworthy of their worship.

As Lauren and Guinevere approached him, Cadence could see Joshua's bright smile. She knew instinctively that he found her friend attractive—that's what she thought any-way. When she thought her worst nightmare was beginning to materialize, fear rose and threatened to devour her. Adrenaline surged as she watched them. Joshua had her heart; there was no controlling him. But she could still control Guinevere and she would. She was not about to give him up; not to Guinevere, not to anyone, but especially not to Guinevere. He pleased her much too much to let any woman get her hooks into him.

Jealous tension began to mount when she saw Lauren go into the stables, leaving Joshua and Guinevere alone so they could chat while she mindlessly stared at them, desperately wanting to know what they were saying. Cadence watched as they chatted back and fourth. From their constant smiling and laughing, she thought they were flirting. To her, this was sexual foreplay. They were carrying on like they had known each other for decades when in fact that had only met twenty-four hours ago. It seemed as if Lauren was taking forever to hitch her team of horses to the wagon, but it hadn't been that long; just a few short minutes. In those minutes, Cadence began to wonder what was *so* funny. She then began to wonder if they were discussing her. When they laughed together, she wondered if they were laughing at her.

It took every ounce of strength Cadence had to keep from literally running down to the stables and putting a stop to it all. But if she had done that, she would expose her dirty little secret; so dirty was the secret that it could never ever be known. Guinevere knew of the affair because she had told her, and thought she could trust her. She also knew she admired her enough to believe that having a sexual relationship with her slave was fine even though she was a well-respected Southern lady and a former member of the Christian Women's Social Club (a club started by the Beauregard women). It occurred to her that perhaps she had offended Guinevere with her comments about being "too old," which made her wonder if her lifelong friend was trying to make a point of showing her that Joshua didn't think she was too old. If she had hurt Guinevere's feelings, she wondered if she would let her knowledge of the affair slip out on the way to New Orleans.

Cadence thought that if Lauren learned of the affair, she might tell her sister-in-law, Marie-Elise Tresvant. Marie-Elise would in turn tell Walker, and they might just put it all together. It might occur to them that she had plotted to have Beaumont killed and then covered her tracks by having the housemen killed too. She began to pace back and forth on the veranda as she watched them, wishing Lauren would hurry up and return with her wagon.

Finally, mercifully, Lauren came out of the stables. She said something to Guinevere and went back in to finish hitching the horses to the wagon, Cadence presumed, when out of nowhere, young Beaumont ran into the stables behind her. Seeing this angered Cadence too, because she knew her son was completely taken with Lauren.

Chapter 25

Another Family Secret

Beaumont Bouvier Jr. had been a highly intelligent, but quiet child for nearly sixteen years. He was dutiful in that he was always a conscientious worker when performing his duties around the plantation he would oversee as Aubrey was grooming him to someday takeover. But he began to change little by little over six months ago, disappearing for hours, leaving the sugar house unattended, basically acting like an irresponsible teenager. When asked his whereabouts, he would tell amusing fables that no one believed. For a while, Aubrey and Beaumont Sr. assumed it was part of the coming-of-age process. Later, however, they learned a very disturbing truth about young Beaumont that necessitated his departure to Tallahassee, Florida.

He had never shown an interest in the opposite sex, until it was discovered that he and his first cousin, Brigitte, the daughter of his uncle, Tristan, had been having forbidden relations of an incestuous nature. Apparently the two had been sneaking off together for months, enthusiastically copulating.

Initially, Tristan blamed young Beaumont for corrupting the morals of his favorite daughter. But he later discovered through rigorous interrogation that it wasn't young Beaumont who had initiated the tryst; it was his pride and joy, Brigitte. She had unashamedly admitted it, going into great detail in her retelling of how she seduced her unwilling cousin. She went on to tell Tristan that young Beaumont wasn't the first boy she had been with; he was the latest of a long list of them; she was far from a virgin by the time she got a hold of young Beaumont. She hated her father for separating them indefinitely.

Tristan and Cadence were consumed with guilt, feeling a sense of responsibility in it all because Tristan was the father of both children. It turned out that while Tristan and Cadence where secretly meeting daily in her office at the dress shop, he was still frequently bedding Christine, and had gotten them both pregnant at the same time. The illicit affair was still unknown at the time and was not revealed until years later. When it was learned that young Beaumont and Brigitte were embroiled in a smoldering love affair, they separated the children for their own good.

But the lust that burned in them both could not be quenched by mere separation, and they continued their affair whenever and wherever they could, just as their parents, Tristan and Cadence had. When it was discovered that Brigitte was pregnant with her "cousin's" child, they were both whisked away from New Orleans. Sending the entire Bouvier brood to Tallahassee was a ruse to cover up why young Beaumont was being sent away.

Brigitte's banishment was of a different variety, which was the norm for white females, as the punishment was always much harsher for the same crime. She was first taken to an abortionist who lived in the Tremé, and then she too was sent away; only she didn't just leave New Orleans or the Louisiana Territory. She was sent to a convent in Italy. And thus the incestuous affair was sufficiently destroyed and neatly covered up—at least to those who were not of the Bouvier family.

Upon returning to New Orleans, young Beaumont went in search of Brigitte to continue the affair, but he never found her, nor would those who knew her whereabouts tell him. He had no idea that Brigitte was his sister, that he had impregnated her, and that she was forced to have an abortion. He missed her terribly. He specifically missed the unbridled passion that drew them together. She was his first love and his first lover. He was completely taken with her and found her to be insatiable. After a few weeks of listless dejection and fruitless searching, he set his sights on the new addition to the family who lived on the third floor—Lauren Renee Bouvier.

Chapter 26

"Tomorrow may never come."

Running at full speed into the barn, wanting to catch her before she left, young Beaumont said, "Good morning, Lauren. I'm sorry you lost your friend, Amir."

Lauren tried not to show her utter contempt for what he was trying to do. He wanted to use her as a cheap substitute for his "cousin" Brigitte. She would much rather he go to Madam Nadine's brothel and take care of whatever sexual yearnings he had. She liked the boy and in many ways she understood him and felt sorry for him too, but she wasn't interested in anything more than making his mother jealous of how he fawned over her. As long as they were in the stables, Cadence, who she had seen watching Joshua and Guinevere, couldn't see what her son was doing. So she led her team of horses out of the stable and when she was sure Cadence could see, she kissed him on the cheek and said, "Thank you, Beaumont. I'm going into town now to put the prince in his final resting place."

"Can I go with you?" he asked. "I have something important to tell you."

"Thanks, but no," Lauren said. "Mademoiselle Delacroix is coming with me."

"Well, I'm leaving in a couple of days and I have something very important to tell you," he said, beseeching her.

She stopped her forward momentum and pretended to give young Beaumont her complete attention. She looked over his shoulder to make sure Cadence was still watching. She was. Then she dazzled young Beaumont by looking into his eyes as he tried to put his thoughts together. He soon discovered that he could not look into her hypnotic gaze and speak coherently at the same time. So he looked at the ground for a moment.

"This is the wrong time to say this, Lauren, but I've fallen in love with you." He waited for her reaction, but she just stared into his eyes, patiently waiting until he finished, knowing the longer they stood there, the more infuriated Cadence would become. "As I said, I'm leaving for Harvard in a couple of days, but when I return, I'll be the master of Bouvier Hill. I'll be in position to take care of you and whatever children you have. I'll gladly follow the rules of plaçage and I'll do my very best to make you happy."

Still looking into his eyes, she could tell his proposal was sincere even if it was naïve and insensitive. She had just told him she was going to bury the prince, the man she still loved fervently. Obviously the young man didn't know that death could never be a barrier to her deep, abiding love for the man she risked all for, particularly since he'd only been dead for one day. Her first thought was to say, "No," but she knew Cadence was watching, wondering what was being said. She also knew that as soon as she left, Cadence would question young Beaumont and he would tell her the truth. She could use that against her as well. So to tell him no and give him no hope at all didn't serve her purposes. While it was cruel to give the young man hope, knowing she would never be his kept woman, she knew he was still hurt because of the separation from Brigitte and that, in all likelihood, was the reason for the proposal in the first place.

Still looking into his eyes, with compassion, she said, "I think you'll find another woman to take the place of Brigitte where you're going, young Beaumont."

"No, I won't," he said, having no idea he was just a pawn in the game of death. "And even if I do, she won't be you. She won't have your smile. She won't have your beauty. And she certainly won't have your kind ways."

"When will you be back?" Lauren said, stringing him along, giving him plenty to tell his mother.

Believing there was hope for a relationship with her, he said, "A year or two. Maybe less."

Her eyes rolled involuntarily before she said, "You expect me to wait that long?"

"You waited for Amir for six months. I suspect you would have waited at least another six months or another year if you had to."

"I would have, yes. But that was Amir, young Beaumont. Did I not tell you all what he and I went though only to be captured and brought to this land against our will? Did I not tell you how difficult it was to leave my mother and my father and all of my family to be with Amir? And now, I don't have him either? Do you really expect me, or any other woman, to wait a year or two for a man who may never return?"

Young Beaumont thought for a few seconds and said, "I understand, I guess. But will you at least think about it?"

She looked at Cadence, who had her hands on her hips and appeared to be fuming. Lauren kissed his cheek again and said, "I'll think about it, but I won't make any promises. And you shouldn't either. If you meet a woman where you're going, marry her immediately. Tomorrow may never come."

Chapter 27

"So you've been bedding her?"

As young Beaumont made his way back to Bouvier Manor, he smiled, thinking there was at least a chance to be with Lauren. Immediately he began to fantasize about the house he would have built for her and the servants he would provide for her. It never occurred to him that he was being used to hurt his mother. It never occurred to him that Lauren had her own money and didn't need to be kept. She was a beautiful girl with a beautiful smile that warmed his heart when he looked at her. But if Brigitte were to return to New Orleans from wherever Tristan sent her, he would drop any idea of being with Lauren. He would whisk Brigitte away somewhere far from her father and marry her immediately.

In the meantime, Lauren was the woman he thought about day and night. He had wanted to make his proposal to her months ago, but didn't because he knew she was in love with Amir and more important, he was afraid. He was afraid because he had never approached a woman before. He had no experience with wooing women. His only experience was with his "cousin" and she was the one who had initiated the relationship. He only found the courage to approach Lauren now because he found out Amir was dead and he was leaving for an extended time. It was now or never. So he took his chances and as far as he was concerned, it had paid off. Even though she had said she wouldn't wait for his return, her promise to think about it was good enough for him.

"What was that all about?" Cadence said, wearing an ugly scowl. Her hands were still on her hips as her firstborn son approached her from the stables.

Having no idea what she was talking about, he said, "What was what all about, mother?"

"Don't you dare play games with me, Beaumont Bouvier Jr.!" Cadence said, almost shouting. "You know exactly what I'm talking about, don't you?"

Laughing, he said, "Mother, I have absolutely no idea what on earth you're talking about. But whatever it is, it certainly has gotten your goat."

"What's going on between you and Lauren?" Cadence asked. "Why was she kissing you? And why didn't you stop her? That sort of thing is improper. That sort of thing is done in New Orleans in the Tremé, perhaps, but never, ever on Bouvier Hill. You got that?"

"You cannot be serious, mother," young Beaumont said. "You and Uncle Tristan have taken Brigitte from me and now you want Lauren too? I will not let her go. And you cannot send her away as you did Brigitte. She is a free woman and you have no authority over her, or me, for that matter. Not anymore. With father gone, I'm the man here now. And you know it. Father only left you in charge until I am of age to take over. The will says so. When I complete my studies at Harvard, I will make all the decisions on Bouvier Hill. You might as well get used to it. So if Lauren will have me, I will have her, and there's nothing you and Tristan can do about it."

"Don't tell me you're in love with her?"

"I am in love with her, if you must know."

"And she loves you?"

"What difference does that make?"

"What difference does it make?" Cadence repeated incredulously. "You were just in love with your own cousin a few months ago, and now you're in love with a nigger wench I used to own?"

Young Beaumont narrowed his eyes before saying, "Be careful what you say, mother. The first grandchildren you have might be niggers if you're not careful."

Cadence's mouth fell wide open. "So you've been bedding her?"

"No. Not yet," Young Beaumont said, feeding into his mother's shock, smiling broadly while he spoke. "But I don't leave for Cambridge for another two days. Perhaps I'll impregnate her before I leave and give you a pickaninny in nine months. Two if she has twins."

With her mouth still wide open, Cadence turned around and stormed off.

Chapter 28

"We have to do it quick, okay?"

In an angry hurry, Cadence continued on down the hill, heading to the stables. She needed to find out what Joshua's intentions were. Feeling like she was about to be abandoned, she was wondering what was going on with everyone. It seemed like all the people she loved were turning against her. Right away she laid the blame at Lauren's feet. She told herself everything was going well until her deceased husband bought Lauren six months ago. But everything wasn't going well.

Everything had gone wrong because she seduced Joshua into killing her husband. Joshua killed Louis, Beaumont's paramour, because Louis wanted to seduce him and have a ménage à trois with their master. Then, being drunk with power, Cadence had seven other men executed by firing squad. There was no way she was going to take responsibility for her own doing though. It was so much easier to blame Lauren and Guinevere for her sense of loss, even though she had lost nothing at all. In fact, she had gained, but because she was insecure where Joshua was concerned, she felt like everything she ever wanted was slipping through her fingers.

She walked into the barn and up to Joshua, who was hammering something on his anvil. "So what's going on with you and Lauren, Joshua?"

Joshua kept hitting the iron he was working with. Ping! Ping! Ping! "With Lauren?" he questioned, and continued working. Ping! Ping! Ping! "What do y'all mean? Nothing's goin' on wit' me and her." Ping! Ping! Ping!

She grabbed his arm and stopped him from working. "You didn't try to bed her the day she got here? And you haven't been trying to bed her for the last six months?"

Joshua shot a hot scowl at her and said, "Who told you that? Her?"

"Yes . . . well . . . she was telling Guinevere this morning and I heard it."

"That wench be lyin' and her knows it," Joshua said confidently. He knew that's what she wanted to hear. He also knew she knew he was lying. But that was how the game was played. So he played along. "Y'all know every woman on this here plantation is just a itchin' to git at me. Y'all knows it, Cadence."

"So you didn't try anything with her six months ago, right?"

"That's right. Why ya takin' her word fo' it? 'Specially when you knows how them wenches be all over me all duh time. Just 'cause she from Africa don't make her no different than the rest."

Having heard what she wanted to hear, she relaxed a bit and said, "You're telling me the truth, right? You're not lying to me, right?"

Joshua smiled. "Naw, Cadence. I won't lie to ya. I don't hav'ta lie, now do I. Y'all know y'all be the only woman fo' me. Don't y'all know that?" He reached out to touch her. She slapped his hand away. "Now what be the matter?"

She put her hands on her hips and said, "I believe you about Lauren. But what about Guinevere?"

"What about her?"

"So you're telling me you're not trying to bed her?"

Joshua's scowl returned. "First it be Lauren I'm tryin' tuh bed. Now it be ya good friend, Guinevere? Y'all must think the worst of me. Thinkin' I would bed yo' good friend like that."

"Well, what was all that talking and laughing about earlier, Joshua? Tell me *that* if you weren't trying to bed her."

"Ya mean when Lauren came to git her horses and wagon?"

"Yes. And don't deny it because I was up on the hill watching it all. You tried to bed her, didn't you? Admit it."

"Cadence, ya say ya watch it all, but ya sho' don't hear it all, did ya?"

"Well, if you weren't trying to bed her, what were you two laughing about then?"

"Just some nigga talk. Y'all know how we be. We be a laughin' all the time about nothin' just tuh be laughin'."

"Well, what was so funny? Tell me. I want to laugh too."

"Well, it probably won't be funny to ya. It was just nigga talk. That's all. Nigga talk."

"Tell me some of the nigger talk then. I'll judge whether it's funny or not."

"Fine, but it ain't gon' be funny to ya." He paused and waited for a second or two to see if she really wanted to hear it. When she stood there patiently, he said, "She was just so excited about goin' into New Orleans fo' the first time, is all, Cadence. I was just pullin' her leg a bit about it bein' her first time. Nothin' serious. She laughed a little bit and I laughed a little bit. That's all there be to it."

Smiling, she said, "That's all there was to it?"

"Yep, that's all."

She looked to the left and then to the right. Seeing nobody, she said, "Close the barn door."

"Cadence, yo' son just left here. I don't think we should.

He could come back. Anybody could come in here and catch us."

"They could, but don't forget who the master is around here," Cadence said with a licentious grin. "They all work for me. They all do what I say or else I'll sell them or I'll kill them."

Joshua walked over to the barn door. He looked out to see if anybody was watching them. "Y'all mean I'll kill 'em. Ain't that what y'all mean?"

"That's exactly what I mean," she said, smiling. "You know me so well."

"Yes, I, do, darlin'," Joshua said, closing the barn door. "I'm 'bout tuh git tuh know ya even better in just a few minutes. Git on in that stall over yonder." He followed her into the stall.

She plopped down on the hay and hiked up her dress. "We have to do it quick, okay?"

Chapter 29

"Why wouldn't I think it, Mademoiselle Delacroix?"

They had left Bouvier Hill half an hour ago and as they rode side by side on the road to New Orleans in Lauren's wagon, Guinevere Delacroix was conspicuously quiet. As Lauren drove a team of four horses, Guinevere couldn't help replaying the verbal exchanges between Lauren and her lifelong friend, Cadence. Their conversation would not let her have one moment's peace. The more she thought about it, the more she knew something was really wrong with their friendship, but she couldn't quite put her finger on it.

For thirty-nine years her mind had been thoroughly trained to think the Delacroix family knew what was best for her. For thirty-nine years she believed in the Delacroix family. For thirty-nine years she loved the Delacroix family. For thirty-nine years she worshipped the Delacroix family. For thirty-nine years they were her deity and she trusted the Delacroix family implicitly.

So absolute was her trust that it made her deaf, dumb, and blind to what they had done to her and what they had done to themselves. She had accepted every word they uttered as if they were the words of God himself. Because the brain-washing process had begun from her birth, she never developed the necessary tools of discernment and could not tell fact from fiction. She was therefore blinded by their deceit and willingly followed them into the murky abyss of a false reality that would handicap them both for the foreseeable future.

The brainwashing was twofold. First, it taught certain members of the Delacroix family to view certain blacks as animal-like creatures who needed them for sustenance and shelter. And in return for their graciousness, they began to think their slaves should be grateful for being fed, clothed, and sheltered. After all, they had done them a favor by taking them out of a hedonistic Africa and transplanting them in Christian North America. Walker Tresvant and other Negroes of his ilk were the only exceptions.

Second, it taught Guinevere to view her white "benefactors" as godlike beings who could do no wrong. It was essential that both master and slave adhere to their respective lines of thinking for slavery to continue. If the master ever saw the slave's humanity, he might develop a conscience and set the slave free. If the slave ever saw his master's humanity, he might hate his miserable condition and rebel against his master—maybe even kill him and his family. Therefore the stakes were high and conditioning for both was crucial for the peculiar institution to continue.

Now though, one of those schools of thought was about to be eradicated—permanently. After having one conversation with Lauren, and then listening to another, Guinevere's faith in Cadence and the Delacroix family had been shaken to its core. She was wondering how a girl Lauren's age could make her question lifelong loyalties with just two conversations. She was also wondering if she should be getting paid for taking care of Cadence's children and other "favors" she did free of charge. Lauren obviously thought she was being paid when she offered her a job at the dress shop.

"Lauren?" Guinevere said in question form, like she had something to say, but didn't quite know how to say it.

"Yes, Mademoiselle Delacroix," Lauren said, fully anticipating their conversation. It was all a part of the plan to get her to first question her loyalties to Cadence and her family and then get her to shift them.

Hesitantly, Guinevere said, "Can I ask you a question?"

Lauren looked at her. "Yes."

With childlike curiosity, Guinevere asked, "Why did you think Cadence was paying me?"

"Why wouldn't I think it, Mademoiselle Delacroix?" Lauren said, looking at her. "When Mrs. Bouvier introduced us yesterday, she said you two had grown up together and that you had since purchased your freedom. Free people don't clean people's houses and *mother* their children without legal tender changing hands. They may do it on occasion, but they don't do it on a regular basis."

Lauren was astonished by the way Guinevere stared at her as if freedom and getting paid for services rendered were foreign concepts. She could only think that Guinevere had to have been a slave for a long time. Then it occurred to her that Guinevere was thirty-nine years old. Offering a bewildered stare, Lauren said, "Mademoiselle Delacroix, how long had you been a slave before purchasing your freedom?"

"Since I was born," she said eagerly, like it was something to be proud of.

"And how long have you been free?" Lauren asked, still wearing the same confused expression.

"Just about ten years, I'd say," Guinevere replied. "Since I was about twenty-eight or twenty-nine, I think. I'm not sure. But about ten years."

Lauren stopped her team of horses, looked at her incredulously, and said, "Are you serious, Mademoiselle Delacroix?"

Shaking her head, she continued, "Please tell me you . . . are . . . not . . . serious."

Now Guinevere looked confused. She said, "I guess I'm not following you, Lauren. Help me understand. Why do you think I'm not serious?"

Chapter 30

"A virtual slave? I don't know what you mean."

Lauren snapped the leather reins against the backsides of her team of horses and they resumed their gallop. She wanted to reveal all to the misguided woman who for all intents and purposes wore the same skin as she, was the same gender as she, who had the same freedoms as she, but she couldn't reveal anything because Guinevere was only a shell of a human being. If Guinevere didn't know or couldn't figure out by now that the Delacroix family had taken advantage of her for a decade or so, telling her all the truths that she knew would put both their lives in jeopardy. Once Guinevere knew the truth and understood the ramifications of those truths, Lauren wasn't sure she would be able to keep her mouth shut.

Lauren also wasn't sure Guinevere could adequately continue to play the fool she had previously been long enough to exact a measure of vengeance if she enlightened her. In all likelihood she would scream, as it were, from the housetops about the injustices she'd suffered. She may even tell someone about Cadence's affair with Joshua. If that happened, and Cadence found out about it, she might have them both killed before "real" justice could be served.

Lauren then wondered if Guinevere knew of Cadence's affair with Tristan. She wanted to ask her, but knew not to. She forced herself to focus on the question Guinevere had posed and said, "Well, Mademoiselle Delacroix, you've been free for ten years, but you've never been to New Orleans. In fact you've never even been off the Delacroix plantation until you came to Bouvier Hill. That just doesn't make sense to me. Weren't you ever curious about life away from the plantation?"

"Yes."

Having been born free and being a slave for only three days could never prepare Lauren for the black men and women she would meet who were born in slavery. They had never been free and had grown to accept their miserable condition without ever questioning its validity because it was the only reality they knew (and it continues today).

Lauren said, "But you never left? Never?"

Feeling the need to defend herself and explain the circumstances, she said, "I wanted to, Lauren, I did. But my father wouldn't let me go. He told me it would kill him if I ever left him, because I would never return."

"How did your father feel when you met the men you had children with. Were they Delacroix slaves too?"

Angrily, Guinevere shouted, "I'm not a whore, Lauren!"

Ignoring her anger, she replied, "So all your children are by one man?"

"Yes!" she said, almost shouting.

"Well, where is he? What happened? Did he get sold off or something?"

"No. He's still there."

"I don't get it, Mademoiselle Delacroix. You had children with the man, but you didn't marry him. He's still on the plantation and he doesn't care that you left him? What's going on?"

"I don't want to talk about him anymore, Lauren."

"Why not?"

"I just don't, okay?"

"Well, what about your children? You don't care about them either?"

"My children, all five of them, are doing just fine."

"Well, what are their names? How old are they?"

Smiling now, Guinevere said, "Well, Javier is my only son. He's twenty-four and studying medicine in France. Then there's my oldest girl, Lacey; she's doing pretty good, I think. Got a fine place of her own, I'm told, in a place called Tremé. Her sisters, Madeleine, Yvette, and Chantal live there too."

"The Tremé, huh? Oh, okay. Now I see."

"You see what, Lauren?"

"Mademoiselle Delacroix, I have customers who did the same with their daughters."

"What did I do, Lauren?"

"You sold your girls to wealthy white men and they paid you handsomely for them, didn't they?"

"I wouldn't say I sold them, no."

"Well, what would you call it, Mademoiselle Delacroix? The men have your daughters and they paid you for the right to have relations with them, right?"

Guinevere's eyes welled. A single tear raced down her left cheek. "Lauren, you're being unfair to me. What I did was a traditional thing. It's been going on for years. I didn't start it. I just wanted to give my girls something better than I had myself. I'm a slave. I mean, I was a slave. My children are free and getting the best that life has to offer. Please don't fault me for that, Lauren."

It broke Lauren's heart to see the tear run down Guinevere's cheek. She thought for a second or two and said, "You know, Mademoiselle Delacroix, I don't know whether to fault you or not. I really don't. The way things are done in this land is upside down. But after a while, I guess a person can get used to anything. I guess after a while, when you get used to everything being upside down, it seems normal. So I guess I can't really fault you at all. If what you did made it possible for your children to be free and produce another generation of free people of color, what can I say?"

She wiped the tear from her cheek while saying, "Just be glad for my children. They're free. They escaped slavery and they are prospering."

Lauren wanted to be glad for the sake of the children and the children's children, but she couldn't. She could, however, shift the subject a little. "Most of the girls who come into my shop to buy dresses for the Quadroon Ball are nearly white though. Many of them have blue eyes and everything. I think their fathers are white men. Judging by the way you look, I can only imagine what your daughters look like."

"They're all beautiful girls, yes," Guinevere said, beaming with pride. "Now that I'm going to New Orleans, I plan to see them from time to time."

That's not the answer I wanted to hear, Mademoiselle Delacroix. I want to know if the father of your children is a white man. But I won't ask you because you didn't take the bait. I sure wish you had though. I really want to know. "That's a good idea. Family should stay together."

"Can I ask you another question?"

Lauren frowned.

"What's wrong?" Guinevere asked.

"You won't answer my questions, Mademoiselle Delacroix, but you keep asking me questions. Don't you think you're being unfair?"

"What questions?"

"I asked about the father of your children and your father."

"I've answered your questions, Lauren. I just don't want to talk about my father or the father of my children. You can ask me other questions if you like."

So the father of your child is a white man, huh? "Okay, Mademoiselle Delacroix, fine. What do you want to know?"

"Please be honest with me, okay?

"Okay."

"Do you really think I'm a good enough cook to open an eatery in New Orleans?"

"What I think really doesn't matter much, Mademoiselle Delacroix," Lauren said sincerely. "It's what you think. More important than that, it's what you believe. It's what you believe about yourself that matters most. When people think less of themselves, their behavior pretty much mirrors what they think. When people think highly of themselves, they behave like it. It's difficult to push people around who are comfortable with who they are and where they come from." She remembered a line from Shakespeare's *Hamlet,* having studied with Captain Rutgers on the voyage to the Americas. She thought it appropriate to quote and said, " 'This above all; to thine own self be true.' So no matter how you cut it, it's what you think." She paused for a second or two while Guinevere considered what she'd heard. "So tell me, Mademoiselle Delacroix, what do you think of yourself?"

After a long silence, she replied, "You know, Lauren, I really don't know what I think of myself. No one ever asked me questions like that before. I guess they never cared to know what I thought or how I felt about anything. And since they didn't care to know my thoughts and feelings, I never bother to think deeply enough about what I think."

"May I be honest with you, Mademoiselle Delacroix?"

"Please."

"Based on what you just said, I see why you stayed a virtual slave. You've been free for ten years, but you still think like a slave. That's why the Delacroix family continues to treat you like you're still their property."

"A virtual slave? I don't know what you mean."

"I know you don't, Mademoiselle Delacroix, and *so* do the people who used to own you. It means to exist in essence but not in actual fact. It comes from the medieval Latin word *virtualis*, where we get the word *virtue*. It originated in the fourteenth century."

Chapter 31

"Captain, do you have your Bible with you?"

By the look on Guinevere's face, Lauren could tell that she still didn't understand. That's when she realized she had revealed too much of herself. It was becoming increasingly difficult to pretend to be less intelligent than she was. Fortunately they were now in the French Quarter and she saw Captain Rutgers crossing Bourbon Street. It looked like he was about to go into a tavern. He was wearing a dark suit, white shirt, bowtie, and a black fedora. It occurred to her that she could simply tell Guinevere where she learned Latin and cover her intelligence tracks at the same time. "There's Captain Rutgers over there, Mademoiselle Delacroix. He's the one who told me about Latin words and such."

Guinevere whipped her head to the left, looking for the man who she hoped would read the Garden of Eden story to her. "Where is he?" she said excitedly.

"Captain Rutgers," Lauren called out.

Rutgers stopped and turned around. He smiled when he saw Lauren. Then he made his way over to her wagon. He tipped his hat before saying. "I was planning to come out to Bouvier Hill today. I need to talk to you about something."

"What?" Lauren said.

Rutgers quickly cut his eyes to Guinevere and then back to Lauren and said, "It's a private matter."

"Captain Rutgers, this is Mademoiselle Guinevere Delacroix. Mademoiselle Delacroix, this is Captain Rutgers."

Rutgers took her hand into his and said, "Pleased to make your acquaintance. You're a lovely woman, Mademoiselle Delacroix."

"Thank you, Captain. It's a pleasure meeting you."

"Captain, I'm wondering if what you have to tell me can wait for a little while. I have to put the prince in a tomb today."

Rutgers bowed his head for a second and sniffed. His eyes watered. Then he said, "You don't have to worry about it, Lauren. I've taken care of everything already. They were going to burn him if no one claimed him. So when I took you to Bouvier Hill, I hurried back to the dock and moved him over to Pierre's Funeral Parlor."

Captain Rutgers had captured her and the prince. Even though they were more than cordial, they weren't exactly friends. She was surprised that he had handled the matter for her.

Lauren said, "You've purchased a tomb and everything?"

"Everything except the tomb. I told the undertaker you'd want to make the choice and you'd want to see him before they took him there."

"How much do I owe you, Captain?"

"Nothing, Lauren. I owe you my life, remember?"

"And I owe you mine, remember?"

"I remember that, too," Rutgers said. "Those were perilous times."

"Perhaps you'll let me buy you dinner sometime."

"I'd like that. Perhaps we can have dinner before I set sail for Europe. If not, perhaps when I return. I'll be leaving in a few days, but I really need to speak with you when you finish your business at Pierre's. Can you meet me at the tavern I was headed to before I came over here?"

"Sure, Captain. It'll be a couple hours or so, I suspect."

Guinevere cleared her throat to remind Lauren she had come to New Orleans specifically to meet the captain and to hear her favorite Bible story read.

Lauren looked at Guinevere for a quick second and then at Rutgers. "Where can I find Pierre's Funeral Parlor?"

"Do you know where the cemetery is?"

"Yes. At the corner of Basin and Conti, right?"

"You've probably passed it many times and didn't notice it. It's about a block away, at Conti and Rampart. Do you know where that is?"

"No, but I don't think I'll have any trouble finding it," Lauren said. "Captain, do you have your Bible with you?"

He tapped his left breast pocket twice. "Right here. Why?"

"I'm wondering if you'll do me a big favor and read Mademoiselle Delacroix the Garden of Eden story. She's a little confused on the details and what happened there."

"For you, Lauren . . . sure," Rutgers said. "Let me help you down, Mademoiselle Delacroix."

Chapter 32

"Looking for me?"

Lauren was apprehensive when she stopped her horses in front of Pierre's Funeral Parlor. She was afraid to go in and afraid not to. She wanted to see the prince, but at the same time she didn't. It was bad enough that she was unable to control the images of the prince being shot that continued to flood her mind whenever she thought of him. So she sat there on the bench of her wagon, trying to get the strength necessary to walk into the undertaker's den. She remembered him the way he was, when she saw him the first time in the marketplace in Dahomey. He was so handsome—too handsome, almost pretty. She remembered his curly hair that rode his shoulders, and seeing his brown eyes, which captured her heart and would not let go.

Though it was improper for a maiden to be alone in a public place, her impetuous spirit tempted her to steal away from her sisters. It wasn't her first time breaking the rules. Breaking the rules was becoming a habit that was absolutely thrilling. When her sisters weren't paying attention, which they were apt to do whenever they were in the marketplace, she slipped away and followed him, watching him, desiring him more and more as she dogged his trail. She never expected to have a conversation with him, but she did want to hear his voice. It was an unladylike thing to do as a matter of etiquette, she knew, but the rebel in her relished the idea of breaking protocol.

Besides, she just wanted to know if his voice was fitting for the god he appeared to be. What was so wrong with that, she wondered. As far as she was concerned her mother and father had too many rules. In fact, the customs for females in Dahomey were far too stringent. She wanted to enjoy what little freedom she had left before she was forced to marry the man her father had chosen for her. She thought she was being so clever, so surreptitious, following the god who had made her heart flutter as he moved from merchant to merchant, totally unaware that he had spotted her long ago. When he looked in her direction, she ducked behind a barrel of apples. By the time she looked again, the prince had disappeared. It was as if he had cloaked himself in an invisible shroud. She couldn't believe she had lost him, the man of her dreams, without even saying hello.

She looked to the left and to the right, hoping to see his black cape flapping in the breeze behind him, which easily stood out among all the pastel colors in the marketplace. She spotted her sisters. They were frantically looking for her. She could tell they were furious with her for leaving them without saying where she was going and when she would return—not that they would agree to let her leave alone. If something happened to their youngest sister, Ibo Atikah Mustafa, they would all have to answer to their mother first and then their father. She watched them, laughing within, knowing they were all blaming each other for not paying attention to the youngest of seven daughters—the daughter who was engaged to marry Prince Adesola—heir to the throne. She did not know at the time that the man she was following was his brother from another mother.

"Looking for me?" the prince said and bit into his apple.

Chapter 33

"Please . . . I'd like to see the prince."

Amir Bashir Jibril had glimpsed her a while ago, but he wasn't sure she was following him. It could have been a coincidence. He wanted to find out for sure; more important than that, he wanted to see more of her. He wanted to see if she was attractive, what kind of figure she had, and if she was a nice girl from a nice family. He had been standing behind her, watching her looking for him. For a minute or so, he watched her watching several women who were in some sort of uproar about something.

Hearing a male voice behind her startled her. She turned around and saw the man she had been following. When their eyes locked, her knees weakened, but her pride held her up. Unable to keep from smiling, almost singing, she said, "It's not nice to sneak up on people, whoever you are."

He found her more than attractive, more than pretty. She was alarmingly beautiful and apparently daring; a combination that drew him to her instantly. For a while time stood still for them both. They stared mindlessly into each other's eyes, and probably would have continued their wanton gaze indefinitely, but a merchant moving a crate bumped into the prince unintentionally and woke them both up. "I am Amir Bashir Jibril, son of the king, captain of the royal infantry."

"May I help you, young lady?" a man Lauren had never seen before said, waking her, reminding her she was not in Dahomey, but in New Orleans.

She wished he hadn't spoken to her. Her thoughts about the day she and the prince met were so real; it was like she was there, back home again. Now though, reality was settling in. She wasn't home again. She was sitting on a wagon in a strange land, about to see the man she was just dreaming about. Only he was dead and would be for a very long time.

"Huh," she said, focusing on the man. His accent was French and thick. He reminded her of Guinevere, who was an octoroon. His skin was very light, acceptably white to any Caucasian who didn't know he was of the Negroid strain. She assumed he had one-eighth black blood too, which, according to the one drop rule, made him black. His hair was dark and naturally straight. He was short in stature, about five feet three inches tall. He wore a thick salt-and-pepper moustache and goatee that matched his gray suit with thin pinstripes perfectly.

"I'm Pierre St. John, the owner of the establishment you stopped in front of. Don't tell me. Let me guess. You're Lauren Renee Bouvier, right?"

Somewhat surprised that he knew her name, she frowned involuntarily and said, "How did you know my name?"

"Captain Rutgers was here yesterday evening and he told me all about you, the prince, and how he met his unfortunate end. I'm terribly sorry for your loss."

"Thank you, Monsieur St. John," Lauren said. "I'm wondering if I can see Prince Amir now."

He extended his right hand. "Sure. May I help you down?"

"No, thank you, Monsieur St. John," she said, and stepped down from the wagon. "Please . . . I'd like to see the prince."

"Sure, sure, Mademoiselle Bouvier," Pierre said as they walked to the entrance.

Chapter 34

"If you don't give him back to me, I'm afraid of what I might do."

Pierre St. John held the door open for Lauren and she entered the funeral parlor. "If you'll follow me please," he said, leading the way. "Captain Rutgers tells me you arrived on his ship and that you've been quite the lucky one." Lauren remained quiet. "He tells me our mutual friend, Beaumont Bouvier, purchased you six months ago."

Again, Lauren didn't respond. She just wanted to see Amir, say her final good-bye, and be on her way. Seeing the familiar stranger who regularly greeted newly arriving ships at the docks murder Amir had been a trying experience. She wasn't interested in small talk.

"And that you recently came into quite a fortune for a girl of seventeen years. Normally, I would have charged more for my services. You won't find a better mortician in the city, I assure you." Lauren was so deep in thought that Pierre's words sounded like a quiet buzz in her ear. "Anyway, since I knew your former owner and Captain Rutgers, I didn't charge him the full price. Rest assured I won't charge you the full price for the tomb and delivering the body to it." He ushered her through the parlor and downstairs where he kept the remains of the dead.

As she descended the stairs, a scent she couldn't identify filled her nasal passages. She looked at Pierre St. John. He was breathing normally as if his nose could somehow filter out the stench that was threatening to asphyxiate her. She opened her purse and pulled out a handkerchief scented with her favorite perfume from the House of Creed. She could breathe again. As they reached the basement landing, she saw the prince lying on a wooden table. She walked over to him, wanting to see if the mortician was able to hide the hole in his head.

Pleased with his work, Pierre St. John said, "As you can see, Mademoiselle Bouvier, we do good work here. You cannot tell he was even shot."

Lauren thought he was going to talk the entire time she viewed Amir's remains. She wanted him to leave, but she did not want to be rude. Quietly, she said, "Monsieur St. John, could I please have a few minutes alone with him?"

"Why, yes, of course. I'm so sorry for the intrusion. I will be at the top of the stairs. Do take your time."

Lauren waited until he climbed the stairs. Then she reached out and touched the prince's hand. Tears sped down her cheeks unceasingly. She kept her hand on his remains as she walked around the table, looking at him from every possible angle, touching him in various places, wanting to get the feel of him. But he didn't feel like himself; he didn't feel alive. He was stiff and unyielding. She closed her eyes for a moment and drifted on the sea of her mind. Touching him somehow transported her back to Dahomey again. Suddenly she was back on her farm, at the end of her father's property. Amir had been waiting for her with two Arabian horses that he had hoped would secure their flight to Sierra Leone.

She opened her eyes and looked at him again, remembering his courage, his defiance, and his indomitable spirit. He had been a warrior and he deserved to wear his uniform to his final resting place. Instead of the uniform, Amir was wearing a suit much like that of Pierre St. John's. It looked good on him. While he looked like himself, he was pale in appearance. His eyes were closed. She so wanted to see them. In addition to his rugged good looks, it was his eyes that drew her to him when they met in the marketplace. She looked toward the staircase. She didn't see Pierre. With both her hands, she lifted his lids and looked into his big beautiful eyes. The light of life was no longer in them. She could see him but he couldn't see her, feel her, touch her, want her, and need her as she did him.

"I'm terribly sorry for disturbing you, Mademoiselle Bouvier, but will you be much longer?"

A scowl came forth. How dare he disturb her while she was with the only man she had ever loved. She took a deep breath and blew it out subtly. Pierre had no idea how he exasperated her with his insincere small talk and his need to interrupt her in her time of bereavement. She didn't let on though. Calmly, she called out, "A little while longer if that's okay, Monsieur St. John."

"It's quite all right. I have another customer or two, it appears. I will attend to them and then I will return to you, okay?"

"Thank you, Monsieur St. John. I shall not tarry much longer."

She could hear his footsteps going away from the top of the stairs. Being totally alone with what was once her prince, she felt the anguish of his sudden and unexpected departure rushing up from the pit of her stomach, into her heart, and then out her mouth. She could be vulnerable now. No one was around to see her mourn. And mourn she did.

Softly, so as not to be heard by anyone within earshot, she said, "Oh, my darling, Amir. My sweet . . . sweet . . . Amir. Oh, how I loved you so." There seemed to be no end of the tears making their way down her face. "Oh, my darling. How did this happen to you? How did this happen to us? Was what we did so wrong that God in heaven would punish us this severely? You're dead and me . . . I'm stuck in a foreign land I dare not leave. Surely God is a God of mercy. Why then? Why did he take you from me? I have nothing now . . . nothing but my hatred for the people who did this to me—to us.

"Oh my God, please, please wake him up. Let me feel the warmth of his touch once more. Just once more." She fell to her knees and wept on his arm. "God if you wake him up, I'll forgive those who wronged me and others. I'll leave them to your justice. Only wake the prince up as you did Lazarus. Lazarus was dead for four days. The prince has only been dead for one day. Surly this is a small thing for the creator of all things. Give me back my Amir. If you don't give him back to me, I'm afraid of what I might do."

She opened her eyes, to see if her petition had been answered. It hadn't. Amir was just as dead when she lifted her head as he was since the bullet entered his cranium. Realizing God would provide no miracle, she wept bitterly. When she heard Pierre St. John's footsteps returning to the top of the stairs, she forced herself to cry no more. She wiped her eyes, looked at her prince one last time and said, "Monsieur St. John?"

Pierre quickly descended the stairs and said, "Yes, Mademoiselle Bouvier. I take it you have finished viewing the remains of the deceased?"

Still looking at her prince, shaking her head, Lauren exhaled and said, "I am finished, yes. Let us take him to the City of the Dead."

Chapter 35

"But that can't be, Captain Rutgers."

It had been one of the happiest days of Guinevere Dela-croix's life. She was finally in the city that would one day be dubbed "The Big Easy" for the very first time. She had found it incredibly difficult to concentrate on any one thing as she and Captain Rutgers crossed Bourbon Street, heading for the tavern. It was nearly impossible to keep her head from swiveling from left to right, seeing all the people dressed in fancy clothes. The thing that enraptured her more than anything else was seeing all the beautiful black women dressed in fine clothes and wearing what looked like new expensive shoes. Their tignons were multicolored and speckled with luxurious jewels.

It was truly a sight. Black men wore fancy suits and ties, much like those that Master Delacroix and other rich white men wore. What fascinated her was the way they walked. It was a strut. They walked with a purpose, like they had something to do, someplace to be. None of them walked around with their heads down. And they all wore big, wonderful smiles—that's the way Guinevere saw them anyway. Those blacks, both light-skinned and dark-skinned, had something she didn't know existed for people of her hue—pride. Yet what she had seen for only a few moments before entering the tavern had her beaming with it.

But that was almost two hours ago. Now the face she wore was one of disappointment and humiliation. Captain Rutgers was hungry, and he had asked Guinevere if she could wait until after he had something to eat before he read the first three chapters of the book of Genesis. She eagerly agreed. She had waited three decades to hear the story. Another thirty or forty minutes wasn't going to make a difference. She had asked him if it was okay to walk around the streets while he ate. He told her she was free to do whatever she pleased. When she returned, she got the shock of her life.

"Hold on, Captain," Guinevere said. "Are you sure you're reading that right?"

"I've read the story a thousand times if I've read it once," Rutgers said. "My parents were Evangelists. This is the true account of the story. Whoever told you that God created woman first and took her rib and made a man lied to you, Mademoiselle Delacroix."

"But that can't be, Captain Rutgers," Guinevere said. "The Delacroix family wouldn't lie to me all my life, would they?"

"Apparently they did," he said and took a swallow of his brandy. "Why they would lie to you about something like that is a mystery to me. They've probably brought a curse on themselves for doing so, to be honest with you."

Chapter 36

Truth's Crystallization

Guinevere was completely befuddled by what she had heard Captain Rutgers read. She sat there shaking her head, trying to make sense of the conflicting stories, which were one hundred and eighty degrees out of phase. Some of the story was exactly as she was told. Other parts were exactly the opposite of what she had been told. It was hard to wrap her mind around a story she thought she knew like the back of her hand. Now she wasn't so sure, but she was reluctant to accept the version he read to her. "Read it again, please, Captain Rutgers."

A little annoyed, Rutgers said, "I've read the same story to you ten times now. I don't see that reading it an eleventh time is going to make one bit of difference. The story will be exactly the same."

She scratched her head, still mystified. "So you're telling me the menfolk are supposed to be in charge of the earth and that God is not a woman like they told me?"

"That's what it says, Mademoiselle Delacroix."

"Hmpf! I wonder what else they lied about," she said, shaking her head. "Can I ask you a question, Captain?"

"Yes, you may, but not about this story." His anger manifested more with each word. She had seriously gotten on his nerves because he didn't understand the shock of hearing the truth. It was simple to him because he read the story when he was a child as it was written. Guinevere, on the other hand, was not afforded the luxury of reading anything for herself. "Either believe what it says or don't. I'm not trying to convince you of the Bible's authenticity. But please, *please*, don't ask me to read it again. I like Lauren and I don't mind doing her a favor and all, but I no longer have the patience to keep answering the same questions about the same story that I've read to you word for word ten times now! I don't, Mademoiselle Delacroix!"

When Guinevere saw Rutgers's frustration, she realized she had been a burden. The last thing she wanted to do was anger someone who was doing her a favor. "I'm sorry, Captain. I really didn't know I was being such a bother. That was not my intention. If you only knew how many times I've heard the story the way I told it to you. And then for you to read me something altogether different? That was just so hard to swallow, you know?"

"I guess I can understand your confusion, Mademoiselle Delacroix," Rutgers said, finally showing some compassion, "And again, I don't know why they would lie to you about it. And I'll answer whatever questions you may have, okay?"

"Okay, thanks so much. Now, tell me something. Do people of color get paid when they work for whites in New Orleans?"

Frowning, he said, "Yes, of course they do. Why do you ask?"

"Because I work for the Delacroix family still and the pay is still the same. Nothing. I've got a mind to quit as soon as we return to Bouvier Hill."

"There's a better way to handle the situation, Mademoiselle Delacroix. You don't have to quit your job if you don't want to. Do you mind working for them still?"

She thought for a moment. "I guess I don't, Captain Rutgers. But I don't know. I feel taken advantage of, you know?"

"I understand. No one wants to feel that way when you're doing someone a favor. The trouble with people is they love taking advantage of others if they can get away with it. They know what they're doing is wrong, but they can usually justify what they do. If you don't mind working at Bouvier Manor, why not negotiate with Cadence?"

"Negotiate?" Guinevere questioned, having a limited vocabulary. "I have no idea what that means."

"It means to bargain. Make a deal with her. She needs you to do something for her and you need her to do something for you. Tell her your concerns and that you want to be adequately compensated."

Frowning again, Guinevere said, "I want to be what?"

"You want to be paid for services rendered. There's nothing wrong with wanting to be paid. You're a free woman now, right? Free women of color get paid for their work in New Orleans. So do the men."

"Do they now?" Guinevere said, smiling. "How much should I get for all the cooking and all the cleaning I do? Besides that, I take care of her children too."

"I don't really know, Mademoiselle Delacroix. That's why you should discuss your concerns with her and then the two of you can come up with a fair amount. Let me give you a bit of advice. Wait until she makes an offer and no matter what she offers you, ask for more. If she really wants you to work for her, she'll give it to you."

Guinevere thought for a few seconds before saying, "If we can't come to an agreement, I don't have to work for her anymore, right? I bought my freedom about ten years ago. So if she doesn't pay me, I can leave, right?"

A pang of guilt shook Rutgers to the center of his being. The woman sitting across the table from him, being perfectly free to do as she pleased, within the bounds of the law, didn't understand her freedom. He knew he and men like him were responsible for her wretched condition. Rutgers's enlightenment process began on the *Windward* when Lauren saved his life. It continued when he recognized her keen acumen. It continued further when he became her teacher and mentor. It crystallized when Amir told him on the voyage from Santo Domingo that he had forgiven him for what he had done. And now his conscience was moved yet again.

He had known from childhood that there was a calling on his life. The calling wasn't just to preach the gospel like his mother and father and brother were doing, but rather to right the wrongs of the peculiar institution called American slavery. "The gospel and freedom are not mutually exclusive," his father had preached too many times to forget. Now he understood. Just as Paul the Apostle had been a hindrance to the gospel by persecuting those spreading it; Rutgers realized he had been a hindrance to freedom by taking it away from those who had it. He needed no further evidence than the woman he was talking to.

Chapter 37

Slavery's Hypocrisy

Lauren had just left the City of the Dead where she had Amir's remains placed in an exceptionally large mausoleum that was first purchased by Sebastian Beauregard. There was no way for Lauren to know she would purchase a crypt that was supposed to be owned by the family of her future white relatives. Had she been able to look into the future, the story that Pierre St. John told her about Sebastian would have been all the more fascinating. Upon learning that Pierre was a black man who could pass for white, Sebastian reneged on the deal. He had paid half up front, but refused to pay the remaining sum. Sebastian had said, "No matter what you look like, *you*, sir, are a nigger. I don't do business with niggers." Yet Sebastian was a distinguished member of the plaçage fraternity, having not one, but two kept black women in the Tremé that were far more dusky than Pierre.

The women were not only sisters, but they were a set of identical twins. Nearly twenty years earlier, both women were of age and had attended the Quadroon Ball with their Creole mother, seeking a white man of means to provide for them. Several French and Spanish men had made impressive pitches to their mother, but when Sebastian saw how stunning they were and that they were only sixteen years old, he was so smitten with them that he offered to take them both.

Being a godly woman, the mother of the twins immediately refused. She had told him it was an abomination to have both daughters. Upon hearing her reason for rejecting his initial offer, refusing to be denied what he thought would be delicious nectar all his own, he then upped the ante and offered her an obscene sum of legal tender, which the godly woman accepted without further contemplation or religious repartee. The identical twins were neighbors and were often pregnant at the same time. Altogether, Sebastian Beauregard sired ten children between them. He loved them all and wanted to keep them together even in death, which was why the mausoleum was exceptionally large.

Pierre had practically given the crypt to Lauren as a favor to Captain Rutgers and in memory of his friend, Beaumont Bouvier, for less than the remaining bill. The mausoleum could easily fit Sebastian Beauregard's two women and ten children in it. When Pierre showed the tomb to Lauren, she knew she had found the right place for the prince. She also knew that one day she and her children would join Amir in that place.

On her way back to the tavern to pick up Guinevere, Lauren saw a white woman standing in front of her Bouvier House of Fine Dresses & Accoutrements shop. She was expensively clad and carrying an umbrella to keep the sun from scorching her delicate white skin. The woman's head deliberately snaked from side to side. It looked as if she was trying to see if someone was in the store. As Lauren's wagon continued down the street toward her shop, she was trying to remember if she had any standing orders due. She was planning to reopen the shop in a few days. She needed at least a day or two, perhaps more, to regain her equilibrium. The death of Amir had taken an incalculable toll on her. Having put him in his final resting place, she knew he would always be near. She would draw upon his strength whenever she needed to. She now knew neither of them would ever see Africa again.

She stopped the wagon in front of her store and said, "May I help you, Mademoiselle? I'm not planning to open the shop for several more days. There's been a death in the family. You understand, I'm sure." The woman turned around and looked at Lauren. She recognized her immediately. It was Christine Bouvier—Tristan's wife.

Chapter 38

"Lauren, trust me. I mean you no harm at all."

Lauren said, "Oh, hello, Mrs. Bouvier. I didn't know it was you. Is there something I can do for you? Something you need in the shop? Some perfume perhaps?"

"Hello, Lauren," Christine said. "I'm truly sorry about what happened to your friend yesterday."

"Thank you, Mrs. Bouvier," Lauren said, thinking, *the story must have spread like wildfire after Captain Rutgers took me back to Bouvier Hill.* "I just left the City of the Dead."

"To tell you the truth, I didn't expect the shop to be open today, but I did hope to see you in the city," Christine said. She paused a short moment, gathering her thoughts, attempting to think of a delicate way to tell Lauren why she had hoped to see her in the city. "I'm wondering if I could speak to you in private about a matter that took place at Bouvier Manor six months ago."

Suddenly afraid that she might be in danger, Lauren frowned and said, "May I ask why, Mrs. Bouvier? I didn't have anything to do with Monsieur Bouvier's murder. Nothing at all."

Christine looked to the left and then to the right to see if any of the many citizens walking past them heard what Lauren had said. No one stopped walking or looked at them strangely. She assumed Lauren's comment about Beaumont's murder wasn't overheard. "Could we please talk in private? This is a very delicate matter."

Still hesitant, Lauren said, "Mrs. Bouvier, whites kill niggers all the time . . . even if they did nothing at all. If you don't mind, I'd really rather not speak with you in private."

Christine thought it ridiculous that Lauren believed she would kill her. It was almost funny, and she would have laughed, but she could tell Lauren was afraid of what might happen to her if they were alone. "Lauren, please listen to me . . . I'm not here to kill you, but I do need to speak to you. Can we go into your store?"

"Do you mind if I get Captain Rutgers? I trust him. He's just down the street in the tavern. Mademoiselle Delacroix is there with him."

A few New Orleanians were approaching them again. Christine waited until they passed and then said, "Lauren, trust me. I mean you no harm at all." She looked her in the eyes while she spoke. "Now . . . open the shop and go to the office and let me in the back door in five minutes."

Chapter 39

The Secret Is No Secret

Christine Bouvier didn't wait for Lauren's response to her request for a conversation in private. She didn't want to keep going back and forth with her on the street where someone could hear their personal exchange. Someone might see her there. What she was planning had to be shrouded in secrecy. Rather than continuing the ineffective urging, she walked off like she was going to a shop down the street. If someone was watching her, they would think the two women had a brief conversation, but that's all.

Lauren watched Christine to see which way she was going to go. She saw her walk a block down Bourbon Street and disappear in the crowd. Lauren thought it was too dangerous to meet her in private. She didn't want to end up dead. As far as she was concerned, white women plotted to kill niggers, and she had too much to live for now.

Despite Amir's death, she was going to find a man, get married, and have children. She needed her offspring to tell the fantastic tale of her life. She was about to head over to the tavern and meet with Captain Rutgers, but a voice inside her head told her to go in the store and hear what Christine had to say. After a few moments of indecision, she stepped down from the wagon, walked up to the door, and opened it. She locked it behind her and made her way through the store and to the back office. A minute or two later, Christine arrived. Lauren opened the door for her.

Christine said, "Thanks for meeting me, Lauren. I know how afraid you are, and your fear is justified, given what Cadence did to Aubrey and the housemen."

Lauren ignored the reference to Cadence having Aubrey and the others murdered. She didn't want Christine to be able to say she had said anything at all about Cadence. She was what whites called a nigger. Cadence was white and Christine was her sister-in-law no matter who she killed. From what she'd seen so far in New Orleans, niggers could be killed for any reason; suspicion alone was good enough reason to kill a nigger. Besides that, she was still living in Cadence's house.

Lauren said, "I'm glad you understand why I didn't want to meet you in private."

"I do," Christine said nervously. "Believe me, I do."

Lauren sat down and offered Christine a chair. "So what did you want to talk to me about?"

"Six months ago, we sat in Julian Bailey's office and he read a very revealing letter from my brother-in-law, Beaumont Bouvier. You remember that, don't you, Lauren?"

"Yes, Mrs. Bouvier, I remember."

"So then you remember that Beaumont had revealed that Tristan and Cadence were having an affair?"

"An affair?"

"Yes, an affair. They were having unlawful relations." She waited for Lauren to acknowledge that she understood, but she didn't. "Well, anyway, it took a few weeks to get the courage to question him about the letter's authenticity. I wanted to believe my husband, and I tried to believe that he would never do anything like that. Not to his brother's wife, you understand. Anybody that would do something that low is a despicable person, don't you think, Lauren?"

Her words sliced into Lauren's heart because she was guilty of the same crime. While she knew what she had done was wrong, she understood how a person could make terrible choices because the temptation was so great. And in her case, the consequences of her affair, though it was never consummated, did land her on the deck of a Dutch ship. "Mrs. Bouvier, it's not my place to say anything about what white people do to each other. If you decide to beat each other to death and slice off one another's privates and stick them in each other's mouths, I have nothing to say about it. Besides . . . I still live in her house. It would not be right to speak against her."

Christine locked eyes with Lauren and said, "I understand, but I think Cadence may have killed Beaumont."

Chapter 40

"But Cadence is the problem."

Christine Bouvier studied Lauren to see her reaction. She realized that Lauren may not ever admit to what she knew, but her unfiltered reaction would tell the tale, which was the main reason she wanted to speak with her in private. Lauren just sat there like this was her first time hearing the story. Christine continued. "It took six months, but I finally got Tristan to tell me the truth last night. For some reason, he got terribly drunk and became talkative. He confessed to everything Beaumont had written in his letter to us. He admitted that he and Cadence had been seeing each other for nearly twenty years. It all begin right here in this office." Again she paused to see Lauren's reaction, but again, Lauren gave no indication of knowing anything. "Tristan told me all four of her children are his."

Lauren exhaled and said, "Mrs. Bouvier, may I ask why you're telling me, of all people, this? Shouldn't you be talking to Mrs. Bouvier?"

Christine leaned forward and with sincerity said, "Under ordinary circumstances, I would, but we're talking about murder and an awful lot of money."

Without thinking, Lauren said, "But the letter said that Tristan wasn't to receive anything from Bouvier Hill. In fact, it said that if it was ever found out that your husband was not Monsieur Bouvier's blood brother, he was to be cut off without any support, but the children he had with Monsieur Bouvier's wife would be taken care of."

Christine's eyebrows raised, surprised that she remembered the letter in such detail. "You are to be commended, Lauren. You have an excellent memory. Nevertheless, we're talking about incest and other issues. Do you understand that young Beaumont and Brigitte had been seeing each other?"

"Yes, and he got her with child and she was sent somewhere far away and nobody knows where, right?"

Christine took a deep breath and rested her back against the chair. She felt like the wind had been knocked out of her when Lauren acknowledged a truth that she still couldn't wrap her mind around. The idea that so many people knew about her daughter's pregnancy and subsequent abortion was unsettling and humiliating. They were religious people—Christians who believed in the sanctity of life, yet abandoned that belief when their own daughter was found with child by her blood brother. She exhaled softly and said, "That's right. We had to send her to a convent in Italy to be sure that those two never get . . . how shall I say . . . involved again."

Thank you, Mrs. Bouvier. I'll be sure to let young Beaumont know where she is when I get back to Bouvier Manor. Maybe he'll go to Italy instead of Cambridge and make some more inbred children that they won't be able to kill. Either way, in another day, he'll be out of New Orleans and away from me. "Again, Mrs. Bouvier, I'm left wondering why you're telling me this. Your suspicion of murder is something you should be discussing with Lieutenant Avery or someone from the garrison, shouldn't you?"

"I suppose I could discuss it with the lieutenant . . . but . . .

this is a family matter. More specifically, this is a Bouvier matter. And you're a Bouvier too, Lauren. Beaumont said you can never change your name or leave New Orleans, right?"

"Yes, but . . ."

"No buts. You're a Bouvier and we have to resolve this thing on our own."

"Which is why I think *you* should be talking to *your* sister-in-law. As you just said, it is a family matter. Perhaps you would feel more comfortable having the conversation in the presence of Lieutenant Avery, Mrs. Bouvier."

"But Cadence is the problem. If she killed Beaumont, how can I talk to her about it? I can't, can I? It's not like she's going to say she murdered Beaumont, particularly if I have Lieutenant Avery with me. If she killed Beaumont, she'll stop at nothing to keep it a secret, don't you think?"

"And Louis."

"Yes, and Louis."

"And Aubrey."

"Yes, and Aubrey."

"And all the housemen."

"Yes, and all the housemen. And she got rich doing so, didn't she? And so did you, didn't you?"

Chapter 41

"If Lieutenant Avery knew
what I know . . ."

Lauren said, "Wait a minute, Mrs. Bouvier. What are you saying? Are you saying I had something to do with all that killing?"

"Well . . . no, but . . . what would the lieutenant believe if he found out that you knew who actually killed Beaumont and Louis in his bedroom that night?"

Lauren kept her mouth shut tight and waited to see where she was going with this new scenario. She could tell that Christine was desperate. She remembered that desperate people were capable of anything when they felt cornered. Aubrey, when he was trapped and had no other recourse, had accused her of killing Beaumont and Louis. She thought that Christine was capable of the same thing if she were desperate enough.

"Come on, Lauren, we both know Aubrey and none of the housemen did the deed, don't we? And we know they didn't do it because they were all sodomites, weren't they? All the housemen were Beaumont's lovers, weren't they? Come on, now. I know you know something."

Lauren remained quiet.

With new confidence, Christine leaned forward again and said, "Lauren, I have to tell you . . . your silence is speaking rather loudly. The smart thing to do would have been to deny everything. But you didn't do that, did you? For the last six months, Tristan had been denying everything in Beaumont's final letter to us. Well . . . he made the mistake of getting drunk last night and I got him to confess it all. Cadence had wanted him to kill Beaumont, but he refused. He hated his brother, but not enough to kill him. He told her as much and she found someone else, didn't she?"

"Mrs. Bouvier, I have no idea what you're talking about."

Christine was in heaven now, savoring it all like it was a deliciously decadent meal that would put five pounds on each of her hips. "Oh, you have really messed up now, Lauren. You can't say you don't know anything after I tell you that's what you should have said. Saying it now tells me you know a whole lot more than you're letting on. Now . . . I have to believe that it was one of the slaves who killed Beaumont and Louis, right?"

Lauren fell silent again. But she was visibly shaken now.

Smiling broadly now and loving how the interrogation was proceeding, Christine said, "You just made another really big mistake, Lauren. You can't start talking and then suddenly be silent again. All of this tells me I'm right or on the right track, which means you probably know the whole story, don't you? You're such a beautiful girl that the lieutenant didn't bother asking you really tough questions, did he? Besides, he didn't know what I know, did he? He didn't know that Cadence had asked Tristan to kill Beaumont, did he? And you didn't know it either, did you? If Lieutenant Avery knew what I know, he would have questioned Cadence and *you* much more stringently. So who was it, Lauren? Who killed Beaumont and Louis?"

Chapter 42

"What else haven't you told me?"

For the first time in a while, Lauren had lost her confidence. She was in trouble. Christine had figured it all out with the help of her drunken husband. She knew that Christine could get Lieutenant Avery and bring him out to Bouvier Hill. He could ask the same tough questions Christine had just asked and he wouldn't accept her silence. He would force her to tell all or face a firing squad with no blindfold. And if that happened before she had children, who would ever remember Ibo Atikah Mustafa and Prince Amir? If questioned, Cadence and Joshua wouldn't be any help. They would probably say she had somehow killed Beaumont and Louis, and even though Lieutenant Avery had already debunked that theory as nonsensical, she was still a nigger and for that reason, her fate would be instantly sealed. Nevertheless, she offered an almost inaudible, "I don't know, Mrs. Bouvier."

"Its okay, Lauren. Really . . . it is," Christine said, enjoying the question and answer session, but also, feeling conflicted that she put an innocent girl in the middle of her rivalry with her sister-in-law. She also felt bad for approaching Lauren the day after Amir was killed, but she knew, or at least believed Lauren would be shaken by the recent tragedy, making her vulnerable. "I know you're scared, and that's okay too. So take a really deep breath and relax. We're going to get to the bottom of this thing today. Now . . . I think it had to be one of the slaves close to her. Maybe it was her driver. What's his name?"

A visual of Joshua materialized in Lauren's mind, but she wouldn't dare let his name slip out of her mouth. "Her driver's name is Dupre." She was hoping that Christine would accept that answer. If she questioned him, he would of course deny any involvement in the murders and hopefully he'd have an alibi to confirm his whereabouts. With Cadence's denials, the whole thing would go away. But she soon learned that wasn't going to happen when Christine asked her next question.

"Was he the one who drove you two to Julian Bailey's office the day he read Beaumont's letter to us?"

Lauren bowed her head. Each succeeding question was more penetrating than is predecessor, and threatened to put her right in the middle of a war she wasn't manipulating, a war she couldn't control, a war that if not properly managed would spiral out of control. She shook her head and said, "No."

Christine's heart was pumping hard and fast now. She had Lauren off balance and reeling. If she pushed hard enough, she believed she could get it all out of her. She believed the former slave sitting before her was the key to dethroning Cadence and wrecking her life—permanently. Anticipating her response, Christine leaned forward a bit and said, "Who was the driver that day?"

"That day, Mrs. Bouvier?" Lauren said, desperately trying to stay out of white folks' business.

"Yes, that day. I remember seeing him. He was a really big buck of a man. He looked big enough to handle two men at the same time. For all I know, he's handling Cadence in the bedroom now too, because Tristan told me that after nearly twenty years, she's thrown him over. She told him it was because he wouldn't kill his brother. But I'm a woman, and I think Cadence probably threw him over because she had another man to take his place. I would have thought it was some lowdown white man who wanted Beaumont's money, but I'd be willing to bet she hasn't had any white men out to Bouvier Hill, has she?"

Looking at the floor exclusively now, Lauren said, "No, she hasn't."

"That means then that she's probably having relations with one of the slaves. I'm betting it's the slave that drove you two that day. It's not altogether unheard of. White women from time to time get involved with their slave bucks or a rich black with class and intelligence like Walker Tresvant. So tell me . . . what was the name of the slave who drove you that day?"

Lauren exhaled hard. She had tried so hard to stay out of it and in so doing, stay alive. She needed to live and reproduce. But staying out of it was no longer an option. The whole sordid affair was over now. Christine, with the help of Beaumont's letter, had figured it out. Defeated, she said, "His name is Joshua."

"A few minutes ago, you said her driver's name was Dupre. Are you certain the slave who drove you to Julian Bailey's office was Joshua?"

"I'm sure. Dupre drives for me now, but he used to drive for her."

"Being a carriage driver is a coveted job at my family's plantation. I assume it was a coveted job at Bouvier Hill as well. Did Dupre do something to lose his job?"

"I don't know, but I really don't think he did. But then, I was only there one day before the murders. I guess it's possible he did something before I arrived."

"Hmm, I see. So when did Joshua become Cadence's driver?"

"The day after Monsieur Bouvier was murdered."

"Uh-huh. So . . . what else do you know? What else haven't you told me? Is Cadence bedding Joshua?"

Lauren answered the question with cool silence and looked away.

Chapter 43

"You're right, Lauren! You're so right!"

Christine laughed hard and from her belly when she saw Lauren look away. She knew the answer was yes, but Lauren couldn't or wouldn't acknowledge it verbally. This was just too good, Christine thought. She had gone to Lauren, hoping that the death of her fiancé would have her in a vulnerable state of mind. She had no idea she was going to unearth so much information so quickly. A number of questions came to mind and she began firing them immediately. "So she *is* bedding him, huh? How do you know for sure? Have you seen them together? Have you heard them? The children were in Tallahassee for a while. Joshua could have been slipping into the mansion at night and then into her." She was laughing again.

"Mrs. Bouvier, if you know all of this already, why did you come to me? Why did you get me all mixed up in white folks' business. They'll kill me and you if you're not careful."

Sweetly satisfied that her theory proved to be authentic, a wide grin emerged before she said, "I just needed to get it all confirmed."

Shaking her head as she tried to hide her anger, Lauren

said, "Forgive me for saying so, Mrs. Bouvier, but now *you're* not being honest."

Puzzled, Christine's grin disappeared before she said, "What do you mean, Lauren?"

"You said this was a family thing; a Bouvier family thing or something like that, right?"

"Yes, I said that and I meant it. What are you saying?"

Lauren raised her eyebrows and said, "The truth, Mrs. Bouvier?"

"Yes, the truth," Christine replied, unsure of what Lauren was going to say, but curious nonetheless.

"Mrs. Bouvier, maybe you haven't figured it all out, I really don't know, but based on everything you've said so far, I think you already know the truth, but you don't want to face it."

"No, I don't," Christine said, and leaned back in her chair. She crossed her leg and rocked it back and forth, trying to appear calm, but her heart was pounding like she had just run a quarter of a mile. "That's why I came here. I came here to find out the truth."

Without realizing it, Lauren rolled her eyes and said, "Yet you knew so much before I answered any of your questions. I'm afraid that if you heard the truth you appear to be denying, who knows what you'll do to me."

Christine put her hand over her heart and said, "I swear I won't do anything to you, Lauren. Now . . . tell me . . . what are you talking about?"

With renewed confidence, Lauren leaned forward, looked Christine in the eyes and said, "Well, it occurs to me that this isn't about family at all. I'm a woman too, and I think this is about Mrs. Bouvier stealing your husband and making babies with him and then passing them off as Monsieur Bouvier's children." Lauren studied Christine as she spoke, looking for signs that would confirm her premise. "When you found out the truth six months ago, that had to hurt something awful, right? Probably the worst pain you've ever felt in your life, right?" Christine didn't respond, but she lowered her eyes to the floor. "And then to find out that this had been going on for . . . let's see . . . young Beaumont is sixteen . . . so it's been going on for sixteen years right under your nose, right here in this office."

Christine looked at Lauren, her eyes full of tears.

"When your husband told you all this, it had to keep you up all night, didn't it?" Christine uncrossed her legs, leaned forward, nodding rapidly. Tears freely ran down her cheeks. Lauren knew there was no need to continue, but she continued telling the truth she needed to hear. "While your husband slept in the bed you shared with him, you looked at him and you thought about all the times you'd been in this shop, buying dresses from a woman who pretended to be a friend, knowing full well she was bedding your husband; a man you totally and completely trusted, right here in this office."

After those words, Christine completely broke down and allowed the pain she was feeling to gush forth like a busted dam. She covered her face with both hands. Her shoulders hunched synchronously as she cried. She blurted out, "You're right, Lauren! You're so right!"

"But there's so much more, isn't there, Mrs. Bouvier?"

Chapter 44

"No woman wants to face the truth about the female she has given birth to."

Christine was crying so hard, she couldn't speak. So she nodded, giving Lauren permission to continue telling the unadulterated truth she had been denying for six long months. She knew there was more to be told and she wanted to hear every single word. She needed to finally hear what she could never admit to herself. But she could hear it from Lauren because not only was she a woman too, she had suffered great loss suddenly when Amir died from a gunshot wound he never saw coming.

Lauren wasn't unsympathetic to the woman sitting in front of her. While what had happened to Christine had not happened to her, she understood just how devastating it was to trust a man, make him your life, and then watch your hopes and dreams of a wonderful life with that man go up in smoke. Lauren understood that what devastated Christine more was to know that the man she had given her heart to and trusted implicitly was fool enough to set the whole dream on fire and then stand there and watch it burn.

Seeing Christine's reaction to what she had said made it possible to feel what she was feeling. On the verge of tears herself, it was difficult to tell the rest; she no longer wanted to. Lauren said, "Are you sure you want to hear the rest, Mrs. Bouvier?"

Christine sniffed and nodded rapidly.

Lauren shook her head, took a deep breath, and reluctantly continued the illumination. "If all of that wasn't enough, you find out that young Beaumont and Brigitte are having relations and that she's with child. You *think* they're first cousins at the time, and that would've been bad enough. But months later, when you hear Monsieur Bouvier's letter, you learn that young Beaumont and Brigitte are sister and brother, but you didn't or couldn't believe it. When your husband confessed last night, you had to think that Brigitte and young Beaumont turned out to be just like the mother and father that brought them into this world—two whores doing what whores do, yet having no idea they're whores."

Still crying, Christine nodded her head again.

As Lauren listened to her own words, two tears slid down her cheeks. She couldn't help but remember her own sins and what her mother, if she was still alive and well, must be thinking of her; the daughter who was being groomed to be the wife of a king. Because she was rebellious and selfish, her mother and father may be dead. In fact, the king may have killed her entire family. And if they were alive, they probably never lived down the shame she had brought on the entire family. She didn't know if not knowing what happened to her family was a good thing or a bad thing.

The conversation had become therapeutic for them both, and so now Lauren continued speaking not for Christine's sake, but for her own. As tear after tear dropped off her chin, Lauren lowered her head and said, "No woman wants to face the truth about the female she has given birth to."

Christine sniffed before saying, "What truth, Lauren?"

"That she had carried a baby girl in her womb for nine months and that baby girl turned out to be a hussy. I watched your reaction to the letter Monsieur Bouvier left for us all. I have to say I admired the way you handled hearing the news of your husband's relationship with Mrs. Bouvier." She sniffed, wiped her eyes, and continued. "I don't think I would have responded that way if it had been my Amir. You were able to be calm about something like that. I'd say you were probably raised by a really good mother. I have to believe that like me, you were a maiden on your wedding night, so it's hard for you to believe that your daughter would behave so far beneath your standards.

"While you can blame her behavior on her father's lack of morality, you had to think that Brigitte wasn't your husband's child alone; she was yours too. That had to make you look into your own heart for answers. Even though you are not a whore, you may have even blamed yourself because Brigitte is a part of you too. Then it occurred to you that young Beaumont and Brigitte are the same age. So then you had to remember that you and Mrs. Bouvier were with child at the same time. You probably remembered celebrating together because you were both with child. That means that the man you had trusted was going back and forth between you and her, getting pleasure from you both at the same time. You needed someone to blame. So you blamed Mrs. Bouvier." Christine nodded. "You blamed her for taking your husband and for your daughter's debauchery. So really, this isn't a family matter is it, Mrs. Bouvier? It's a personal matter, right?"

Chapter 45

"I don't want to get caught up in white folks' mess."

It was all out in the open now. Christine felt so much better. Crying had done her good, but it was the truth she had been denying that had set her free. It was the bright light of truth that pried open the viselike jowls of denial and snatched away its strength and ability to keep her captive. She raised her eyes from the floor and looked at the young woman who had helped deliver her from denial's bondage. She saw that she was crying too and said, "Why are you crying? This happened to me, not you."

"You're right. It didn't happen to me, Mrs. Bouvier. But I've come to know and understand that we women are often the instruments of our own troubles."

"What are you saying? That I somehow brought all of this on myself?"

"We all bring it on ourselves, Mrs. Bouvier. If we look hard enough, if we look in places we don't want to look, we'll see that we did something or should have done something to avoid most of the things we suffer."

"What do you mean?"

"I mean that your sister-in-law knew your husband was married to you, yet look at what she did to you. And you probably knew your husband was capable of doing what he did to you long before you married him, but you denied it, I suspect. Now look at your situation. It's critical, isn't it?"

Christine sniffed before saying, "You're a smart girl, Lauren. What tipped you off?"

"Monsieur Bouvier didn't leave your husband any money. Since there was nothing to gain, that meant you wanted more than legal justice. If legal justice was your *real* motive, you would have gotten Lieutenant Avery to go out to Bouvier Hill to shoot Cadence and Joshua for their crimes. You wanted female justice, which is a thinly disguised version of revenge. Female justice demands more than a firing squad. That's too good for her, right? Killing? With few exceptions, that's a man thing. If a man is humiliated, he kills. Suffering? Now that's a woman thing. You wanted to make her pay somehow for the humiliation you've suffered, right?"

"Like I said, you're a smart girl, but you missed one thing."

"What did I miss?"

"It is about money, but not the way you think. I'm going to blackmail her. She's going to pay to stay alive. I don't need the money, but that's what she wants. The best way to hurt her is to make her pay to stay alive. That's exactly what I'm going to do. And each time I collect my booty, she'll have to look me in the eyes and know I'll own her until the day she dies. So you're right, suffering is a woman thing."

"What about me, Mrs. Bouvier?"

"What about you, Lauren?"

"Are you going to tell her I told you her secret?"

"Does she know you know about her and Joshua?"

"I don't think she does. I've been pretending not to know anything. I don't want to get caught up in white folks' mess."

"Well, keep your mouth shut and you'll stay alive. I was never here and we have never ever had a conversation. You got that?"

"Yes, Mrs. Bouvier. I got it."

"Now . . . one last thing. When the opportunity presents itself, I want you to make another secret known. This will throw Cadence off balance and crush her heart. Her good friend Guinevere Delacroix is staying at Bouvier Hill now, right?"

"Right, but how did you know? She just arrived."

"I know. Young Beaumont told us yesterday. I think Guinevere's arrival sent a strong signal to Tristan that she no longer needed or wanted him. He thought Cadence was moving on with her life without him. He actually had the nerve to tell me that. I think that's what made him go on a drinking binge. I think he really loves her, and that infuriates me. If you could have heard him crying all night as he confessed it all. You have no idea how that made me feel." She covered her mouth as more tears rolled down her face. She sniffed and then opened her purse and pulled out a handkerchief. She took a deep breath and gathered herself. "Now listen to me. Here's what I want you to do at the right time, and you'll know when the right time is."

"What do you want me to do, Mrs. Bouvier?"

"I want you to expose the best kept secret. The men usually keep these kinds of secrets from their wives and daughters, but Tristan told it all last night. I know everything he knows. Everything."

"A better secret than murder, Mrs. Bouvier?"

"To me, yes."

"Okay, what is it?"

"Her best friend Guinevere is really her sister."

Stunned, Lauren said, "Mrs. Bouvier and Mademoiselle Delacroix are sisters and Mrs. Bouvier doesn't know it?"

"Yes."

"Does Mademoiselle Delacroix know?"

"I'm sure she does. But you can find out. You said she's waiting for you with Captain Rutgers, right?"

"Right."

"On the way back to Bouvier Hill, ask her about it. But that's not all."

"There's more?"

"Not only is Monsieur Emile Delacroix Guinevere's father, he is the father of her five children also. You can ask her about that too. She probably won't answer, but her reaction will tell you everything you need to know."

"I don't think I need to, Mrs. Bouvier. On the way into town, she pretty much admitted that the father of her children is a white man. I didn't stop to think that her best friend's father is her father *and* the father of her children."

"Well, it's all true. It may be a secret to Cadence, but I guarantee you it's no secret on the Delacroix plantation, just as it was no secret that Tristan was the real father of Cadence's children on the Bouvier plantation. I didn't know about her and my husband, and she doesn't know that one of her sisters is a nigger. Guinevere has five children, so she is the aunt of niggers. And if we're lucky, Joshua will get her with child and then she'll be the mother of a nigger."

"So is that why Mademoiselle Delacroix was able to sell her daughters? Is it because Monsieur Delacroix felt he owed his daughter something for getting her with child five times?"

"Yes. The fool is so decadent that he started sleeping with Guinevere, his own daughter, when she was just fourteen. He felt an obligation to let her make all the money from the plaçage system. If he wanted, he could have kept all the money, but I guess he has some conscience left."

"I must say, this has truly been an interesting day. I wonder what else is going to happen. The day is still young."

"Well, I have other business to attend to in the city. I best be on my way."

"Before you go, I'm wondering if you can do me a favor, Mrs. Bouvier."

"Sure, if I can."

"Captain Rutgers wants to speak to me in private too. And Guinevere would like to visit her daughters in the Tremé. I'm wondering if you can come by the tavern in a few minutes and take her there before you go about your other business."

"Okay, Lauren. I'll do that for you."

Chapter 46

"I'll take you to see your daughters now."

Lauren watched Christine leave the same way she came into her shop. She noticed that Christine was being very careful, looking to the left and to the right, as if someone was following her. It was all so strange to Lauren. White folks ruled, but they seemed to be at each other's throats all the time. And there seemed to be no end of secrets. As she sat in her office, she thought about the things Christine had told her about Guinevere and Cadence. They were stunning and potentially devastating.

Lauren was beginning to like Guinevere, but she forced herself to remember that in the game of death, everyone was a pawn and could be used to meet her own ends. Nothing and no one was off limits as far as she was concerned. If there would be one exception, it would be Josette because she genuinely loved her from the heart. She quickly reminded herself that she had just met Guinevere. They were not friends and she owed her no allegiance. As far as she was concerned, Guinevere could be just like Aubrey, whom she liked right away, yet when his life was on the line, he served her up like a Thanksgiving Day turkey. She had realized that just as whites were constantly at one another's throats, so were the people whites called niggers. Neither could be fully trusted, she learned. As she was about to leave her office, she saw a man walk past her office door. She couldn't help thinking that maybe Christine was being followed. Or maybe it was a coincidence and she was imagining it.

After locking the front door, Lauren climbed up on her wagon and headed back to the tavern. By the time she'd gotten there, she saw Christine getting out of her elegant carriage. It was all white and the slave who had driven her there was dressed in a fancy black suit. She stopped right behind Christine's carriage and stepped down from her wagon. She was about twenty seconds behind Christine, who had already entered the tavern. By the time Lauren entered, Christine was approaching the table where Captain Rutgers and Guinevere were sitting. They were at a table next to a picture window. She watched them for a moment, expecting Guinevere to leave with her. Seconds later, she saw Guinevere grabbing her things, preparing to leave.

Lauren made her way over to the table.

"Hello, Lauren," Christine said. "I was just telling Guinevere that you'd asked me to take her to see her daughters in the Tremé."

Lauren looked at Guinevere and said, "I hope you don't mind riding in Mrs. Bouvier's beautiful carriage."

"No, I don't mind at all, Lauren," Guinevere said. "I have a lot to tell you on the way back to Bouvier Hill."

"I'm sure you do," Lauren said. "I'm looking forward to hearing it all."

Christine said, "Well, if you two will excuse us, I do have an engagement or two. If you'll follow me, Guinevere, I'll take you to see your daughters now."

Chapter 47

"It's better that you don't know."

Rutgers was sitting there quietly taking it all in. He was so proud of his protégé, though he wasn't sure how much influence he'd actually had on her. While they were on the *Windward*, he'd taught her to read and write, sure, but she was already a brilliant young woman when he met her. She could already speak five languages and could pick up others easily. He watched her slide into her seat with grace and poise. She was such a beautiful girl and her eyes still captured him. Now that Amir was dead, it was hard for him to restrain his feelings for her. But decency demanded that he be a gentleman and he would be.

Lauren locked eyes with him and said, "So . . . Captain Rutgers . . . what did *you* need to talk to me about?"

Smiling, Rutgers said, "You know I've just had the most interesting conversation with Guinevere."

"There have been lots of interesting conversations today, it seems. I wonder what insight this one will have."

Confused by her response, Rutgers said, "What do you mean by that, Lauren?"

She shook her head. "I don't mean anything, Captain. Please . . . go on with what you were saying."

Rutgers stared at her for a few seconds, trying to figure out what he was missing. He shook his head slightly, dismissing his thoughts and said, "It appears that someone told Guinevere some very erroneous tales concerning the word of Almighty God."

Lauren looked at the people walking the streets through the window and said, "Yes, she told me all about it last night. I didn't have the heart to tell her the truth."

"Really? She discussed it with you already, huh? And you said nothing about what the text actually says?"

"Nothing at all."

"Hmm, so you decided to bring me into your caper."

She stopped looking out of the window and returned her eyes to his. "My caper, Captain?"

"Yeah, I know you're up to something at Bouvier Hill."

"Hmpf. And that's what you had to tell me privately, Captain? That you know I'm up to something at Bouvier Hill?"

"Of course not, Lauren. I was just making a little small talk. That's all."

"Okay, so . . . tell me . . . what did you need to talk to me about? I'm so much in need of sophisticated stimulation as you can imagine, I'm sure. Conversing with individuals who are far behind me intellectually and having to pretend that I'm the plantation idiot can be quite taxing."

Rutgers laughed heartily. "I can imagine." He laughed a little more and then became serious. He leaned in and whispered, "I suspect that someone hired the man who killed the prince."

Without thinking, Lauren yelled, "What do you mean you think someone hired him?"

Rutgers looked around to see who was paying attention. No one was, not that he could tell anyway. In a hushed tone, he said, "I don't know for certain, okay?"

Following the captain's lead, Lauren leaned forward and lowered her voice too. "Well, what *do* you know for certain, Captain?"

"I know for certain that the murderer is not Helen's brother."

The murder of Amir flashed vividly in her mind again. She heard his assassin yell, *And this is for you. POW! That was for François and Helen Torvell! Helen was my sister and you savages raped and killed her!* She returned to the present, and said, "Are you sure? That's what the man said after shooting Amir. I hear those words over and over in my dreams. I'm sure that's what he said."

"I've known the Torvells for nearly half my life, and Helen doesn't have a brother."

"*Really?*" Lauren said, calculating where Rutgers was going with this information.

He scanned the room again to see if anyone was paying attention. Satisfied no one was, he said, "Now . . . I've got to believe that any enemies the prince may have had are not on these shores, you agree?"

"I agree."

"To my knowledge, the man's never been here before yesterday, right?"

"Right."

"Do you see where I'm going with this?"

"I believe I do. Someone was trying to hurt me, weren't they?"

"Exactly. From what you've told me, if you die, Walker Tresvant's wife, Marie-Elise, gets your ten percent of the Bouvier fortune, right?"

"Right."

"If they kill you, they would be the immediate suspects because they get your money. The problem, however, is this: Walker Tresvant is very rich. And his wife inherited sixty percent of Bouvier Hill. They don't need the money. Your ten percent of Bouvier Hill is not going to matter that much when they control the estate already. So I think we can rule them out. Do you agree?"

"Let's just say it certainly looks that way. Given all that I've seen and heard, nothing's impossible here."

"Fine, but consider this: Marie-Elise hates Cadence, so she wants you to live forever, or at least as long as Cadence lives so she'll know that Beaumont had left a nice hunk of his money to a servant he had only owned for three days. She was his wife for over twenty years and she only got thirty percent. That's a slap in her face. Now, on the other hand, Cadence wants you to stay alive too, because the last thing she wants is for Walker Tresvant and Marie-Elise to get another ten percent of the money she thinks is rightfully hers. At some point, she'll probably try to befriend you in hopes of you putting her in your will so she'll have forty percent of Bouvier Hill at your death. So they both want you alive, but for different reasons."

"Go on, Captain. I'm intrigued. What do you think is going on?"

Rutgers exhaled hard and said, "I think Cadence hired the man to kill the prince to hurt you. Which tells me she wants to kill you, but can't."

"Why do you think she would want to hurt me? I've done nothing to harm her in any way that I can think of. I've done nothing to make Mrs. Bouvier want to hurt me that much."

"Maybe it's not just about hurting you. Maybe she needs you to live long enough to get a will. I think she's trying to show you that life is short and that you should have a will and she should be in it. Or maybe she thought that if you married the prince, whatever monies you left at your death would go to him and your children. Perhaps she was trying to prevent that for as long as she could so that she could perhaps persuade you into leaving the money to her. She thinks you're a dumb nigger and you might fall for something like that. I'm not sure what she was thinking, but she was Beaumont's wife for over twenty years, and she probably thinks she deserves that ten percent."

After hearing that, Lauren leaned back in her chair and thought about what she'd heard. A few seconds later, she said, "Hmm. Tell me, Captain . . . what led you to this conclusion?"

"To tell you the truth, I think she had something to do with Beaumont's death too."

"*Really*. And why is that, Captain?"

Rutgers smirked and then stared at her unflinchingly for five seconds. "These ignorant locals don't know your mind the way I do, Lauren. You're way ahead of them intellectually, so don't sit there and treat me as if I'm like them. It's insulting."

"I have no idea what you mean, Captain."

"Come on, Lauren. Are you going to sit there and tell me you haven't suspected as much? Are you going to tell me it's never even crossed your mind?"

Lauren tried to fight off a burgeoning smirk, but couldn't. "No, Captain. I'm not going to tell you that."

"Okay, then. Now we're getting somewhere. So then if she did kill Beaumont, she's more than capable of killing you or the prince. I'll say it again: If she could get her hands on that ten percent, you'd already be in your grave."

"I can't argue with you on that, Captain."

Rutgers frowned. "How can you be so nonchalant about this?"

"Am I being nonchalant, Captain?" she said flippantly.

"Yes, you are! And frankly, I don't understand it!"

Sarcastically, she said, "I'm a nigger here, Captain. What else can I do other than be nonchalant with the possibility of being whipped to death or looking down the barrel of a firing squad?"

"Your life is in danger. Don't you care?"

"You just pointed out, brilliantly I might add, that my life isn't in any danger at all. Cadence can't kill me because she wants to make sure the Tresvants don't get my money. So how can my life be in danger?" She paused for a half a second and said, "It can't be, can it, Captain?"

Rutgers locked eyes with her and said, "You got something up your sleeve, don't you? You've already set something into motion, haven't you?"

Lauren smiled.

"Tell me about it."

"It's better that you don't know."

Chapter 48

The Nimburu Sanction

Over one hundred years before city alderman Sidney Story wrote the legislation that would set up a prostitution district called Storyville, there was a bordello in the two hundred block of Basin Street, called Madam Nadine's House of Infinite Pleasure. The bordello's architecture was that of the pagoda and boasted four floors. It was luxurious throughout and cost ten thousand dollars to build, a substantial sum at the time. The décor was that of the Orient, complete with sliding doors, and a well-maintained Japanese garden, and transplanted cherry blossom trees. It even had an opium den in the basement for those who required that sort of escape. Black-and-white color schemes could be found in every room and corridor, along with jade, cobalt blue, and white vases wherever one looked. There were even imported bamboo hardwood floors. It was a place where anything could happen and often did.

The proprietor was a slender, forty-two-year-old Japanese woman whose name was not Nadine, but that was the name she went by. Her real name was Pearl Nimburu (Nimbooroo). Except for a select few, no one knew much about her or where she was from, but there were always rumors about her background, which she herself started. She understood that people had a desire to know things that really didn't concern them, but they wanted to know anyway.

So from time to time she would tell someone a fascinating tale about her origins, knowing the person couldn't wait to spread the latest rumor about her. The rumors always brought in more business. She had told so many fables that when she told people the truth about where she was from, no one believed her. The real truth of her origins was only known by a few people—Madam Nadine, her son, Solo, a select few of the Japanese people who worked for her, and Walker Tresvant.

Pearl Nimburu was eighteen years old when she met Walker, who was taking classes at the Sorbonne in Paris. She was alone and on the run. Her parents had been trained assassins in the Ninjutsu arts and were killed because they tried to leave the secret Nimburu sect that had been in existence for over three hundred years. They didn't want their daughter to live the kind of life they had lived. They wanted her to have the choice they didn't have.

Any children born in the Nimburu sect were automatically taken from their parents and trained to become assassins on their fifth birthday. Pearl was nearly five years old when they escaped, and had been at large for thirteen years before the sect found them. The assassins had been sent to kill her parents and return Pearl to the sect for reeducation. She narrowly escaped. She had gone to the market to get some food and when she returned to their apartment, she found her mother and father lying side by side on the floor dying.

Shuriken (eight-sided throwing knives) were in their heads and their throats had been sliced open by blades dipped in poison. Their blood was still pumping out and intermingling when she entered the apartment. They had fought hard to stay alive, it appeared, as the apartment was in total disarray. There was blood in different areas all over the apartment. Judging by the amount of blood spilled, Pearl thought her parents must have killed or at least maimed some of their assailants. Blood was still dripping off their swords. She packed her clothing as quickly as she could and fled.

Chapter 49

Birthing a Madam

The Nimburu sect was persistent and above all, ruthless. Pearl's parents knew they would eventually find and kill them even though they had taken meticulous precautions. They often moved from continent to continent, attempting to stay ahead of their unforgiving pursuers. They had lived all over the world in exotic places like Korea, Thailand, the Philippines, India, Egypt, Malaysia, Singapore, and finally France.

From the time they set up a new home in Paris, the Nimburus prepared their daughter for their deaths, as they knew the sect would one day find them. Pearl, though, had grown weary of the necessary safety measures and the instructions on what to do just in case their enemies found them. She listened to them talk about the dangerous sect for thirteen years and nothing ever happened. She thought it was silly to continue to be afraid of what amounted to ghosts who never darkened their doorsteps—until they did.

She had to stay on the move. Her parents had told her not to stay in one place too long. She couldn't afford to take a job that required her to establish habits that could be traced by the sect. She had nowhere to go and the stash of emergency money her parents left for her eventually ran out after a few months.

Though it was difficult for her, she resorted to begging. Some days she was able to secure enough money to eat for the day, and some days she went without eating. She was a very attractive girl, and when men made it clear they wanted something extra for the money they gave her or the meals they paid for, she initially refused. Sometimes she didn't eat for days, and was often dizzy from hunger.

She eventually resorted to selling the one commodity she had that would never fail her. It was hard to allow her body to be used, but she didn't see any other way. She told herself she would only do it long enough to get a meal. After a while, though, she no longer begged for money; she was now offering her body exclusively in exchange for money or a meal. It was so much easier that way.

One day, she literally bumped into Walker Tresvant. He was about to get a seat at an outdoor eatery a few blocks from his apartment. He had only been in Paris a few weeks and didn't have any friends or family there. She offered herself to him for a meal. He thought it a shame that such a good-looking girl found herself in such dire conditions. He bought her something to eat, but refused to take the sex she proffered. While they ate, he inquired about her situation and she told him everything. He felt sorry for her and gave her a few francs and left after their meal together.

To his surprise, later that evening, she knocked on his door. She had followed him home. This time she offered to cook and clean for him, if he would feed and clothe her. He agreed and they became fast friends. However, because she was his live-in maid, they became close and eventually they became lovers.

Fearful that something could happen to him and she'd end up on the streets again, she turned to prostitution to earn extra money. When he attended classes at the Sorbonne, she used his flat to "entertain" men. She made sure the men were long gone before Walker returned. She was very careful and he probably would have never known what was going on in his absence if he hadn't accidentally found her stash of money. When she was confronted about the cash, she tearfully told him the truth and her fears of him one day never returning. He was very fond of Pearl and promised to take her to New Orleans with him when he returned.

When his ship set sail for America, he kept his word and took Pearl Nimburu with him. Walker had explained to her that it would be improper for him to keep company with her publicly because he had a family vendetta he had to settle with the Bouvier family before they left Paris. It had fallen to him to do to Marie-Elise, Damien Bouvier's granddaughter, what he had done to Jennifer Tresvant, his grandmother.

She was the only Japanese in New Orleans, and while men wanted to bed her, none would hire her. A few months later, she discovered she was pregnant with Walker's son, but she did not tell him it was his child until after the boy was born. The child's complexion was darker than usual, a darker shade of olive, but his physical characteristics were such that he could pass as fully Japanese. Solo was their eternal secret and their everlasting bond.

Besides, Pearl Nimburu understood Walker's need to settle the score with the Bouvier family because she wanted to get even with the Nimburu sect for what they did to her parents. She took revenge on the sect when she returned to Japan with her five-year-old son in tow. She explained who she was and that she wanted her son to be trained according to the sect's tradition. The sect took her son in and let her go and told her the debt had been paid in full. Thirteen years later, after having been thoroughly trained, Pearl's son skillfully killed Lord Ishido, the sect's leader, and Hoshi, his concubine, but made it look like a murder suicide just as his mother had instructed him.

Before their child was born, before she told Walker Solo was his firstborn son, Pearl had asked Walker to loan her the money to open a house of prostitution. He asked her to let him take care of her, but she flat-out refused, citing he could die and she would still have to take care of herself. Reluctantly, he agreed to loan her the money, but suggested that she create a fictional madam named Nadine and pretend to work for her until she was well established. Soon all the men who wanted to bed her were now loyal customers. Over time, her "business" blossomed. And thus Madam Nadine's House of Infinite Pleasure was born.

Chapter 50

"Solo will show you the way."

Christine Bouvier's carriage stopped in front of Madam Nadine's House of Infinite Pleasure. She, like most New Orleanians, had heard any number of rumors about the madam and her house of ill repute. It was the place where the men of the city went to play unusual sex games with girls young enough to be their granddaughters. They paid Madam Nadine a handsome booty for experiences they couldn't get anywhere else in the city. Normally, Christine wouldn't dare darken the doorstep of an enterprise that dealt almost exclusively with fleshly pleasures, but according to Tristan, Walker Tresvant spent much of his time there, and that's who she was there to see.

In his drunken state, Tristan had told her that many of New Orleans's leading citizens frequented the brothel. He also told her that Walker was the only lover Madam Nadine had and that he visited her regularly during daylight hours.

After dropping Guinevere at her daughter's home in the Tremé, it occurred to her that the best way to hurt Cadence was to hand her over to Marie-Elise Tresvant. Christine believed that Marie-Elise, being Beaumont's sister, and the recipient of the bulk of the Bouvier fortune, would push Walker to make sure that justice was served.

She couldn't be sure the authorities would indict Cadence once they learned that she didn't commit the actual murders. She thought the authorities would take the path of least resistance and lay everything at the feet of Joshua because he was the easy target. After leaving Lauren's shop, it occurred to her that taking Cadence's money wouldn't hurt her, it would only anger her. But having to look Marie-Elise in the face, knowing that she not only knew that Cadence had given birth to four children who were not Beaumont's, but that she murdered him as well might just lead to a public execution.

Christine hoped the bombshell about her father and Guinevere would do irreparable harm, which was the only thing that would bring a measure of satisfaction. She wanted Cadence to feel the full weight of the devastation she had felt when she learned the awful truth about her husband, before looking down the rifle barrel of a squad of soldiers. After she had suffered awhile, Walker's political connections would see to it that the judge deliver the death penalty. An evil grin emerged as she opened the door of her carriage and got out. Then she climbed twenty cement stairs and knocked on the door.

An elegantly dressed and well-educated Japanese man opened the door and said, "May I help you?"

Although the man was from Japan and had an Oriental accent, he could be clearly understood. Madam Nadine understood that her customers' experience didn't begin with meeting her selection of scantily clad girls, or in the boudoir, but at the door. She knew that a well-dressed, well-spoken man, no matter what his origins, would put her customers at ease and set the tone for the rest of their visit. She further knew that the first impression would be lasting and often resulted in sumptuous spending. More important than anything else, the doorman had to understand discretion. It was the life's blood of doing business with New Orleans's elite gentlemen.

"Yes, you may. I'm looking for Walker Tresvant," Christine said. "I'm told he's here during daylight hours."

"We don't open for business for several hours, but on the off chance that someone by that name is on the premises, whom shall I say is calling?"

Who do you think you're fooling? I know he's here, Christine was thinking, but instead said, "Would you please tell him that his sister-in-law, Christine Bouvier, is here and that it's urgent that I speak with him immediately."

"I will check and see if such a person is here. Can you wait for just a minute or so?"

She exhaled and said, "Yes. Be sure to tell him . . . *if* he's here . . . it's quite urgent."

He bowed and closed the door. A few minutes later the door opened. This time there were two Japanese men. Both men bowed. The first Japanese man said, "Monsieur Tresvant will see you in Madam Nadine's office. Solo will show you the way."

Chapter 51

"The Needles Arrived Yesterday"

Pearl thought Solo would be the perfect name for her son. The name served a dual purpose. First it reminded her that she was all alone in the world before Walker came along, which was why she hoped he would be the father when she discovered she was pregnant. He was the only man who had shown real concern for her. Second, the named reminded her of where she could end up if she didn't take decisive control over her life.

Solo eyed Christine for an unnoticeable second before saying, "Come with me, please."

Christine followed him through a series of corridors before they reached their destination. Solo slid the door to the left, bowed, and then gestured for her to enter. The smell of jasmine was suddenly in the air. She inhaled deeply and then stepped inside the room. The décor immediately transported her to the Orient. Through a large picture window she could see a lush green garden, complete with a waterfall, and a small pond full of fish. Fresh flowers were meticulously placed around the room. Dragon masks along with Japanese artwork covered the walls. Imported porcelain figurines from Asia were everywhere she looked.

Walker Tresvant was sitting comfortably in a chair in front of a large hand carved wooden desk. A gorgeous Japanese woman with flowing shoulder length hair, who looked to be in her twenties, was sitting behind the desk. She was wearing a silk black-and-gold kimono. A chessboard with expensive hand carved jade and onyx pieces was between them. Behind the woman was a set of four ivory-handled swords mounted one on top of the other, nestled inside a black built-in bookcase full of books. Each sword was longer than the one beneath it. The woman was studying Christine carefully. Her hands were in steeple formation with her fingertips pressed together.

While she was taking it all in, she heard Solo, who also had a Japanese accent, say, "Would you care for some tea, Mademoiselle Bouvier?"

She offered a quick, friendly smile and said, "No, thank you."

Solo bowed and left the room.

Walker threatened Pearl's king with his queen and said, "Hello, Christine."

She looked at Tresvant, who didn't seem to be put off at all by the fact that he was married to a respectable white woman from an elite family, but was in a whorehouse during daylight hours, acting as if he were sitting in an eatery in the French Quarter. "I need to talk to you about a family matter."

Still studying the chessboard, wondering what move Madam Nadine would make to get her king out of danger, he said, "What's wrong? Did something happen to Marie-Elise?" Then he swiveled his body around and faced her.

Christine cut her eyes toward the Japanese woman sitting behind the desk and then back to Tresvant. She could tell the woman was still sizing her up as the woman's eyes took in her physical appearance. Her penetrating gaze was intimidating and left her feeling vulnerable. "Walker, please. I said this is a family matter. I don't mean to be rude, but could we please talk *in private.*"

"Christine Bouvier, I'd like you to meet a good friend of mine, Madam Nadine. For some reason she allows me to call her by her birth name, Pearl. I've known her for twenty years now, right, Pearl?"

"Twenty-four years, my friend," Pearl said, correcting him, while still glaring at Christine. She spoke with a slight Japanese accent. "Longer than you've been married, right, Walker?"

"Right, Pearl. They've been good years, too," he said.

Still looking at Christine, in a sultry voice, Pearl said, "Yes, they have. Very good years. And I'm looking forward to many more to come."

"As am I," Walker said, smiling without shame.

Christine felt the sting of the virtual backhand and nervously said, "Pleased to meet you."

Pearl Nimburu stood up and bowed. "Nice meeting you, Christine." She looked at Walker. "I'll leave you two alone." She bowed to Walker and then to Christine and turned to leave. Then, as if she remembered something she had forgotten, she turned around and said, "And, Walker, don't forget that the needles arrived yesterday on the *Seaquest* along with my servants. I'm dying to try them out on you. It is said that if done correctly, a centuries-old secret form of acupuncture can make a man stiff indefinitely."

Walker couldn't contain an emerging salacious grin.

Pearl looked at Christine. Her eyes narrowed. Her face tightened, smirking as she relished the awkward position she put Christine in by making such a candid sexual innuendo. Keeping her eyes on Christine, Pearl bowed again and then left. She went into the adjacent room, where her son was waiting. Together they watched and listened to Walker and Christine's conversation through dragon masks mounted on the walls.

Chapter 52

"What could I do?"

Walker, knowing where Pearl and Solo were and what they were doing, said, "Have a seat."

Christine sat in the empty seat a foot or so from him and said, "I just found out that Cadence killed Beaumont."

"Finally figured it out, huh?" Walker said, devoid of emotion.

Stunned that he knew already, Christine said, "How long have you known?"

"I suspected she had done it the night I went there with Lieutenant Avery. There was no way Aubrey or any of the housemen killed Beaumont. They were all sodomites. People kill for a reason, Christine. People have to have a strong motive to kill; especially the way those men were killed. Unless they knew what Beaumont had left in the will, none of those men had a motive. Even if they did know he'd left them something in the will, it still wouldn't be motive to kill him. They needed him alive because Beaumont had the power to keep the authorities from prosecuting them for sodomy. As you know the penalty for such a crime is death. So if they had motive, it was motive to keep him alive. Cadence, on the other hand, did have motive to kill him. But who was going to believe a white woman with her pedigree killed those two men?"

"Well, why didn't you do something about it?"

"What could I do? I didn't have any proof she had done the deed. These things often have a way of working themselves out." He thought for a moment and then said, "You said you just found out. Did someone tell you about this or what?"

Christine locked eyes with him and said, "Lauren told me about an hour ago."

Chapter 53

"What have we gained and what have we lost?"

Lauren was still sitting at the table in the tavern next to the picture window when she said, "Captain Rutgers, I didn't get the chance to talk with Amir, as you know. He told me he had forgiven you for what you did to us. He said he understood his mother's willingness to die and that he had found peace. Please give me the details of what happened aboard the *Windward*."

A single tear dripped out of Rutgers's left eye and slowly glided down his face. He shook his head and tried to gather himself as the memory of what happened on the island resurfaced the moment her question vibrated his eardrum. He opened his mouth to speak, but nothing came out. Another tear fell. He took a deep breath and exhaled. Finally, he opened his mouth again. "I knew two years ago to get out of this business when the people I knew on the Isle of Santo Domingo started getting killed." He exhaled hard. "But the money was just too good to pass up. I kept telling myself, just one more load, just one more load and I'll have enough money to open my own brandy shop. I had been planning to get out for years and I had seen a spot in the French Quarter that I wanted."

Lauren sat there patiently as he rambled on about things of which she did not ask. She figured he would get there in his own time.

"I guess I can still open it. I was going to call it Joseph Rutgers's Vintage Brandies and Fine Wines." He looked at her and hoped she would respond to his idea, but she didn't. She just looked at him and waited for him to continue. "Anyway, I might as well tell you up front that the lawyer you sent over there to retrieve Amir won't be coming back. He was killed by the Maroons on the way back to the ship."

"But he had already found Amir? Or did you find him?"

"He found him in the stockade. The white planters and the free mulattos had joined together to save their plantations, but they were losing to the Maroons. French soldiers got to the island in time to save them and restore peace, but the peace didn't last very long."

Lauren was losing her patience. She decided to help him get to the point. "Okay, Captain, so my attorney, Phillip Winslow, found Amir in the stockade and . . . ?"

"Winslow found out that Amir and a number of other rebels were sentenced to death. They were going to burn them at the stake. Winslow bribed the commandant and secured Amir's release. The commandant told us we had to come back later that night to take him to the ship. His men wouldn't understand why he was letting him go when several of the Maroons had confessed that one of the reasons they had been so successful was because Amir had vastly improved their fighting skill and tactics.

"Because of Amir, the Maroons weren't just hitting and running anymore. They had become sophisticated overnight, according to the commandant. They were no longer attacking only at night. They had become incredibly organized and were getting more and more aggressive, slaughtering French soldiers and disappearing into the hills where the soldiers didn't dare go. Were it not for the mulattos who were pretty much forced to join the whites or be killed by the Maroons, the island would have been lost by now. The Maroons are determined to win their independence and in time, I think they will prevail."

Trying to keep Rutgers focused, Lauren said, "Did you ever learn what changed about him? Did he ever tell you about his mother?"

"Yes. He told me all about her and her sacrifice. It was a brave thing she did to help you two escape." He wiped another tear from his face. "It's so much easier to enslave people you don't know and don't understand. I realize that now. When you don't understand the language, it's easy to justify what you're doing by passing people off as animals. But when you get to know them, when you realize they have family, people who care about them, just like you have family, it awakens the conscience and forces you see the truth about what you've done and what you are doing. That's why I knew I should have gotten out two years ago.

"Anyway, I let Amir live in my quarters just as I had let you live there. He had already learned to speak English, so it was easier to have conversations with him. I told him I had taught you to read in my quarters. He asked me to teach him to read and everything I had taught you. So I did. The more I talked to the man, the more I admired him." His face was wet with tears now. "I regret it all now. I swear to God Almighty, I regret it all! If I could just go back in time, I'd make a lot of different decisions."

"I think we all would, Captain," Lauren interjected. "The problem with being in charge of your life is that you don't know or don't want to know what the consequences are going to be from the decisions you make. I thought by running away with Amir, I would be gaining my independence."

She closed her eyes and shook her head. Then she opened them and looked at Rutgers. "I did gain my independence, but it only lasted three days. And even then, we were on the run, hoping the king's men had gone south instead of west. I remember being so excited about what Amir and I were planning. We were going to show everybody they couldn't tell us what to do anymore. We were going to do things *our* way and we didn't care what they thought. And now look at us. What have we gained and what have we lost?"

Chapter 54

"Okay, well, let's go meet him."

Rutgers stared at Lauren for a few seconds, realizing how much she had grown in his absence. She had become much more than she was when they were aboard the *Windward*. He wanted her now more than he ever had. She was a prized possession to be cherished above all things he owned or ever wanted; even more than Tracy Combs, his former wife. "I've gained wealth," Rutgers said, "but I've lost my life. I have no wife and no children. I only recently regained my brother."

"I've lost everything, Captain," Lauren said solemnly. "I've lost father and mother; sisters and brothers, people I loved dearly and may never see again. I've lost dignity and have brought shame on all those that I left as I stole away in the middle of the night to find the man who I thought was the very air I breathed. Finally, I lost him too. I have lost even the name that I was born with—Ibo Atikah Mustafa—all in an effort to do what I wanted to do regardless of who I hurt in the process. In the end, I hurt myself more than I hurt anyone else. Now I, like you, have wealth and no one to share it with. But unlike you, I dare not take the name I was born with or leave the city of New Orleans or I will lose even that."

After hearing Lauren take responsibility for her own decisions, another pang of guilt shot through him like a ball of lead fired from a musket. So far, he had not heard her blame him for her condition. He decided to change the subject before she realized that he had as much to do with her being in New Orleans as she did. "To answer your questions, I think Amir found peace in the cargo hold of the ship on the way to Santo Domingo."

"Why do you say that?"

"He told me that you came down there and were going to set him and the others free, but he told you to wait until a better time."

Stunned by that revelation, she said, "Amir told you that?"

"Yes, he did. He also told me that after you left, he prayed to the God of his mother, Asenath, and a great peace came over him. He told me he had a conversation with his mother before he left; it was a conversation that would play over and over in his mind while he was in the cargo hold. His mother had told him to trust in God when the bad times come. He had told his mother that he trusted in his sword, his shield, and his spear, but that he realized those things did not save him or you. He realized that his mother was right when just minutes before he was supposed to be burned at the stake, you, through Phillip Winslow, saved his life. The commandant had made him watch all but one of his friends become a human torch."

Tears were free-falling out of her eyes now. She sniffed and said, "I bought a mausoleum for the prince today. I wanted to bury him in his uniform, but they had a suit on him instead. When I asked your friend Pierre St. John, the mortician, about his uniform, he didn't know anything about it. Do you know what happened to it?"

"Yes, I was getting to that. He told me he had figuratively put his sword and shield away the moment you saved him through Winslow. He told me he had no further need of them and had given his uniform to his student. A man called Rokk Baptiste."

"Where is this man?"

"He's here. He was aboard the ship too. The prince talked Winslow into buying his freedom too. Winslow said no at first, but the prince said he would not leave his friend to burn at the stake. He said he would take responsibility if you had a problem with it. Only then did Winslow agree. I think he agreed because you had told him the story of how it all happened and that you two were going to get married. He didn't dare return to New Orleans without him."

A quick smile emerged before Lauren said, "That sounds like the prince. He could talk a person into anything."

"After talking with him day after day in my quarters, as I said, I admired him." Rutgers wept again after saying this. "You know what's really sad, Lauren?"

"What?"

"I had enslaved a man and that man had forgiven me. I thought I had made it up to him by teaching him to read and write."

"You did, Captain."

"No, Lauren, I hadn't." He sniffed a few times and wiped his eyes. "When we docked, my brother Jonah came up to me like usual, wanting me to forgive him for what he did to me. I pushed my way past him. I wasn't ever going to forgive him for bedding my wife, a woman he knew I loved. Not in a million years would I ever forgive him, I had told myself. Now . . . Lauren . . . you have to understand that I have enslaved tens of thousands . . . only God above knows the number. Amir had forgiven me, but I didn't forgive my own brother." He wiped his eyes again as the tears continued to flow. "But I felt good about teaching one of my slaves to read and write? That was supposed to somehow make it up to you and Amir and the countless others? I had taken a bit of solace when I saw you two together, embracing one another. It made me feel good about myself. I had done something righteous and it alleviated a considerable amount of guilt. But when I watched Amir get killed, I realized that the man who had forgiven me was now dead and gone in a blink of an eye. My brother was still alive, and I knew then it was time to let go of what he had done to me."

When Lauren heard that, she knew she too had to forgive and let it go. Otherwise she would have no peace. She wanted to, but she couldn't. Too much had happened to let it go. People had been murdered all around her. She had seen it all and now, she was expected to just drop it? She couldn't do it. She wouldn't do it. They were going to pay. However, after hearing Captain Rutgers's story, she decided she would forgive him. He would be the one concession. Everybody else would get what they get. She had followed Amir's lead in life, and she would follow his lead in death.

"What will you do now, Lauren?"

"As I said, I just put the prince in a really nice mausoleum. I guess the next thing I'll do is try to find the man who has Amir's uniform. What's his name again?"

"Rokk Baptiste."

"What does he look like?"

"You can't miss him. He's about the same height as Amir. He's a little bit smaller, but strong and solid." Rutgers looked out the window. "As a matter of fact, here he comes now. He's wearing the uniform. Would you like to meet him?"

"Yes, I would," she said, all of sudden excited by the prospect of getting Amir's battle gear. "What kind of person is he? Do you think he'll sell me the uniform?"

"I don't know if he'll want to part with it. Who knows though; he might. You're almost Amir's widow. He just might give it to you. You paid for his freedom. He probably wouldn't feel right selling it."

"Okay, well, let's go meet him."

Chapter 55

"I should have never freed him."

After introducing Lauren to Rokk Baptiste, Captain Joseph Rutgers went back into the tavern to finish his brandy and to keep close eye on them as they talked. While he would never admit it, he was afraid that given enough time, they would fall in love. It would be easy for them given the circumstances they found themselves in. Lauren had been alone for six months and her prince was dead. He sensed that she was extremely vulnerable and susceptible to falling in love with the first man she found attractive—only he hoped it would be him. For six long months he thought about her and their conversations and how effortless their exchanges were on nearly every subject. Even though he was three times as old as she, he thought they would be perfect together.

Now that the prince was dead, he thought she would remember how well they had gotten along and how important it was to her to have a man in her life who was her intellectual equal. He took a sip of his brandy and looked at them again. He noticed something he should have noticed long ago. Lauren was black and so was Rokk. It wasn't that he didn't see her color before; her beauty and intelligence trumped her color—love had a way of doing that. There was no way to fight love. No legislation could ever ban love in all of its forms and colors. Nevertheless, marriage was out of the question. Not only were there laws against such unions, but it was improper for a white man to marry a black woman. The plaçage system was the only allowance and it was mainly for the rich elite who circumvented the law with their money whenever it suited them. He could, however, put her in a house and live with her and have babies with her, he thought as he watched Lauren and Rokk through the picture window.

He wondered what they were talking about as he stared at them, hoping nothing would come of their meeting. He assumed they were talking about the only thing they had in common—Prince Amir. What else did they have to talk about? From what he could tell, the conversation was going well. As far as Rutgers was concerned, there was no way Lauren would ever be interested in a man like Rokk. The man was too ignorant. He probably couldn't hold his own in a conversation of depth and reasoning. He thought that if it weren't for Prince Amir's death, she wouldn't think twice about having a prolonged conversation with a man whose intelligence was miniscule at best. That's how he saw Rokk anyway.

It had been twenty years since he had last seen Tracy Combs, the only woman he had ever loved prior to meeting Lauren when her name was still Ibo Atikah Mustafa. Tracy was a gorgeous blond Aussie he and his brother Jonah had found irresistible. The brothers had been in competition all their lives, but when Tracy decided Joseph was the man she wanted to marry and spend the rest of her life with, Jonah should have backed off. And he did back off, at least for a while. When Tracy and Jonah saw each other, they felt an electrical charge neither of them could resist—not for long anyway. Eventually they gave into their carnality and Joseph walked in while they were in the throes of passion.

Joseph had hated both of them and the God he once served. He had even hated love. However, love had arrested him again and there was nothing he could do about it. Lauren Renee Bouvier was a prize to be won, he knew, and now it looked as if Rokk Baptiste would be in the best position to win her because he was black and Joseph was not. He took a gulp of his brandy and continued watching. Jealousy began to mount when he saw them laughing. He knew then that his chances of making her his were dwindling. He took a large gulp of his brandy as he watched closely. They were smiling at each other flirtatiously—at least that's the way it appeared to him. Full of envy now, he slammed his fist on the table. The silverware rattled.

"I should have never freed him."

Chapter 56

The Christian Holy Wars

Even though Lauren had been introduced to Rokk, she didn't *see* him at first. She saw the uniform he was wearing; the leather vest and kilt, and the black cape that flapped when the slightest breeze blew. She thought the uniform rightfully belonged to her. After all, she was Amir's widow. Never mind that they never married nor had they taken occasion to consummate their relationship.

She wanted to offer Rokk a tidy sum for the uniform right away, but she believed he would be reluctant to part with it, especially since the prince was dead. She believed the uniform would now have a measure of sentimental value to Amir's friend and accepted student. As they stood on Bourbon Street talking about Amir, remembering who he was, his fierceness, his bravery, and his cunning battlefield tactics, she felt an immediate kinship with Rokk. She could tell that he loved Amir by the way he talked about him.

"So, Rokk . . . how did you and the prince meet?" Lauren said in French.

In a voice so deep it vibrated, Rokk said, "The prince was

one of the men I set free when we set the first and the biggest plantation ablaze."

"You mean the Torvell plantation?"

"Yes."

"Captain Rutgers knows nothing of you burning the Torvell plantation, does he?"

"I don't think so. I never said a word. I suppose the prince never said anything to him either."

Intrigued, Lauren said, "So how did you get to the island?"

"I was born on Santo Domingo. I am the son of Tarik Baptiste. My father was a wealthy planter on the island. He told me that we are descendants of the Moors."

"The Moors?"

"Yes, my people are north Africans. My father says we invaded Europe over eleven hundred years ago. I think he said the year was 711. I cannot remember all the details. Anyway, he said that after conquering the southern peninsula, our people civilized the land and ruled for seven hundred years."

Fascinated, Lauren said, "So what happened? How did the Moors lose control?"

"According to my father, who was told by his father, and his father before him, there was infighting among the leaders, but it was the Crusades that finally ended it all."

"The Crusades?"

"Yes, the Christian Holy Wars against Muslim rule. Anyway, my father wasn't too certain of all the details because much of what happened had been forgotten, but there was a lot of race mixing between the African and the European women for hundreds of years. I've only been here for two days, and I can tell that race mixing is going on here too, much like what happened on the island. My family settled on the island several generations ago. My father was an educated man. So was his father before him and so on. My family came to the island by ship. Which one, I do not know, but they were free."

"Again . . . what happened, Rokk?" Lauren asked, riveted by the story that rang in her ears as if it were a bell tolling, awakening her to a truth she would otherwise never know.

Rokk exhaled loudly before saying, "When my father converted to Christianity, he told us we had to either set our slaves free or pay them for their labor. My mother converted also and she agreed with my father, but feared that if they set their slaves free or paid them, the idea would spread throughout the island and create unrest. My father knew this too and told my mother that if given the choice between doing what's righteous and continuing what he had learned was wrong, it was better to do what was righteous, even if it cost him his life. He told my mother that true Christianity demanded it. He told her that to consistently live any other way would be the equivalent of self-deception."

"I see. So what happened?"

Chapter 57

"Do you blame your father for his decision?"

The look in Rokk's eyes suddenly changed and hardened as he seemed to be remembering the events of what he was about to say. "I could live another five hundred years and never forget it. When word spread among the slaves that the Baptiste family was paying their workers, the slaves on other plantations wanted their freedom or to be paid too. The other planters learned that my parents were primarily responsible for the unrest, so they got together and came to our plantation.

"At first the planters tried to reason with him, but my father's mind was made up. When reason didn't work, they tried using the Bible to justify slavery. He told them he could no longer call himself a Christian while at the same time be a practitioner of slavery. The two lifestyles were incongruent. When their attempts to undermine his faith didn't work, they probably felt they had no other choice but to kill him or lose everything they had worked for. One night, the plantation owners, most of them Christians, mostly white, some Negro, came back and killed my entire family. I only escaped because I was with a girl at another plantation.

"I was on my way back to our home when I saw the flames. At first I couldn't believe what I was seeing. It was like a bad dream you hope to wake up from. I was seventeen years old and was scared they would capture and kill me too. I could hear my mother and my sisters screaming as my father's Christian brothers sat atop their horses and watched the blaze engulf the house I lived in. I wanted to help my family somehow, but there was nothing I could do. So I hid. I listened to their horrific screams as they burned alive.

"When I could no longer hear them screaming, I saw the planters ride off into the night. By the time I made it back, the house was gone, but it was still smoldering. I saw the charred remains of my mother and father, my sisters and brothers. All of them dead because my father, when he realized the error of his way, stood up for what was right when few others would. I later learned that when the planters left our home, they went to the Deville plantation and killed him and his whole family too.

"Deville was a white man. He converted my father. He was paying his laborers too. My father was following the example he set. A month or so later, Francois Torvell, the leader of the mob that killed both families took over both plantations and made them his own."

Lauren remembered meeting the Torvells. She remembered thinking they appeared to be very nice people. She shook her head and asked, "When did all of this happen?"

"About seven years ago."

"And you're sure it was Francois Torvell?"

Rokk frowned and blurted out, "I saw him and his lackey, Herman, sitting side by side on their horses, Lauren. Yes, I'm quite sure." He took a deep breath and calmed down a bit. "As I said . . . I will never forget that night. And I will never forget the faces I saw, either."

"Do you blame your father for his decision?" Lauren asked.

"At first I did. At first I hated him because my mother had told him what would happen and he didn't listen to her. He had to do what he thought was right. But later, fearing for my life, I fled to the hills where I was taken in by the Maroons. They became my family. While they never claimed to be Christians, they agreed that slavery was wrong and it had to end. From that day forward, I saw my father as a hero because he would rather die than continue doing what he knew was wrong.

"When I thought my life was in danger, I ran away. My father knew they were going to kill him and he didn't run. He stood his ground. I wanted to be brave like he was, so I joined the Maroons and they taught me how to use my fists. After a while, I became the best of all the brawlers. When our leader thought I was ready, I went on raids with them."

Chapter 58

"He could have taken whatever you delivered, Rokk."

Lauren liked Rokk right away. He seemed to be everything she thought Joshua was upon meeting him. Rokk seemed to be different in that he was a warrior and had seen action. Like Lauren, he also was born free. From what she had observed over the course of six months, Negroes who had never been slaves had a totally different mindset and so did their progeny. She had learned that people born into slavery had a difficult time changing the way they saw themselves, even after being given their freedom. Guinevere was the best example of this.

Guinevere had been free for ten years, yet she still acted as if she were a slave. For Guinevere to change, her thinking had to change, which meant she needed a new mind, new thoughts, and new ideas. Lauren observed that people with new minds, new thoughts, and new ideas appeared to be uppity or arrogant to those who still had the slave mind, no matter what color skin they lived in. Lauren had inadvertently started Guinevere's mind-changing process the previous night and continued it the following morning. On the way home, she would continue the process.

Seeking a way to ingratiate herself, Lauren said, "So, Monsieur Baptiste, where are you staying?"

"Captain Rutgers is courteously allowing me to stay aboard the *Windward* for now."

Right away, she wanted him to join her at Bouvier Hill. Cadence had told her that she couldn't use Bouvier slaves indefinitely. She had also told her she would have to buy her own slaves or hire someone to drive for her. Lauren had paid for Rokk's freedom, and that would be her argument if Cadence had a problem with it. Lauren wanted Rokk near her. That way she could make him feel beholden to her so that when she offered him money for the uniform, he would take it.

Even though her money had secured his freedom, she didn't feel right using that fact to get the uniform. Besides, the uniform had been a gift from Amir. She wanted him to give it to her without being made to feel guilty. She locked eyes with him, knowing no heterosexual man could resist them. She then offered him a friendly smile and said, "Well, you can't stay on the *Windward* forever."

Lost in her eyes for a few seconds, Rokk remembered what the prince had said about them. Now he was looking into those same eyes, being drawn to the person they belonged to, and had almost forgotten his friend had only been dead for a little more than a day. And here he was looking at the woman his friend and teacher loved like he wanted her to be his. He forced himself to break the trance he was in by looking across the street and then back to her, but not into those eyes. Those eyes threatened his loyalty to the prince. He said, "I know I can't stay on the ship forever. But I must first find suitable work."

"What kind of work do you want to do?"

"I'm very strong. I suppose I can do just about any job available."

"I suppose you could, but I asked what you *wanted* to do."

"It doesn't matter, I guess. I'll be glad to do anything that pays a wage that will allow me to make a life for myself here. I saw a number of ships being unloaded on the docks. Perhaps I can do something like that for a while."

"That's why I asked you what you wanted to do. It would be so much easier to prosper if you did the thing you enjoyed most, don't you think?"

"I suppose you're right."

Lauren thought trying to find out what he liked doing was like pulling teeth. She wanted to get to know him a little better, perhaps help him in some way before asking to purchase the uniform. "Tell me this, Rokk: If you could do anything you wanted, what would it be?"

He thought for a few seconds and said with noticeable excitement, "Brawling. I like mixing it up with my fists. I thought I was the best brawler on the island until I was soundly beaten by the prince." His eyes lit up as he spoke. "I had never seen anything like him. He was so fast with his hands and feet that I couldn't see his fists coming. His movements were precise, yet unpredictable. It seemed like his punches were coming from every angle. After a while I realized he wasn't even trying hard. I was sweating just trying to keep up with him.

"But not one drop of sweat beaded on his forehead. I was breathing heavy and he was breathing normal, like we are right now. It was the most fascinating thing I've ever witnessed. I was taking the beating of my life, yet I was admiring the man who had bloodied my nose and mouth while he was doing this to me. After taking so many punches, I wanted him to knock me out so the fight would be over. Even though I wanted to quit, I couldn't; not in front of a crowd of friends, not in front of the family who took me in when I was alone in this world. They had never seen me lose, so I had to keep fighting. Pride demanded it. I had to keep taking blow after blow, knowing I would never catch him."

Rokk's story made Lauren feel good on the inside and produced a gleeful grin. "So how did it end?"

"He quit."

"He quit?" Lauren asked, puzzled by Rokk's answer.

"Yes. I think at some point he knew I couldn't win, but no matter how many blows he delivered, the crowd kept cheering for me. I think the prince knew I would die at his hands if he didn't quit." He laughed a little. "The funny thing is . . . when the prince quit . . . the crowd cheered for me as if I had won. I looked at them, blood was all over my face, my body felt like I had been hit five hundred times with a piece of iron, and they were cheering like I had done to him what he had done to me with ease."

"That's my prince," Lauren said, laughing with Rokk.

"Even after I became his student, I still could not touch him. But no one on the island could touch me. We trained every day up in the hills. I learned more in a day from him than I had learned in the seven years I'd been with the Maroons. We had plenty of time to train when we weren't attacking the planters because the soldiers didn't dare come up there. It felt good knocking men out with little effort. But to be honest with you, Lauren, I wanted to punch the prince in the face at least one time. If for no other reason than to see how he reacted to a good strong punch. Although I never tasted the full power of his blows, he knew I could take a good punch." He laughed again. "I had taken so many of them I lost count. He probably did too."

Full of pride, Lauren said, "He could have taken whatever you delivered, Rokk."

"You think so, huh?"

"I know so. I saw him kill ten men before they had a chance to move against him. Come to think of it, he didn't sweat then either."

Chapter 59

This is getting better all the time.

Rokk Baptiste paused for a quick moment as he remembered the story Amir had told him about the Dutchmen he had killed in seconds. He also remembered the stories Amir had told him about other battles he waged and came out of victorious. He offered Lauren a wide inviting smile and said, "He told me he had killed ten Dutchmen before being captured when you two were in Africa, but I didn't believe him. It sounded impossible. So I asked him to show me. He agreed. I picked five men I knew that were tough. Men I had trouble with, but had defeated in a one-on-one brawl. Before I knew it, all five men were out cold—quick, decisive blows to the chin. I had seen it, but I couldn't believe it. It had happened so quickly, with very little effort on his part." He was shaking his head as what he had seen materialized in his mind. "It was simply amazing what he could do. One blow each and they were all on their backs with their eyes closed. I knew then that when we fought, he had held back—a lot. The interesting thing was that he was only eighteen years old."

"How old are you, Rokk?"

"I'm twenty-four."

Lauren smiled wickedly. Now she definitely wanted him to come back to Bouvier Hill and give Joshua some competition. Joshua was the reigning plantation stud. She thought Bouvier Hill could use another one—a fresh one. She thought the women on Bouvier Hill would love a chance at him. *If I'm lucky, he might even bed Cadence. And maybe she'll turn against Joshua. After hearing the real Garden of Eden story, I'm sure Guinevere is ready to turn against her and the Delacroix Family.*

"I saw him prove himself in several battles with the French soldiers about a week after I freed him," Rokk continued. "After our leader saw the prince effortlessly killing men in battle, one after another, he asked him to train us. The prince agreed. With him leading us, we became more confident, and bolder. We believed we could win. We believed we could take over the entire island in time. It wasn't long before we started engaging the soldiers in the daytime when they least expected, when they thought they were safe and could rest. We'd sneak down there and kill a few men and steal their weapons before returning to the hills."

"So how were you two captured?"

"We think we had a traitor in our ranks. We never found out who it was. One night we had swooped down on the soldiers again, but they were not where we thought they were. By the time we realized they had outmaneuvered us, we were surrounded by hundreds of soldiers, maybe thousands. Whatever their numbers, it was a whole lot more than our raiding party of twenty."

"What made you think you had a traitor? Wasn't it possible they had figured out the prince's battle strategy?"

"It's possible, but I don't think so. But assuming they figured out what we were doing and anticipated us being there that night, how were they able to figure out the prince's name? How did they know he was the leader of the raiding party and that I was his best friend? Amir told me that he had only been at the Torvell plantation for one day before I set him free. It is highly unlikely the Torvells told anyone who he was before we set the plantation on fire. The irony of it all is that because they knew who we were, we were supposed to be the last to die. Your attorney, Winslow, got there just in time to save us. And here I am."

Lauren had heard enough. She definitely liked Rokk. "How would you like a job working for me for a while?"

"Doing what?"

"Whatever needs doing. Can you handle a team of horses?"

"I can."

"What kind of work did you do on Santo Domingo?"

"Nothing important. I was one of several blacksmiths."

This is getting better all the time, she thought, smiling. "Really," she said. "I think you're going to work out nicely. I want you to come on out to Bouvier Hill with me. Tomorrow you start working for me. I'll pay you a good wage. When we come into the city to the dress shop, I'll have you do whatever I need done and you'll pick up whatever shipments I have on the dock and around the city. You'll make deliveries as well once you learn where everything is, okay?"

For the second time, she saw his smile. It was very big and very bright. It made her uncomfortable because all of a sudden, she realized that Rokk Baptiste was a big, strong, virile man, not a uniform.

He said, "Okay, Lauren. I will work for you. I will tell the captain."

"Wait a minute," she said and grabbed his arm. She felt the thickness of his bicep, but ignored the feeling it gave her. "Can you keep a secret?"

"Yes."

"I want you to do me a favor."

"Anything."

"There's a man named Joshua on the plantation. He offended me. I want you to do to him what the prince did to you."

"You mean brawl with him."

"Yes. I want his face to be a bloody mess."

"Why, Lauren?"

"Because he offended me," she said, frowning.

"Really? Show me where he is and I'll deal with him."

"No, no, no. I don't want anything to happen to him until I say, okay?"

Rokk frowned. "Why?"

"Can you please just trust me on this?"

"Okay."

"Now . . . he'll probably start something with you, but pretend like you're afraid. And then later, when everybody's watching, bloody him up good, okay? I'll pay you a good wage for doing so."

"Okay, but you don't have to pay me to thump him. I will do it as a favor and because he offended you."

"Now . . . you can fight, right? You're not just wearing the uniform, right? It makes you look like a warrior, but it will not fight for you."

"Unless he's as hard-hitting a brawler as the prince or at least as quick, I'll take care of him for you. Trust me."

Chapter 60

"You knew the real truth all along, didn't you?"

While Lauren and Rokk were still speaking, a fancy carriage stopped where Lauren was standing. Rokk politely excused himself and entered the tavern to tell Captain Rutgers he would no longer be staying in his quarters on the *Windward*. The door of the carriage opened. Guinevere Delacroix and her four daughters descended the steps one by one. Just as Lauren suspected, Lacey, Madeline, Yvette, and Chantal were all very pretty and shapely women. All of them could pass for white women—their eyes were an assortment of blues, grays, and greens. Were it not for the tignons the law required women of color to wear, one would have to have a discerning eye to tell the difference.

As she looked at each of Guinevere's daughters, she couldn't help but think of the conversation she'd had with Christine in her dress shop a few hours ago. *How sick is Monsieur Delacroix? It's bad enough to be Guinevere's father, but to have relations with your own daughter? And when she was only fourteen? You would have thought he would have stopped after he got her with child the first time, but five children? How sick is that? Hmm, I wonder if he was still having relations with Guinevere all the way up until the moment she packed her bags to leave. She doesn't want to talk about her father or the father of her children, which are one and the same. I'll bet they are still sleeping together and she knows the whole thing is sick. That's why she doesn't want to talk about it. She's too ashamed of herself to talk about it.*

Rokk Baptiste and Captain Rutgers came out of the tavern. After the introductions were made, Guinevere's daughters got in the carriage and returned to their homes in the Tremé. Rutgers wished them all well and returned to the tavern for more brandy. It was nightfall by the time they started back to Bouvier Hill. Rokk Baptiste was in the wagon, stretched out. He was tired and had fallen asleep. Lauren and Guinevere were sitting on the bench.

Lauren couldn't wait to hear Guinevere's thoughts on what Captain Rutgers had read to her, but she wanted her to bring it up. Guinevere had been quiet again, much like she was on the way into New Orleans. She decided to start a different conversation, hoping it would lead to what she really wanted to know. "So, how was your visit with your daughters, Mademoiselle Delacroix?"

Guinevere, bubbling with joy, said, "First let me say, thank you so much for bringing me to New Orleans for the very first time. And the visit with my daughters was wonderful, Lauren! Just wonderful!"

"*Really?* It doesn't seem like it went well at all."

Unsure of what she meant by that, Guinevere said, "Whatever do you mean, child?"

"Well, you're quiet for someone who had a wonderful time with her daughters."

"Was I quiet?"

"City of the Dead quiet."

"Oh, well, I was just thinking about a few things."

"Things like . . ."

"Well, for one, my oldest girl wants me to leave Cadence and come live with her. She says the Delacroix family has taken advantage of me long enough. And when I told her that they had lied to me about the Garden of Eden story, she got mad and said, 'Mama, if they would lie to you about that, they have probably been deceiving you your entire life. How can you trust people like that?'"

"What did you say to that?"

"I told her I was thinking the same thing." She looked at Lauren. "You knew the real truth all along, didn't you?"

Chapter 61

"Please don't bring anything up tonight."

Lauren hesitated for a moment, unsure how the conversation was going to flow. If Guinevere was glad to finally hear the real Bible story, Lauren could confess that she had known. But if she was the type who would rather not hear the truth, the type who would much rather embrace ignorance than hear the hard truth, she could be facing a firing squad. She decided to continue playing dumb to see how Guinevere responded. She said, "The truth about what?"

Guinevere smiled and hit her playfully. Then she said, "Come on now, I figured it out already. I'm not angry with you. You know I'm talking about the Garden of Eden story."

Solemnly Lauren nodded and said, "Yes, Mademoiselle Delacroix, I did."

"Why didn't you say something, Lauren?"

"If I told you the truth instead of a white man reading you the truth, would you have believed me? Besides, I told you, if anything goes wrong, I don't want to get in the middle of whatever happens between you and *your* friends. And don't forget you promised to keep me out of it *and* you owe me a favor, remember?"

Guinevere exhaled. "I remember. What do you want me to do?"

"Right now, I want you to use whatever influence you have with Mrs. Bouvier to get her to let Rokk stay on the plantation until I'm ready to leave."

"As long as he pulls his weight, that shouldn't be a problem."

"He won't be working for her. He'll be working for me. I'm paying him a good wage to drive my carriage and to do whatever I need done."

"Okay, is that all I have to do?"

"For now, yes."

"Okay, I'll do that, but you've just reminded me that I'm not getting paid."

"Are you going to say something to Mrs. Bouvier about me paying Rokk?"

"You don't want me to?"

"No."

"Why not? You're paying him, aren't you?"

"Yes, but, again, I don't want to be in your mess with her. If you want her to pay you, that has nothing to do with me paying Rokk. Rokk was a good friend to the prince when they were on the island. He's a free man now and he needs money to survive. One day he's going to want to start a business or something. He's going to want a family. All of that takes money. Now you tell me . . . what does any of that have to do with you, Mademoiselle Delacroix?"

"Nothing, I guess."

"You *guess?* Forgive me, Mademoiselle Delacroix, but if your own daughters are telling you you're being taken advantage of, why not bring them into the conversation instead of me? I never said they were taking advantage of you. Your flesh and blood did. Why bring me and Rokk into it when you know we're living on her property?"

"I won't bring you into, but it's so unfair for him to get paid and I'm getting nothing for all the work I do."

With a hint of anger in her voice, Lauren sighed heavily and said, "Mademoiselle Delacroix, didn't I offer you a job this morning? Didn't I?"

"Yes."

"And didn't I promise to pay you a good wage?"

"Yes."

"And what did you say?"

"That was before I found out the Delacroix family was deceiving me."

Remembering that Guinevere couldn't be fully trusted, she watched her, studying her facial expressions as best she could in the dark. It could all be a setup to get her to divulge something that could get her executed. She quieted herself and let Guinevere talk, hoping she would reveal whatever truths that may lie beneath her deaf, dumb, and blind exterior.

"Now that I know they can't be trusted, I want to work for you and get paid. Is the job still open?"

"Do you promise not to bring me into it?"

"I promise."

"Okay, the job is yours. And Mademoiselle Delacroix . . . whatever you do, please don't bring anything up tonight. Let's all sleep on it and if you feel the same way tomorrow, bring it up then. Tonight though, I just want Rokk to get some of your delicious food and get a good night's rest, okay?"

"Okay."

Chapter 62

"I had to make sure they had finished."

Lauren drove the wagon through the gates, up the hill, and over to the stables. She woke Rokk up and showed him where he would be sleeping for the night. Then she showed him where her horses' stalls were. She promised to bring him something to eat as soon as they returned to Bouvier Manor. Lauren and Guinevere then left the stables and headed over to the big house.

Guinevere was quiet again for a while and then reluctantly, it seemed, she said, "Lauren, I have to tell you something."

They stopped walking and faced each other.

"I'm listening, Mademoiselle Delacroix."

She lowered her eyes to the ground before saying, "I don't know how to say this, but, I was brought here to be a thorn in your side."

Lauren was beaming inside. She had hoped this confession would come one day, but she didn't know it would happen so soon. Nevertheless, she had to continue to act like she had no idea what was going on, hoping she'd get a full confession now. "What do you mean to be a thorn in my side?"

"Cadence hates you, Lauren!"

"Really? Why?"

"She hates the idea of you getting all that money her husband left you. She hates the fact that her children love you; especially Josette and young Beaumont. She hates the idea of you living in the mansion. She hates you because you now own what was once her dress shop. She hates you even more because you have made it grow in the last six months when she thought it would fall apart in her absence. She hates you because you speak so many languages and she doesn't. She hates you because you're pretty. She hates you because she thinks Joshua likes you. She hates everything about you, Lauren. Everything!"

Smiling within, Lauren said, "I can understand her hating me for most of that. But what does Joshua liking me have to do with anything? I'm confused." She hoped that last question would be enough to get her to tell all she knew about Cadence's affair with him.

Still looking at the ground, she said, "I was also brought here to cover for what's going on between her and Joshua."

"Between her and Joshua?" Lauren repeated, believably pretending to be unaware of the liaison. "What are you talking about?"

Guinevere took a deep breath and said, "They are seeing each other in secret."

"What?"

"You heard me right, Lauren. I'm being totally honest with you. I wouldn't lie about a thing like that. If it ever got out, there would be hell to pay. That's why I told Josette to have a piece of the crème brûlée last night when you two were about to go up to bed. They were in the room next to mine going at it. When you and Josette were about to go to bed last night, I had to make sure they had finished. I didn't want Josette to hear them. I don't know how long it's been going on, but I'm starting to wonder if it was going on before Aubrey and the housemen killed her husband."

Chapter 63

"Why are you telling me all of this?"

Upon hearing that someone other than Christine had figured out what really happened in the mansion the night of the murders, Lauren, trying her best to keep the smile within from bursting forth, asked, "Why would you wonder about that?"

"Well, I don't know if you know this, but her husband was what they call a Molly! Did you know that?"

"I heard his brother call him that in Monsieur Bouvier's attorney's office, but I don't know what it means."

"It means that he's perverted, Lauren! It means that he likes men, not women!"

Still playing the dumb role, knowing Guinevere could still be working in concert with Cadence, Lauren knew not to say a word about Beaumont's proclivities. If Guinevere called him names, that was up to her. She had Cadence's protection. They needed each other, but Lauren was still expendable. She wasn't going to offer anything just in case Guinevere turned out to be just like Aubrey and Herman Torvell. She said, "Oh, okay, well, what does that have to do with what you're telling me now?"

Guinevere exhaled hard. "Don't you see, Lauren? Aubrey was a Molly and so were the housemen."

Lauren still looked confused, wanting her to confess it all herself.

"Lauren, I wondered about this when Cadence told me she was bedding Joshua. She wanted me to cover for her. I've known her since we were children and with her husband being a Molly, well, I guess I didn't see anything wrong with her hiding the horn with Joshua. I mean the menfolk seem to hide the horn with as many women folk as they can and nothing is ever said about it. Nothing! So I thought if Cadence is doing the same, so what? But now, though, I'm wondering if she had something to do with her husband's death."

"Hiding the horn? What do you mean by that?"

Guinevere smiled and then stuck her index finger through the circle created by the thumb and index finger of her other hand. "You know."

"Oh!" Lauren said and laughed. Then she thought for a second and said, "Mademoiselle Delacroix, that makes no sense. Hiding the horn with Joshua doesn't mean she killed her husband. Besides, Mrs. Bouvier couldn't have killed two men. She's not strong enough."

"Lauren, have you heard one word I've said?"

"Yes. I've heard everything."

"Don't you realize Joshua could have killed her husband and the other man by himself? He's a really big man!"

"Hmm. I suppose he could have . . . but . . . what made you think of all of this?"

"When I was telling my daughters about it, they all thought the same thing I was thinking. To be honest, it crossed my mind when I heard what happened, but I didn't believe Cadence would do something like that. Lacey, my oldest girl, said, if she could deceive me about a small matter like a Bible story when there was no reason to, she could deceive me about a big matter like murder, when there was every reason to; especially if she profits from it."

"Well, assuming it's all true, what are you going to do about it?"

"Nothing."

"Nothing?"

"What can I do? I am a free woman, but I'm still a nigger, Lauren. What I think happened does not matter. Not at all. If white folks don't stop her, no nigger, no matter how fancy, ever will. This is something white folks have to handle. If they don't, I guess the good Lord up above will have to in the hereafter is all I can say."

"Why are you telling me all of this?"

"I've known you all of one day, Lauren. And you did right by me from the very beginning. I've known Cadence and the Delacroix family all my life and they deceived me from the very beginning. I trust you more than I will ever trust them again."

When Lauren heard Guinevere declare her trust, she felt a pang of guilt. Her plan had worked and she had successfully turned the tables on Cadence, but it didn't feel right. It felt wrong to continue deceiving a woman who had told her the truth while she offered nothing, no confirmation of any kind. She felt like confessing all, but she couldn't. She wanted Cadence to pay and now it was all coming together. Christine knew about the murder and so did Guinevere. That meant other people might know too. She began to wonder if Walker Tresvant knew and hadn't said anything. She thought he must have. If Guinevere could figure it out, an educated man like Tresvant had to, too.

"Is there anything else you want to tell me, Mademoiselle Delacroix?"

"Yes. I want you to call me Guinevere from now on. We're going to be good friends, I suspect." She reached out and hugged her. "Thank you for having the captain read the story to me. Like Eve, my eyes are open now, too."

They continued up the hill until they reached the mansion. They entered through the kitchen door and to their surprise, Guinevere's father was there waiting for her.

Act 3

End Game

Chapter 64

"This ain't over, son."

"**P**ack your things. It's time to come home to plantation Delacroix," Emile Delacroix said, as soon as Guinevere, his daughter and concubine, walked through the door. His hair and full beard were white. He was a handsome man and it was clear that Cadence had gotten both her looks and her attitude from him.

"Don't pack anything," Cadence said defiantly, but smiling all the while. "You don't work for the ol' goat anymore. You work for me now. You're not going anywhere."

Lauren knew then that all her plans may have been for naught with this unexpected development. Amir had explained the intricacies of combat. She knew that war, even a concealed war, like the one she was waging, was and always would be a fluid situation; meaning it was always unstable, always unpredictable. No matter how well one planned, the unexpected could happen and dramatically shake things up suddenly and irrevocably. Amir went on to explain that battles are often won because of momentum. One army could be routing another army, but something unexpectedly happens, and they end up retreating or they get slaughtered for standing their ground in a no-win situation.

With this in mind, Lauren went to the cabinet and got a plate, listening intensely to everything being said, knowing that if things went bad, they could go bad quickly and her life would be in danger if Guinevere said too much. She went over to the stove and started piling food on it for Rokk.

"Is this the heifer you were telling me about, Cadence?" Emile asked, while glaring at Lauren.

"Yes, Daddy," Cadence said. "That's the one Beaumont left a small fortune to."

"I'm not going anywhere, Master Delacroix," Guinevere said with rancor. "I'm staying right here. And if not here, I'll stay with one of our . . . one of my four daughters in the Tremé."

Lauren's eyes bulged, sensing disaster.

"Now you listen to me, Guinevere Delacroix," Emile began again. "You do what *I* say and nuthin' else. You got that?"

"I'm a free woman now, Master Delacroix. I paid you in more ways than one for my freedom. I'm not coming back to your plantation—ever!"

Emile grabbed her by the arm. Guinevere snatched away.

Watching all of this, Lauren knew all bets were off. It was all about to come out whether Guinevere planned it to come out or not—that's what she thought anyway. She watched them to see where it was all going, ready to make a dash for the door and escape if necessary.

"What's gotten into you?" Emile said and snatched her by the arm again. "You do what I tell you! Now you get up them stairs and you pack your bags right now!"

"Don't you move, Guinevere," Cadence commanded, no longer smiling. She was all business now. "You're not going anywhere!"

Emile turned around and eyed Cadence. "Just who in the hell do you think you are, missy, to contradict me?" Smack!

He backhanded her and she fell to the floor. He whirled around and he eyed Guinevere. "You still here?"

"Master Delacroix, I told you . . ."

Emile backhanded her. Smack! She was now on her backside too.

About this time, all of Cadence's children came running into the kitchen. They had heard the shouting and the blows.

When she realized what was going on, Josette ran to Lauren and wrapped her arms around her, crying uncontrollably. "Please make him stop, Lauren!"

Young Beaumont screamed, "Grandfather, no!"

Smack! Emile backhanded him too. Now he was on the floor.

"What the hell is going on around here?" Emile screamed. "When I say something . . . that's the end of it! Now . . . if I have to . . . I'll kill every last one of ya." He looked at Guinevere again. "For the last time . . . get your things. You're coming back to plantation Delacroix where you belong. I don't care if you *are* free. You're mine and you're always going to be mine. Don't you know that, Guinevere? I'll never let you leave me. Never! I'll see you dead first!"

Young Beaumont got up and ran out of the room. He came back seconds later with a loaded musket. He pointed it at his grandfather's head and said, "I'll say this only one time, Grandfather. I'm the man of the house now that Father's gone. Me! Not you! Now . . . you get outta here right now, or I won't be responsible for what happens to you."

Emile stared at his grandson for about a minute, trying to figure out if young Beaumont had the guts to shoot him. He looked into his eyes, hoping he'd see some hint of reluctance, but what he saw was unflinching resolve. He knew young Beaumont would shoot him. His tone changed. "Would you kill your own flesh and blood?"

"If I have to, Grandfather. Let's not find out. Walk out the front door and we'll both be happy. You'll be glad to be alive and I'll be glad I didn't blow your brains out. Now . . . what's it going to be?"

Emile went back to the kitchen table, snatched up his hat, and angrily secured it to his head. Then he fast-walked toward the kitchen doorway. He stopped and turned around. "This ain't over, son! I'll be back and when I come back, Guinevere will be leaving with me!" Then he stormed out of the kitchen. A few seconds later, they all heard the front door open and slam shut.

Chapter 65

"So Lauren had nothing to do with it?"

Guinevere looked at Lauren and said, "Could you please take the children to their rooms? I need to have a talk with their mother."

"Sure, Guinevere," Lauren said, loving it all. "Just let me take this plate out to Rokk. I'll be right back."

"Can I go with you, Lauren?" Josette said, no longer crying.

"Sure, sweetie. Come on."

"Who is Rokk?" Cadence asked firmly.

Feeling sure of herself, Guinevere said, "Lauren's friend. He'll be staying here for a while. He's working for Lauren now."

Looking at Lauren, Cadence said, "Nobody asked my permission."

Guinevere said, "Young Beaumont, you did good, son. Now you put that musket away and come on back to the kitchen." He did exactly as he was told and came right back. "Now, I have to talk to your mother in private. Go on out to the stables with Lauren and when you return, I want you to go around to the front door and on upstairs to your bedrooms. Do not come back through the kitchen door or I'll skin all of you alive."

"Yes, ma'am," the children said, and followed Lauren out the back door.

Angry now, Cadence said, "What in the world has gotten into you, Guinevere?"

"What's gotten into me?" Guinevere replied, glaring at her like she wanted to slap the taste out of her mouth. "The truth. That's what's gotten into me."

Frowning, Cadence said, "What do you mean the truth has gotten into you?"

Noticeably angry, Guinevere said, "I mean you and your family lied to me."

Having no idea what her longtime friend was talking about, she put her hands on her hips and said, "We lied to you? We lied to you about what?"

Guinevere folded her arms and looked Cadence directly in the eyes. "You told me God was a woman!"

Cadence laughed out loud for a few seconds and let her hands slide off her hips. "Oh, that. That's nothing. It was just a private joke among the Delacroix women. Is that what's bothering you?"

"A joke, huh?" Guinevere said and tightened her folded arms. "So you and your family have been laughing at me for almost forty years? I thought we were friends and then some. Now I see we were nothing . . . nothing at all."

"Oh, Guinevere, come on. It was just a little joke. That's all. You're taking it much too seriously."

"Am I? Am I really? If I'm taking *your* joke much too seriously, you're taking too much advantage of me."

Feeling the pressure of the attack, Cadence folded her arms and said, "What do you mean I'm taking advantage of you?"

"I mean if I'm to continue working here, I want to be paid a good wage. As a matter of fact, I'm not sure I want to work for you anymore, given that you are capable of lying to me about something as small a matter as a Bible story. It's the small sins that lead to the bigger ones. Your mother has been telling us that for years. For all I know, you could be lying about a host of other things."

Suddenly Cadence realized what was really going on. "This is all Lauren's fault! I can't believe you would let her come between us! You've known me all your life, Guinevere. You've only known Lauren for two days. How could you let her do this to us? How could you let her ruin our friendship so easily?"

"This isn't about Lauren, Cadence. It's about *you* and *your* family taking advantage of me for the last ten years. I worked for you as a slave and I continued working for you free of charge when I bought my freedom. Now . . . since you and your family thought it was funny to lead me astray for better than thirty years . . . I need a good wage to continue working for you just like any other free Negro in New Orleans. That's why your father never wanted me to go in town. He knew I'd find out how things *really* work. He knew I'd find out that free Negroes own their own businesses and everything. He knew I'd find out that free Negroes get *paid* and live well. Now . . . I need to get paid for all that I do around here. Otherwise, I'll be leaving in the morning. Tonight, if Lauren will take me to my daughter's house."

"I can't believe you're serious about this, Guinevere."

"Believe it. I'm very serious."

"If this isn't about Lauren, why does her name keep coming up?"

"If Lauren's name keeps coming up, it's because *you* keep bringing her name into this. Not me."

"If Lauren hasn't influenced you to talk to me like this, how is that you want *her* to take you to your daughter's home instead of asking me? Joshua or Dupre could take you over to your daughter's home. Why did you say Lauren would do it? Have you asked her already? Have you already discussed this with her?"

With her arms still folded, Guinevere tightened them a bit

more and said, "I only asked Lauren about a job on the way home. I had already discussed leaving here and living with Lacey or with one of my daughters. Lauren agreed to give me the same job I turned down this morning because I didn't know then what I know now."

"What didn't you know this morning?"

Guinevere exhaled hard. "I didn't know that you and your family have been shamelessly taking advantage of me. All four of my daughters agree that I can do better on my own. So on the way back to Bouvier Hill, I asked Lauren if she would still give me the job she had offered this morning."

Deflated, Cadence said, "Okay, Guinevere, fine. If you want to be compensated for your work, I'll pay you a good wage. Now, will you stay here and help me with the house and the children?"

"One other thing. I'm going to be working in New Orleans at the dress shop for Lauren too. I start tomorrow."

"Tomorrow? You start tomorrow, Guinevere? But I thought you decided you didn't want the job. I thought you just said you were only taking it if I didn't pay you."

"I didn't want the job at first. Now I do."

It suddenly occurred to Cadence that this all started with a Bible story that she and her mother had fabricated three decades ago. She was wondering how she had learned the truth. "Wait a minute. Who told you about the Bible story? Your daughters?"

Remembering her promise, she said, "A white man I met in New Orleans today. He had a Bible with him and I asked him to read the story to me. I had him read it to me ten times because what he was reading wasn't the same story you had been telling me for years."

"So Lauren had nothing to do with it?"

Chapter 66

"What is there to think about?"

The question was penetrating and it put Guinevere further on the defensive. She wanted to get it all out in the open, but she also wanted to keep her promise to Lauren. Faced with that dilemma, she thought the best course of action would be to match Cadence's aggression with her own. To accomplish that without being threatening, she changed the subject. "Are you jealous of her or something?"

Cadence looked away. "No."

"Hmpf! You sure act like it."

Cadence folded her arms again and said, "What do you mean?"

"When she offered me a job this morning and mentioned she would pay me, you didn't like it. And when she told you that Joshua had tried to bed her six months ago, that angered you too."

Pacing the floor now, Cadence said, "I can explain that. It wasn't jealousy. It's just that I wanted you to work for me. She was trying to take you away from me. As far as Joshua is concerned, she has it all mixed up or she's lying. And that's what made me angry. It wasn't jealousy."

"Call it whatever you like, but it sounded like you were angry. And I'll tell you another thing. It doesn't look good to be bedding Joshua. People might think he killed your husband for you."

Guinevere was so full of herself she didn't realize the position she had just put herself in. She didn't realize that Cadence was capable of killing her too, if necessary.

"Guinevere!" Cadence shouted. Then she took a deep breath and gathered herself. "I have indulged you because I've known you all my life. You have forgotten your place. I'm your friend, but I'm also the master of Bouvier Hill. Now, I said I would pay you for your services, but . . . don't forget your place."

They heard the front door open and close along with lively chatter. They couldn't quite make out what was being said by Lauren and the children, but they were laughing as they climbed the stairs.

Whispering now, Cadence said, "Now . . . I don't want to hear any more talk about me killing Beaumont, do you understand?"

Guinevere realized that Cadence was indeed the master of Bouvier Hill. She also realized that no matter what truths she had unearthed, she was still a nigger, whether she looked like it or not, which meant Cadence could kill her for any reason and nothing would be done about it. It was one thing to quit working for her and quite another to accuse her of murder. That was way out of bounds. With Beaumont being dead, and believing her lifelong friend engineered it, she humbled herself and remembered her lowly status in life. She unfolded her arms and lowered her head before saying, "Yes, I understand."

"Good. Now, what is Lauren paying you?"

"We haven't discussed money yet."

"Including room and board, I'm willing to pay you ten cents a day. How does that sound?"

"What about the ten years I've worked for free? Can we add that in too?"

"You cannot be serious. You expect *me* to pay *you* for the ten years you worked for Mother and Father? Why don't you ask them to pay you all that money?"

"I just might. Your father just demanded that I return to plantation Delacroix. He might just pay me all that and then some if I return."

"Good luck getting any money out of him!"

"I'll think about your offer."

"What is there to think about?"

"To be honest with you, I'm thinking about opening an eatery in the Quarter someday. If I do, I would have to leave here anyway." She remembered that Captain Rutgers had told her not to accept the first offer; he had told her Cadence would be willing to pay more. "Besides, I don't think I could work for less than fifteen cents a day."

"You expect me to pay you fifteen cents a day? Are you serious, Guinevere?"

"I'm very serious. It's fifteen cents or I move out of here first thing in the morning."

"Okay, I'll pay you what you're asking, but won't it take a few years to save up all the money you'll need to start your business?"

"I have plenty of money to start now, if I want to."

"Okay, do what you want, but you've got a lot to do here. I don't see how you can do both. Beaumont had seven men running this place. You need to find the people to help you run the place as efficiently as they did. And that might require a lot of time." She looked at the clock and realized that Joshua would be coming to Aubrey's room soon. She needed to prepare for his arrival. "So you think about it. I'm going to bed. Good night, Guinevere."

"Good night," Guinevere said, smiling from ear to ear. It had been one of the best days of her life. A wonderful day indeed!

Chapter 67

"See to it that it doesn't!"

While Cadence didn't show it, she was still very angry when she left the kitchen. She had known Guinevere for nearly forty years and she had never ever spoken to her so boldly before. Although Guinevere had denied it, Cadence knew Lauren was behind it all. Lauren had taken just about everything away from her. Now she had taken her best friend too. There were only three things left to take: her home, her man, and her life. As far as Cadence was concerned, she wanted all three; especially her man. The way she saw it, Lauren wanted Joshua more than anything. She thought this because she herself wanted him more than anything. After that first sexual encounter with him, she was hooked.

I don't understand why I'm the only one who can see how conniving the little witch is. It's like she's cast some sort of spell on everybody but me. I'm going to put a stop to it. I wish I could just get rid of her and be done with it. But if I do that, Marie-Elise and Walker Tresvant will collect another 10 percent of the money that rightfully belongs to me. It's so unfair! And all of it happening right under my own roof. And where does she get off thinking she can bring a nigger man to Bouvier Hill without asking my permission first? She's smart. I'll say that much for her. She only hired Guinevere to work for her because she knew that would put pressure on me. I can't get rid of her, but I can give her a piece of my mind and that's exactly what I'm going to do right after I say good night to my children.

She climbed the stairs in an angry huff, but when she opened the door of each of her children's rooms, she forced herself to smile and say, "Good night and sweet dreams." Then she climbed another set of stairs and went to Lauren's room. She didn't bother knocking. She just opened the door, went in, and closed it behind her. She shouted, "I know what you're doing! But it won't work!"

Lauren grabbed her clothing and covered her exposed chest. She was washing herself before going to bed. She turned around and said, "Mrs. Bouvier, I realize this is your house . . . but I do have a right to be here. So please . . . from now on . . . would you please knock before coming in here?"

Cadence ignored her request and said, "I know what you're doing to Guinevere, my children, Joshua, and everyone on this plantation. They may not see you for who you really are, but I do."

"Mrs. Bouvier, I have no idea what you're talking about. I've been nothing but courteous to you and everyone else since I arrived. I've done nothing to harm you in any way."

Cadence rolled her eyes and shouted, "You must think I'm a fool, Lauren! You love the idea that you're turning everyone against me!"

Lauren offered a confused frown. "Turning everyone against you? Why would I do that? I have a lovely place to stay and a good business thanks to you. What have I done that I need to apologize for? Could you please tell me that? And I'll gladly do it."

"You turned Guinevere against me!"

"Did she tell you that?"

"She didn't have to! She was fine until she met you, and now she wants me to pay her to work for me!"

"I never told her to ask you to pay her. I never said anything to her about money other than I wanted her to work at the shop and I would pay her. I thought you were paying her already because you two had been friends since you were children. I didn't know you weren't paying her until she said you weren't. I only told her I would pay her because the other free blacks in New Orleans get paid. Mrs. Bouvier, I've only been here a short while. I still don't understand how everything works. I'm sorry if I caused you any trouble with your friend. If you think she listens to me, I'll go and tell her right now that she should continue working for you free of charge, because that's how things are done on Bouvier Hill."

Cadence exhaled hard. "No. It's too late now."

"No, it isn't. I'm sure she's still awake. I'll go right now."

"No. I meant that she already knows you were going to pay her, so now I've decided to pay her too."

Lauren smiled within. She knew all along Cadence wasn't talking about the lateness of the hour. "Are you sure you don't want me to talk to her?"

"No. Don't say anything to her." She took a deep breath and tried to calm down. "Also, just so you know, she won't be working for you at the shop. She'll be working for me here."

"Okay, that's fine with me."

"And another thing, don't you ever bring another nigger out here to live without checking with me first! Do you understand me?"

"Yes, Mrs. Bouvier. I understand you, but you were the one who told me I couldn't use Bouvier slaves forever. So are you now saying I can use Bouvier slaves until I'm ready to move?"

Cadence had forgotten that she did in fact tell Lauren that. Lauren had found a way to use her own words against her; that, too, vexed her. She stared at Lauren for a few seconds as the day she had said those words washed over her.

Shaking her head, Cadence said, "I did say that. But . . . even so . . . you still should have checked with me before bringing him here."

"You're right, of course," Lauren said, loving every minute of it all. "It won't ever happen again."

"See to it that it doesn't! You can thank Guinevere for why I'm allowing it this time."

And with that, Cadence stormed out of the room and slammed the door.

Chapter 68

"Just come with me now and be very quiet."

As soon as Cadence left, Lauren laughed hard and from her belly, albeit silently. She had Cadence right where she wanted her. She believed that Cadence had no idea what was going on. She was being blamed for everything because it was convenient. She believed Cadence had to blame somebody for the mess her life was becoming.

She understood that people rarely took responsibility for their own nonsense. It was always somebody else's fault when the consequences of their decisions pursued them and wreaked havoc on their lives and their children's lives. She had seen it in Africa and now she was witnessing it in the New World. She also knew that people tended to blame the person they knew was innocent of the charges they were levying against them.

Some of her best lessons were learned by watching the interaction of American women who came to her shop. Nothing, however, topped the interaction of the Bouvier and Delacroix women. In this case, Cadence happened to be right about Lauren, but she did not know she was. Cadence blamed her because it was convenient. By laying everything at Lauren's feet, she didn't have to look at herself and see the wickedness of her own heart.

Lauren waited for about a half an hour and then crept down to Aubrey's former room. She put her ear to the door and listened. Cadence and Joshua were going at it again something fierce. She shook her head and whispered, "What a whore." Then she crept down the stairs and entered young Beaumont's room. She sat next to him and woke him up.

It was dark in the room and he couldn't see her. Groggily, he said, "Is something wrong, Lauren?"

She whispered, "Earlier today you wanted to take care of me. Did you mean that?"

"Of course I meant it, Lauren," he said. With renewed hope, he asked, "Have you made up your mind? Are you going to let me take care of you for the rest of your life?"

She wanted him to know that what she was about to say was sincere and heartfelt. She sighed and softened her voice to get his attention. "Well, you might change your mind when I tell you what I have to tell you."

"What's going on?" he asked, more alert, yet apprehensive about what she was going to say.

She hesitated for a brief moment and then sighed again before saying, "Let me ask you this. Do you still love Brigitte?"

Young Beaumont was silent while he searched his heart for a second or two while resting his head on his palm. Then he said, "I suppose I'll always love her. But I love you too."

"That's what I thought. Thanks so much for being honest. Now, let me ask you another question. And please . . . young Beaumont, please be honest with me, okay?"

"Okay, Lauren," he said from the heart. "I'll be honest with you."

"Thank you. Now here's the question. If you knew where Brigitte was, who would you rather spend the rest of your life with? Me or her?"

Young Beaumont hesitated for a few seconds. As much as he wanted to be totally honest with her, he realized he couldn't be. Not if he wanted to win her heart and make her his own. He thought that if he told the whole truth, his answer would offend her. He chose what he thought was the safe route by saying, "I'd love to spend the rest of my life with both of you."

Lauren exhaled hard, knowing he was being dishonest with her. She could have told him what she wanted him to know, but the game of death was still afoot and she was playing it step by step. "Okay, but if you could only have one of us for the rest of your life, which one of us would you rather be with? Please be honest for both our sakes."

Young Beaumont exhaled and said, "Lauren, I don't want to hurt your feelings. You believe me, don't you?"

"Yes, I believe you. But I want an honest answer even if it does hurt me. I have a big decision to make. I want to make the right one."

Young Beaumont quieted himself. He thought he loved Lauren. He certainly wanted to bed her, but what she was asking for, he wasn't sure he could give because he knew his heart still belonged to Brigitte. He exhaled again and then said, "I don't want to hurt you, Lauren. I don't."

"I just want the truth regardless of my feelings. If you don't tell the truth now, you may end up regretting it for the rest of your life. Be totally honest with me, please."

He hesitated for a few more seconds, believing his answer would crush her. His answer would make it nearly impossible to make her his. He looked away and said, "Okay then, to be honest with you, if I had to choose one of you, I'd have to choose Brigitte."

Relieved, she sighed, pleased that he chose Brigitte instead of her. She said, "That's what I thought. Thanks for being honest. I know how difficult it can be to tell the hard truth. Now . . . what if I knew where she was? What if I could tell you where she is? What would you do?"

Stunned, he looked at her and said, "You know where she is, Lauren?"

"I don't know her exact whereabouts, no. But I do know where she is. I found out today."

Excited, he said, "Where?"

"She's in a convent in Italy."

"How did you find out?"

"Promise not to tell?"

"Of course."

She looked at him for a few seconds, and then said, "Swear."

"I swear I won't tell a soul you were the one who told me," he said before she could finish her request.

"Your aunt Christine told me today. I don't think she intended to, but she did."

Upon hearing what he had been fruitlessly seeking for months, he sat up in his bed and said, "I'm going to go there and find her."

"Good, but, don't tell anybody what you're doing. They'll try to stop you. Pretend to go to Cambridge as planned. Do not change your destination here in New Orleans. Someone may know your family and tell them. Go on to Cambridge first and then book passage to Italy. No one will know what happened until you've found and married her. Stay in Italy until she is with child and has the baby. That way no one can force her to get rid of it like they did the last time, understand?"

"Yes, but why are you helping me?"

"Have you forgotten so quickly, young Beaumont? The prince is dead. I understand exactly how you feel. Brigitte is still alive. Find her! Marry her! Be happy with her!"

"I will. Thanks so much, Lauren."

"You're welcome."

He quieted himself, suddenly realizing that Lauren had not only revealed information that he couldn't find, but she had told him something he had not known. "Wait a minute. Brigitte was with child? My child? And they made her get rid of it? They made her kill my child?"

"Yes. And then they whisked her away from you so that you would never see her again. Now, come with me," she said before he had a chance to ask questions she did not want to answer. "I want to show you something."

"What?"

"Just come with me now and be very quiet."

"Okay."

Chapter 69

Time to go!

Young Beaumont slid into his trousers and followed Lauren down the long hallway and up the stairs, wondering where they were going, but hoping she was leading him to her room to have relations. They crept up to Aubrey's room and listened. He heard a woman's fever-pitched sighs. They reminded him of how Brigitte sounded when they were intimate. He snickered quietly and asked, "Who's in there?"

"I think it's Joshua and Guinevere."

Young Beaumont laughed heartily, but quietly, so as not to be heard. "Let's bust in there and catch 'em in the act."

"No. I don't think we should." She tugged and pulled at his arm. "Come on, let's go."

"Come on, Lauren. It'll be fun. We won't tell on 'em. Come on."

"No. Don't do it. Let whoever's in there have a little fun."

Young Beaumont crept over to the other side of the hall and took a lit oil lamp off the wall. Then he crept back over to the door and silently counted, *one . . . two . . . three.* Then they burst into the room.

"Hi, Joshua! Hi, Guinevere! We caught you two!" He saw a

woman's legs on a man's shoulders. She was folded like an accordion. The room fell suddenly silent. Only the synchronous gasps of the caught man and woman could be heard. Without thought, it seemed, the man and the woman turned their heads to see who had interrupted their coupling. That's when young Beaumont saw their faces.

For a few seconds, everything stopped and quiet consumed the room as the shock of the moment saturated their minds. Lauren was the only one in the room who wasn't in shock. She was in absolute heaven, seeing the look of utter humiliation on Cadence's face. Joshua snatched himself out of Cadence, quickly grabbed his clothes, covered his privates, and ran out of the room.

Totally blown away by what he had seen and heard, young Beaumont said, "Mother?"

Cadence was completely undone. She pulled the cover over herself and screamed, "Get out of here!"

"What the hell is going on, Mother?"

Although Lauren hadn't planned to burst into the room, it had happened and there was no going back. She had seen Cadence's face when she realized that her firstborn son had seen her nakedness and her shame. That's why she went into the room too. For a few precious seconds, it felt so good to know that Cadence would never be able to explain what young Beaumont had seen with his own eyes and heard with his own ears. She knew it was time to go.

Chapter 70

"So now we don't have a place to stay?"

Lauren ran out of the room and bumped into Guinevere, who was awakened by Cadence's scream and on her way into the room. She pushed her way past her and ran down to her room. She could hear young Beaumont and Cadence screaming at each other. She knew the other children were bound to hear it and they would soon be running up the stairs to see the spectacle. Dressed now, she ran down the stairs, two at a time, and ran into Josette, knocking her down. She apologized and kept moving; her life hung in the balance. She took the next set of stairs as quickly as she could and ran through the kitchen and out the open back door Joshua had just bolted through like an Olympian.

Down the hill she ran at full speed, gravity pulling her along at record speed. She opened the stable door and woke up Rokk. "Get up! We have to leave now!"

Still half asleep and groggy, Rokk said, "Why? What's going on?"

"Move it, Rokk! Or die where you lay! It's up to you!"

Rokk jumped up and was helping her with the team of

horses when out of nowhere a fully dressed Joshua jumped on his back and shouted, "Where do y'all think y'all goin'?"

While Lauren quickly hooked the team of horses to the wagon, the two men fought, but it wasn't much of a fight. Lauren watched for a few seconds to see who would prevail. Rokk was busting Joshua up good, just as he said he would, but she was too scared to enjoy it. She continued hitching the horses to the wagon again. She kept hearing vicious licks being delivered with awesome precision. There seemed to be a rapid rhythm to the blows. Smack! Smack! Smack! She heard grunts and groans. She climbed on the bench portion of the wagon and watched from there. "Bloody his face, Rokk! Bloody his face good!" she screamed. Then she laughed. "He earned it and then some."

If Rokk somehow lost, she was in position to take off, but he wasn't losing at the moment. He was punishing Joshua with bone-crushing punches, but he would not fall. Rokk backed off a little and let him swing and miss to take away his energy and whatever wind he had left. Joshua was desperate now and swinging wildly. Rokk ducked, bobbed and weaved, and delivered thunderous blows to his body. Boom! Boom! Boom! They sounded off and then he punched him in the face again. Smack! Smack! Smack! Rokk hit him with three wicked left hooks in a row, yet Joshua was still on his feet, still coming forward for more. He seemed determined to kill Rokk. But in his haste to get his hands on the man that was literally reshaping his face, he walked into an uppercut that ended it decisively. Rokk jumped on the back of the wagon.

"Hah!" Lauren yelled and snapped the leather reins on the backs of the team of horses and they took off. They sped out the gate and down the road at full speed.

"What happened, Lauren?" Rokk asked calmly. The prince had taught him how to breathe when brawling, which gave him a distinct advantage.

"It got crazy in there."

"I thought everything was okay. One minute you're bringing me food and the next you're saying we have to leave. What happened?"

"I showed young Beaumont who his mother really was," Lauren said, and snapped the reins again.

"What do you mean you showed him who his mother really was?"

"The man you just beat up was Joshua."

"The same man you wanted me to bloody in front of others."

"Yes."

"Hmpf . . . okay . . . so . . . what happened?"

"Well . . . he is Cadence's lover."

"The woman who owns the place?"

"Yes."

"So her son saw her with the slave? He saw them together?"

"Yes. He has a quick mind. It won't take him long to figure it all out."

"Figure all what out?"

"That his mother and the man you just tussled with killed his father and several other men on the plantation."

"What?"

"Yes. I was planning something else, but I let her get to me and I took her son up to their love nest. I only wanted him to listen. I told him I thought it was Guinevere and Joshua. He was going to find out later anyway and when he did, he would know exactly who his mother was. He would know that the woman who brought him into this world was a liar. He would know what she was capable of no matter what excuse she came up with.

"No woman wants her son to know she's a whore. Having her son, her favorite son, her heart and soul, know that she could hide the horn with the niggers, but he couldn't, would expose her as the ultimate hypocrite. This truth would then separate mother and son for a long time, perhaps forever. Cadence's heart would be shattered into a thousand pieces. She would never be the same. Having him listen was supposed to be a foreshadowing of a future revelation, when either Christine or Guinevere used their knowledge of it against her. But unfortunately, he wanted to have some fun by busting in on them. I didn't count on that."

"Why didn't you stop him?"

"I tried, but he was determined to see them. He busted in and here we are. I have to tell you, Rokk, seeing the look on Cadence's face, seeing the shock and the shame, seeing her fear and hurt all at the same time gave me more pleasure than I've had in a long time. And to be honest with you, looking back on it, I'm glad her favorite son busted in on her. It serves her right after all she's done. She should have never busted into my room like she did, talking to me like she still owned me, and it wouldn't have happened. Her favorite son would have learned of it, but he would have never seen it. If she somehow survives what I'm about to do to her now, maybe next time she'll knock before entering someone's private dwelling."

"So now we don't have a place to stay?"

Lauren kind of laughed and said, "I'm hoping we'll be welcomed where we're going."

"Which is where?"

"Château Tresvant."

Chapter 71

"Come in, come in, dear girl."

Lauren pulled the team of horses up to the front door of Château Tresvant and stopped. Everything had happened so fast she hadn't had time to really weigh her options, which was one reason why she should not have let her anger control and dictate her course of action. She should have responded to Cadence's tirade with undisturbed serenity. Refraining from comment or action would have given her the rest of the night to think of a way to make her enemy pay for speaking to her like she was a slave. But because she reacted instead of responding, she was on the run and was no longer welcome in the house she had every right to be in. More important, her life was on the line.

Now she had to improvise and deal with people she had no faith in. She could go to Captain Rutgers, but she didn't know how much sway he had with the authorities, and he was over an hour away on the docks if he was aboard the *Windward*. She could have also gone to the garrison commandant, but she was black and the soldiers were white. They may not have even allowed her to see the commandant. Even if they had, she didn't think he would believe the story she was prepared to tell him. The third and only real choice was Walker Tresvant and his wife, Marie-Elise.

Walker and Marie-Elise had more to gain and more motivation than the other two combined. They also had enough wealth between them to be respected by the authorities. If nothing else, Marie-Elise had three things going for her. She was white, a lady, and wealthy; a combination that demanded attention and respect by all. Besides those three things, Beaumont Bouvier was Marie-Elise's brother, and she didn't like Cadence. Then there was Cadence's 30 percent of the Bouvier fortune. If the law meted out righteous justice for murder, the Tresvants would collect it.

Lauren told Rokk to wait in the wagon until she returned. Then she trotted up the stairs to the double doors of the mansion. When the doorman answered, she said, "I'm Lauren Renee Bouvier. It is of vital importance that I speak with Marie-Elise Tresvant right away."

"Please wait here for a moment," the doorman began. "I'll check with Mrs. Tresvant and see if she'll be able to accommodate you."

The doorman returned a few minutes later and invited her into the mansion. She followed him down the corridor to the parlor where she expected to wait for Marie-Elise, and possibly Walker, given the lateness of the hour. She waited for the man to open a pair of wood framed glass doors, but stopped in her tracks and gasped after entering the parlor. Walker, Marie-Elise, Christine Bouvier, and Lieutenant Avery were sipping drinks out of crystal glasses while they quietly waited for her.

"Come in, come in, dear girl," Marie-Elise said. "We're all dying to know what's so urgent."

Lauren eyed them one by one. They all wore intimidating, somber faces. "Uh, I think I should tell you in private, Mrs. Tresvant."

Walker said, "Is it about Beaumont's murder?"

Chapter 72

"There's no need to be afraid, dear girl."

When Lauren heard Walker Tresvant ask if what she had to say in private was about Beaumont Bouvier's murder, her mouth fell open and she felt faint. She looked at Christine, who was unmoved by the question. Caught completely off guard, she wasn't sure what she had walked into. She managed to say, "Uh," several times while her eyes shifted from one person to the next. When she had talked to Christine in her dress shop earlier that day, she had said she was planning to blackmail Cadence. Now Christine was in a room with the Tresvants and Lieutenant Avery openly discussing the murder? It made no sense. *Did they tell her? Or did she tell them?*

"That's it, isn't it Lauren?" Marie-Elsie said. "Christine told us all about it."

Wondering what she told them, Lauren looked at Christine again and said, "What did she tell you?"

"She told us that she talked to you about this earlier today in your dress shop," Lieutenant Avery said. "Is that right?"

Still looking at Christine, Lauren tentatively said, "Uh, I guess so."

"Either she talked to you earlier today or not," Walker said sternly. "Which is it?"

Unnerved now, Lauren said, "If Mrs. Bouvier said we talked, we talked."

"She said you told her that Joshua killed Beaumont Bouvier," Lieutenant Avery said. There was much skepticism in his voice. "Is that right?"

"I never said anything like that," Lauren said, looking at the floor. "Mrs. Bouvier told me that's what she thought."

"And do you agree with her?" Marie-Elise asked.

"It's not for me to agree or disagree, Mrs. Tresvant," Lauren said. "This is white folks' business."

Marie-Elise said, "There's no need to be afraid, dear girl. Have a seat. I'll pour you a glass of cognac. It will relax you."

Chapter 73

"He didn't have to die the way he did."

Lauren sat down and tried to gather her thoughts while Marie-Elise went over to a liquor table and poured tea-colored cognac in a glass. From the previous questions, she knew there was no point in lying. It would be easy to trip her up with Christine sitting in the room with them. Either they would believe Lauren or they wouldn't. She looked at Christine again, trying to ascertain if she had been duped earlier that day when they talked about "family" matters. As best she could tell, Christine was calm, which told Lauren that she probably wasn't interrogated into giving up the information. *Maybe they were all in it together. Maybe they got together and decided to send Christine to my shop to confirm their suspicions without implicating themselves.*

Marie-Elise handed the glass of cognac to Lauren and said, "Here you are, dear." Then she returned to her seat.

Lieutenant Avery began again. His skepticism was more apparent than before when he said, "Now . . . did you tell Christine Bouvier that Cadence was having a liaison of a sexual nature with one Joshua Bouvier, a slave of Bouvier Hill?"

Lauren's hand was visibly shaking. She took a swallow of

her cognac, her first ever alcoholic beverage. Then she closed her eyes and rapidly shook her head as the burning sensation warmed her chest. Then she looked at the floor, wondering what they were going to do to her. She was in a room with very powerful people. All of them had the right to take the life of a nigger on a whim. All of her plans had gone wrong so incredibly quickly. She wished she had stuck to the plan. Then it occurred to her that maybe they were going to do something about what Christine had told them because they were all sitting in Walker Tresvant's house discussing what was said. She wasn't sure of their intentions, so she decided to play it safe.

Lauren took another swallow of her cognac. Again it burned as it went down. She looked at Lieutenant Avery. "Six months ago you didn't believe I could have killed Beaumont and Louis. Do you still believe that today?"

"I do," Lieutenant Avery replied.

"And do you still maintain that it would take someone very strong to have killed both men?"

"Yes," Lieutenant Avery replied.

"And do you maintain that it was Aubrey that did the deed?"

"I never accused anyone, Lauren," Lieutenant Avery said. "I simply told Mrs. Bouvier to choose one of her niggers and *she* chose Aubrey."

"And we all know that Aubrey, Beaumont, Louis, and the housemen were all sodomites, right?" Lauren said and cut her eyes to Christine. "That's what Christine Bouvier told me today."

"All right, that's enough," Walker finally said. "All of this dancing around what happened that night is a ridiculous waste of time."

Lauren looked at Walker and replied, "I suppose it is, since one of your female slaves said that Joshua was here that night." She drank the rest of her cognac, wiped the residual beverage off the corner of her mouth, and handed the glass to Marie-Elise, who took it, refilled it, and handed it to her. "Before he was murdered, Aubrey said that *you*, sir, had motive. And at the reading of the will, your wife got the bulk of the estate."

"Are you accusing me of something, Lauren?" Walker asked.

"Not at all, sir," Lauren said. "I'm accusing the woman who vouched for Joshua. She's the guilty party. Not you."

"You mean Natalie?" Marie-Elise asked.

"I mean whoever said Joshua was here, Mrs. Tresvant," Lauren said. She looked at Lieutenant Avery again and said, "Did you actually talk to the woman Joshua was with that night?"

"Of course I did," Lieutenant Avery said. "Are you suggesting I don't know how to conduct a thorough investigation?"

Lauren gulped her cognac again and looked the lieutenant up and down before saying, "I'm not only suggesting it, Lieutenant Avery, I'm flat-out saying it. We wouldn't be wasting Monsieur Tresvant's time if you had been more thorough, sir."

Astounded by her uncharacteristic bravado, Lieutenant Avery said, "Why, this is an outrage!"

"Oh, shut the hell up, Lieutenant," Marie-Elise said. "The only outrage is that you failed to question the one person who could have committed the murder—Cadence Delacroix Bouvier. You were in all likelihood put in a trance by her exquisite bosom, no doubt."

Lauren hadn't eaten since breakfast, which meant she was drinking liquor with nothing in her stomach to slow down the absorption rate of the alcohol. She was feeling the effects of the ninety proof brew and vindication when she said, "Do you still believe her story, *Lieutenant?*"

"Just what are you getting at, Lauren?" Walker asked.

"I'm saying that if Natalie lied, she had to have a really good reason," Lauren said, and gulped her cognac again. "I'm wondering if she may have lied that night and if she did, why? Natalie says Joshua was with her that night. That might be true, but I know for a fact that Joshua is bedding Mrs. Bouvier now. That's one of the reasons I'm here now. Young Beaumont and I walked in on them less than an hour ago. They were as naked as newborn babes fresh out of their mothers' wombs."

"What?" Marie-Elise yelled.

"You heard me right, Mrs. Tresvant!" Lauren said, and took another gulp. "I saw them and so did young Beaumont! We were standing at the door, listening to them howl!" she said. "Well, it was mostly Mrs. Bouvier." The cognac was telling her what to say now. "I told young Beaumont not to go in. He thought it was Joshua and Guinevere."

"Why did he think that?" Lieutenant Avery asked.

" 'Cause that's what I told him," Lauren said.

"Why would you tell him that?" Christine asked. "Didn't you know it was Cadence and Joshua?"

"I sure did," Lauren said. "I told him not to go in there though. I even tried to stop him."

"Okay, but why did you tell him it was Joshua and Guinevere in the room?" Christine repeated.

"I told him that because Mrs. Bouvier blames me for all of her trouble with her children and her friend, Guinevere. I just wanted him to hear his mother and think it was Guinevere. And later, when it all came out, young Beaumont would know just how long it had been going on. I didn't know he was going to bust in the room." She finished the cognac and handed the glass to Marie-Elise. She refilled it and handed it to her. "I tried to stop him, but he just laughed and went in anyway. It was a sight, let me tell you." She laughed hysterically. "Joshua took off running. You could see all he had to offer, that's for sure."

"So what happened after that?" Lieutenant Avery asked.

"Well, I knew I was going to be blamed for it all so I ran too," Lauren said. "I thought that if she would kill her own husband, she would kill me too. The only safe place I could think of was here." She looked at Marie-Elise and took a swallow of her cognac. "Beaumont Bouvier was your brother. He didn't have to die the way he did. He deserves justice and you being his sister, I thought you would be the one person who would want to see to it that he got it."

Christine said, "I think we better get over there before they have a chance to get their stories straight."

"Yes. And bring your firing squad," Lauren said. "You're going to need it, Lieutenant."

"I brought them with me," Avery said. "They're out back waiting for us."

Chapter 74

"She's a whore!"

Less than an hour later, Lieutenant Avery, Walker, Marie-Elise, Christine, and Lauren barged into Bouvier Manor, leaving Rokk out front with the horse and wagon. They could hear young Beaumont and Cadence screaming at each other. They quietly followed the voices to the kitchen and listened to them from the hallway to see if they might hear a confession.

"Lauren knew I was in there with Joshua and she wanted you to see it!" Cadence screamed.

"Whether she wanted me to see it or not doesn't excuse what you did, Mother! It doesn't matter what her motives were, either! You were the one caught doing what you didn't want me and Brigitte doing. Didn't you tell me this morning that this kind of thing doesn't go on here? Never ever at Bouvier Hill! Wasn't that you, Mother?"

A loud slap sounded off and was quickly followed by Cadence's apology. A desperate plea for forgiveness was heard next.

"You can slap me, you can beat me, you can kick me until I bleed, Mother, but I'll never forget what I saw! Never!"

"What can I do to make this up to you?"

"Make this up to me? You think you can somehow make this up to me?"

"You just remember that this is my house!" Cadence screamed, offering the only defense she could think of at the moment. "I can do whatever I want to do in it!"

"That obviously means you can hide the horn in my father's house with a nigger slave if you want to, right, Mother? And that obviously means you can be as scandalous as any woman working in Madam Nadine's brothel, right? Or better yet, why not turn Bouvier Manor into a low-rent bordello since the resident nigger blacksmith gets his milk free of charge." He looked his mother up and down, assessing her, before saying, "And he gets his milk directly from the cow, who thinks she's the bull. As a matter of fact, in just a short while she'll be removed and returned to the pasture from which she came, and become nothing but a common hussy!"

With that, another slap sounded off and the shouting between mother and son began anew.

When Cadence and young Beaumont kept going back and forth and getting nowhere like arguments tend to do, the Tresvants, Christine, Lieutenant Avery, and Lauren walked into the kitchen like *they* owned the place, and stunned mother and son as the argument raged on. The silence was piercing and the looks on Cadence and young Beaumont's faces were priceless. Cadence took one look at Lauren and ran full speed at her.

Marie-Elise stepped in her path and said, "Don't you dare touch her!"

Cadence came to an abrupt halt. She was breathing hard like a bull chasing a matador's red cape. Her eyes were fiery red. Dry tear streaks were visible. She would have broken Lauren's neck while strangling her if she could have gotten her hands around her throat.

When Lauren realized that she had the protection of

Marie-Elise, she looked at Cadence and doubled over with laughter. She tried to stop laughing but couldn't. She didn't realize the white folks and Walker Tresvant were giving her a pass for two reasons. First, they believed Cadence and Joshua were guilty of murdering Beaumont Bouvier. Second, they realized the cognac was in charge of Lauren's mouth and her actions; otherwise, they wouldn't stand for her defiance.

Clearly in charge, Walker Tresvant walked over to Cadence, got in her face and yelled, "Where's Joshua?"

"Huh?" was her timid response.

"Lieutenant!" Walker yelled while still nearly nose to nose with Cadence and gazing deeply into her bloodshot eyes.

"Yes, sir!" Lieutenant Avery responded, coming to the military posture of attention as if Tresvant were his commanding officer. The lieutenant was no fool. He knew Walker Tresvant was very wealthy and he had friends—white friends—in high places that included the mayor and the garrison commander among others. Even Walker's enemies respected him. Avery knew and clearly understood that how he handled this situation could make the difference on whether he was promoted or demoted. He also knew he had botched the original investigation in the first place. If Aubrey and the housemen were white, he might be standing in front of his own firing squad for that kind of mistake.

"Have your men search out back," Walker said in an even tone. "Find Joshua and bring him to me immediately. We're going to find out what's going on around here tonight!"

"Yes, sir," Lieutenant Avery said and left the kitchen without fanfare.

"Now . . . Cadence," Walker continued, "have a seat."

Cadence walked past her sister-in-law without looking at her. She could not look into her eyes. Embarrassment was threatening to consume her. She sat in a chair at the table and tried to appear confident when nothing could be further from the truth.

Walker looked at his wife and said, "You and Christine take young Beaumont upstairs with the rest of the children and see to it that they stay up there. They don't need to hear the truth about their mother."

"It's too late!" young Beaumont yelled as he left the kitchen. "I have both seen and heard the truth! She's a whore! It's a good thing my father is in his grave. He wouldn't be able to stand the sight of you! And frankly, neither can I!"

In her heart, Lauren said, *Your father is very much alive, young Beaumont! But they won't tell you, and neither will I.*

Chapter 75

"That's the *real* reason he came here tonight."

Walker waited a few moments before saying anything to Cadence. Even though young Beaumont had seen his mother doing scandalous things, he didn't want the young man to hear any more. As far as he could tell, young Beaumont didn't know his mother was the main suspect in his supposed father's murder. When he was sure they were alone and couldn't be heard by the children, he walked over to his sister-in-law and locked eyes with her. "It's over, Cadence. You know that, don't you?"

"What's over?" Cadence asked, knowing she didn't dare acknowledge the terrible truth.

"Your life," Walker said without compassion. "You had to know you were going to get caught, right? Tell the truth now. You knew that, didn't you?"

"Caught? What do you mean, caught? Caught doing what?" Cadence said, determined to play the dumb role to the very end.

Lauren was still high from the cognac. She sat down at the table with her nemesis. Her eyes were glassy. She looked at Cadence and smiled. "You might as well tell the truth. They know all about it, Cadence. We all do. You shouldn't have treated Tristan so badly. You might have gotten away with it if you had just handled him better. But you didn't. He was the one who told on you."

Cadence still didn't know how much trouble she was actually in. She thought they were only there because Lauren had told them she had caught her in bed with Joshua. It was unsettling, awkward, and embarrassing, but that was about it. Joshua, on the other hand, was probably going to die for the same crime because he was a nigger. They both knew the stakes were very high if they were caught. She had no idea this query was about murder. Tentatively, she said, "What did Tristan tell you?"

"He didn't tell her anything," Walker said. "He told Christine everything last night. Apparently he loved you very much."

While she did not show it, Cadence's heart was racing, pounding, and ready to explode. Ba-boom! Ba-boom! Ba-boom! Her voice cracked under the stress when she said, "He told Christine what *exactly*?"

Walker looked at Lauren who was beside herself with glee. "Do you want to tell her, Lauren? Beaumont saved you from the rigorous life of being a bed wench. He saved you from a life of uncompensated servitude. He set you free and made you rich in the process. Everything that you have, you owe to him."

Lauren took a deep breath to try to calm down. It felt so good to have Cadence right where she wanted her. It was time for more illumination in this final act of the game she had played. She was going to enjoy every bit of this. She smiled again and said, "You know, Cadence . . . can I call you Cadence?" She laughed so hard her jaws hurt. "Hear the wisdom of King Solomon: 'There is nothing new under the sun' and 'To every thing there is a season, and a time.' Cadence, your time is at hand." She laughed again. "Do forgive me, dear girl. I believe my giggling has been brought on by my consumption of a wonderful drink called cognac. My first time trying it. It produces an amazing feeling." When she saw how her continued laughter angered Cadence, she laughed even more. "Anyway, what was I saying . . . oh, yes, yes . . . your time is at hand, dear girl. Tristan told Christine, who hates you with an intense hatred, by the way, that *you*, dear girl, tried to get *him* to kill one Beaumont Bouvier, your beloved husband. Now . . . what do you say to *that?*"

"That's a lie!" Cadence said with rancor.

"Really, Cadence?" Lauren said, realizing now would be the perfect time to drop a bomb she never expected.

"Really!" Cadence said, showing no fear of what Tristan may have told Christine.

Lauren smiled, knowing, or at least believing that Cadence had absolutely no idea what she was going to say and how devastating it would be when she heard it. She studied Cadence carefully, calculating every word, waiting for the precise moment to release the bomb so that it would do the most damage. Having locked eyes with her, she knew she had her complete attention when she said, "If I were you, I wouldn't worry too much about being caught with Joshua. It may be in your blood."

Snarling, Cadence said, "What do you mean by that?"

"Since it may be in your blood, how about this tidbit of information?" She paused for a couple of seconds for maximum effect, allowing silence to become a key ingredient of the conversation. "Did you know that Guinevere is your blood sister?"

An ocean of silence filled the kitchen.

Cadence leaned back and thought for a short second before saying, "No. It's not true," she said as if her words could make what she'd heard go away.

"Yes," Lauren said. "A thousand times, yes. And deep down, you know it. You've always known it, haven't you? You always wondered who fathered Guinevere's children, didn't you?"

Cadence shook her head. Her face first twisted into absolute shock and then into a mask of horror as the truth broke through all the lies.

In heaven now, Lauren added to her misery by saying, "Yes, she's your *sister*." She paused again to let it settle and then added, "Your father is also the father of her children. That's the *real* reason he came here tonight. That's the *real* reason he wanted her to return to plantation Delacroix. He was probably still bedding her until the day she left to come and work for you. So maybe, just maybe, this thing with you and Joshua was bound to happen. You like to tell Bible stories, so I'm sure you know what I mean when I say, maybe it's a sins of the father kind of thing." Then she laughed in her face.

Chapter 76

"I wonder how that happened."

When Cadence learned the awful truth about her father, and understood that Guinevere was in reality her sister, and that her father was the father of her newfound sister's children, the pain was too great to bear. She dove over the table and attempted to strangle Lauren, who was laughing wildly. The chair Lauren was sitting in flipped over backward with her in it. Walker pulled Cadence off Lauren and sat her back in the chair. Cadence had thought it strange that Guinevere had no husband and no man in her life, yet she kept getting pregnant. She had asked her mother about this strange phenomenon, and was told by her that it was the overseer's children.

Cadence's mother then made her swear to never ever reveal the awful truth. If she did, it would bring shame on the overseer and his family, and in due course, on plantation Delacroix. Cadence didn't know she was swearing to keep her father's secret, and consequently, the family secret. She didn't know that while she was lying to Guinevere about a biblical story that in the grand scheme of things meant next to nothing; at the same time, her mother was lying to her about a matter that in the end meant there were niggers in their family tree. Unfortunately there was more bad news on the horizon.

Still laughing, Lauren sat back in her chair and said, "They also know you killed Beaumont and Louis, Cadence. It's all over."

"I didn't kill anybody!" Cadence screamed.

"We know, Cadence. We know," Walker said, pausing to put her at ease before dropping yet another bombshell. When he was sure she was relaxed, he added, "You had Joshua and Lieutenant Avery do your killing for you, didn't you?"

Avery and several of his men brought Joshua in through the kitchen door. When Walker saw his battered and bloodied face, he said, "He tried to run, huh?"

"No. Someone else did that to him," Avery said. "We found him on the ground outside the stables."

When Lauren saw just how badly he looked, she laughed and said, "Rokk did that to him before we left. He tried to stop us from leaving and took a sound beating for his trouble."

"Rokk . . . the man in your wagon?" Lieutenant Avery asked.

"Yes. He's a friend of the prince—my fiancé. The man I was going to marry before he was killed on the dock yesterday."

"Sit down, Joshua," Walker commanded. He waited until he complied. "What happened the night Beaumont was killed?"

"Don't tell them anything!" Cadence yelled.

"Ya know what happened, Massa Tresvant," Joshua said, ignoring Cadence's desperate plea. "Ya knew this here was bound tuh happen. I comes to ya fuh help, suh. I comes to ya, and told ya 'bout it. I told ya 'bout this here thing."

Lieutenant Avery looked at Joshua and said, "What do you mean, Monsieur Tresvant knew all about it? Knew all about *what*?"

Joshua locked eyes with Lieutenant Avery. "He knew what Cadence, uh, what Mrs. Bouvier made me do the night she comes tuh muh cabin, suh."

"The night Beaumont Bouvier was killed?" Lieutenant Avery asked.

"Naw, suh. Long b'fo' that there night," Joshua said. "She had beena eyin' me fo' a long spell b'fo' she comes tuh muh cabin wit' a itch she wanted me tuh scratch."

Lieutenant Avery was stunned by Joshua's rendition of what had been going on at Bouvier Hill. He had been skeptical when Walker came to the garrison and repeated what Christine had told him. The lieutenant had told Walker he wanted to hear it directly from Christine. He turned and looked at Cadence, who was obviously embarrassed, and said, "Is any of what he's saying true, Mrs. Bouvier?"

"He's lying, Lieutenant!" Cadence shouted, recognizing that the lieutenant was the one person who didn't believe a word of the fantastic tale he had been told. She would play that angle for all it was worth, hoping to somehow extricate herself from certain execution. "Why would someone like me, a refined white woman, even get involved with someone like him? An *ignorant* nigger!"

"I be sho' nuff ignorant and a nigga," Joshua said sincerely. "But I don't be lyin' 'bout this here thing between us. She don' told me little while ago she got my chil' in her belly."

Lauren laughed out loud. "I wonder how *that* happened."

"Is it true?" Walker asked, looking at Cadence. "Are you with child?"

Cadence looked as if she could keel over and die. Her head lowered. Her eyes found the floor and diligently searched it. But Lauren's unrestrained laughter felt like someone had poured acid on her heart. She used the only believable defense a white woman in her position could use. She screamed, "That good-for-nothing nigger raped me time and time again."

Chapter 77

"But the nigger won't be afforded the same."

When Joshua heard Cadence claim he had violated her, it angered him. "Rape?" he repeated with rancor. "If there be a rape, it be tha otha way around. Told me if I don' do what she wanted, she'd tell Massa Bouvier I don' raped her. What could a nigga do? Ya rememba me tellin' ya 'bout this a long time ago, Massa Tresvant?"

"I remember. I told you to do as you were told, remember?" Walker said, secretly enjoying Cadence's figurative dismemberment.

Beaumont was dead and Cadence was in serious trouble with looming murder charges. Walker was going to do everything he could to facilitate her swift execution under the guise of getting his wife the long-awaited justice she had asked him to get for her brother's untimely demise. While he was interested in getting justice for Marie-Elise, the family vendetta was still in play. His real motivation for the pursuit of justice was so that he could finally and irrevocably mete out his own brand of justice by taking over the plantation that had once owned his family. If that meant Cadence had to face a firing squad in order to achieve that end, so be it.

As far as Walker was concerned, the murderous seeds Cadence had sown had taken root, germinated, then grew up and divinely worked in his favor. Being pregnant only added to the revenge he sought for Alexander Tresvant Bouvier, his grandfather. When word got out, and he would personally see to it that it did, the scandal would be devastating. Young Beaumont, being the heir to his father's fortune, might be eager to step aside. If young Beaumont did relinquish control of the company, Marie-Elise would take over. If that happened, a merger between Bouvier and Tresvant Sugar with Walker being at the helm was within his grasp.

"Yea, suh. I sho' do," Joshua said. He knew that if he admitted to not only bedding Cadence, but that he was a more than willing participant in a double murder, his admission would hasten his departure from this world. He thought the best course of action was to do what she was doing—blame her. What did he have to lose? "Ah did just that, too. Near 'bout every day we beena goin' at it. Even when it her time of duh mont', she told me tuh do it and I did. After a while, she begin tuh say she wanted Massa Bouvier dead and she wanted me tuh be the one tuh do it."

"To do what, Joshua?" Lieutenant Avery asked in an attempt to solicit a confession that would give him reason to show him the receiving end of a firing squad while simultaneously releasing Cadence of all wrongdoing.

"Tuh kill 'im dead, suh!" Joshua said, looking him in the eyes.

"And did you kill Beaumont Bouvier?" Lieutenant Avery asked.

"Yea, suh," Joshua said. "I sho' did. Just like she told me to."

"And Louis, too?" Lauren asked.

Joshua's lower lip quivered and his eyes welled before he nodded several times, admitting to the murders he committed. Now that Cadence had served him up as her rapist, he was fairly certain they were going to kill him. He wanted them all to believe it wasn't his idea to kill his master and to bed his wife. He didn't think there would be much of a penalty for killing Louis. That was just one nigger killing another one. Who cared about that? Killing his master on the orders of his wife was one thing. But regularly bedding his master's wife and impregnating her sealed his doom.

"That's it then, Monsieur Tresvant," Lieutenant Avery said. "I'm satisfied we have our killer."

"Yes, we do," Tresvant said, "but what about the slave girl at my plantation, Lieutenant?" He looked at Joshua. "Why did she say you were with her?"

"I was wit' her. After I kilt 'em. If she wants me, she say whateva I tells her tuh say, suh. That how womenfolk be once I don' been up in 'em, suh. They do whateva I tells 'em." He looked at Cadence. "Even she do what I tell her now that her husband be dead, and she be the massa of Bouvier Hill."

Walker looked at Lieutenant Avery and shook his head, pretending he wasn't absolutely elated by the revelations. He had wanted Cadence in an impossible position all along. "What about Cadence? What are we going to do with her? She's with child. We can't put her to death without killing the child inside her, can we?"

"Monsieur Tresvant," Lieutenant Avery began, "even if she were not with child, she is still a white woman, sir. I'm not altogether convinced she's guilty as you and Christine assert. She deserves the benefit of a trial. But the nigger will not be afforded the same. We'll shoot him right now."

"Noooo!" Joshua's anguish gushed forth. "I don' told the truth! I has no choice in the matter, suh! I got tuh do as she say or I git kilt! And if I don't do what she say do, I git kilt!" He was referring to the initial sexual encounter. In his mind, one thing led to the other. "Ain't no way a nigga can win this here thing, can he, suh? I guess if a nigga got tuh git kilt fo' somethin', I guess it's bes' he enjoy his self while it las', huh, Massa Tresvant? I guess that's whatcha be tellin' me, huh? The day she comes into muh cabin, I knew muh days was numbered."

Chapter 78

"You know how we women can be sometimes."

Though he hid it well, Lieutenant Avery was annoyed that there was a bona-fide possibility that Joshua had been bedding Cadence. He thought she was attractive, beautiful in fact; too beautiful for an ignorant nigger like Joshua. It was too disturbing to even contemplate what could have motivated her. And she had money, too; lots of money. He wanted to bed her himself, and if there was any way he could save her, he would. On the chance that he could save her, he planned to make a play for her himself.

Now that her husband was dead, he saw nothing wrong with her taking a lover, but he thought her lover should be an intelligent white man like him, not some brainless nigger who could be barely understood when he spoke. He thought even Lauren, with her advanced linguistic skills, would have trouble deciphering such gibberish. He looked at Cadence and thought: *If you were going to have a black man as a lover, why didn't you pick someone like Walker Tresvant? The man was educated at the Sorbonne in Paris, for Christ's sake.*

"Sergeant!" Lieutenant Avery shouted, looking at Joshua

like he wanted to shoot him in the face for daring to do to Cadence what he wanted to do to her himself.

"Sir!" a man wearing a three-stripe chevron on his sleeve said and saluted.

"Take this *nigger* outside and have him dig a grave for himself," Lieutenant Avery said. "I'll be out in a little while to execute sentence."

Suddenly sober, suddenly focused, angrily, Lauren said, "Wait a minute! You're going to shoot him and let her go? She was the one who told him to do it, Lieutenant."

Cadence was conspicuously quiet. She knew that her white skin, her elitist pedigree, and being with child would win the support she needed to escape the firing squad justice demanded. She had hoped it would never come to this, but if it ever did, like Aubrey had served up Lauren to be executed when he was in an identical position six months earlier, she would serve up her nigger paramour just as coldly. She had decided before the affair began that if they were ever caught, she would try to save Joshua if she could; but if it came down to her or him, her life would be more important than his. After all, she was a woman and a mother.

Angry now, Lauren said, "If he was raping her time and time again as she has said, why didn't she tell somebody? With her being white, someone would have done something about this the moment she made it known."

Cadence was more than ready to defend herself. She had been preparing for this drama almost from the beginning. She knew when she decided to get involved with Joshua that she might have to defend herself if they were ever caught. She knew that men believed women to be weaker and far less intelligent than men. She knew she was a very real exception if their line of thought was true. She knew she could use their ideology against them.

Looking at Lieutenant Avery exclusively, knowing he was her advocate, Cadence said, "I would have said something sooner, but he told me he would rape Josette if I didn't let him do what he had been dreaming about all his life." She said this, knowing that a lot of white men thought Negro men thought that way, and because they did, it might save her life. "While he raped me, he kept saying, 'I've been wanting to do this to you since the first time I laid eyes on you. You're the most beautiful woman I've ever seen. I can't control myself when I see you. I just have to have you every day,' he would say. He, of course, didn't speak nearly as clearly as that, but I understood very clearly what I had to do or my only daughter was next. With my husband dead and gone, I didn't know what to do. After a while, I was so ashamed of what was going on that I kept my mouth shut and prayed to God that he didn't get me with child.

"Besides, nobody thought I could run this place without Beaumont, and Joshua is the best blacksmith around. I couldn't report him. Where was I going to find a replacement with his skill? So I gave him what he wanted. I thought he would grow weary of me and move on to a younger woman sooner or later.

"He wanted me every day and I was getting tired of giving into him. What I found particularly deplorable and downright despicable was that I would tell him that I was on my cycle. He was so taken with me that he didn't care. He'd say, 'So what? It'll just be slipperier. That's all.' Imagine my shame of being in the position of resisting a huge man like him or being made to watch him do to Josette what he had done to me over ten thousand times.

"I was going to tell Walker what was going on, but I couldn't when I realized that he had gotten me with child. It was stupid of me not to get help sooner. I know that now, but what could I do? You know how we women can be sometimes. You understand, don't you, Lieutenant Avery?"

Chapter 79

"White women are as innocent as the day they were born."

Joshua cried out, "She be a lyin', suh!" He looked at Cadence. "Why ya doin' this tuh me? Y'all know ah tol' ya this'll happen tuh me if'n ah gives ya whatcha itchin' fo', didn't ah?"

"Lieutenant Avery," Lauren said, realizing that the pendulum was starting to swing the other way and that she was now in danger of facing the firing squad that Cadence was supposed to face. "I saw them, Joshua and Cadence, together in Mrs. Bouvier's room doing it. I saw her rip off his shirt and everything."

Calmly, Cadence said, "If I ripped off his shirt it was because it was all I could do to keep a nigger buck his size off me."

"But I heard you admit to killing your husband and Louis!" Lauren shot back angrily.

"You have it mixed up, Lauren. You heard him say he'd killed Beaumont and Louis and that I was next if I didn't let him do what he wanted."

"Lieutenant, I saw them the night after she had Aubrey and the housemen killed," Lauren said, desperate to convict

Cadence before them all. "She told you to shoot them in the face when she knew she had planned to murder them all. She used you, Lieutenant, as her instrument of death. Aubrey and the housemen were innocent just as they claimed. If you let her get away with this, knowing what you now know, their deaths, all six of them, will be on your eternal soul, sir!"

"Lieutenant," Cadence said, prepared to rebut Lauren's conclusions. "*You*, sir, told *me* to choose one of my niggers. If you recall, I did not want to do it. But, in order to get justice for my beloved husband, I took *your* advice, sir. So, to blame *me* for *your* suggestion is something you have to live with too."

"Come to think of it, I did make the suggestion," Lieutenant Avery said, wanting to believe what she was saying. But at the same time, he knew that Walker held his career in his hands. Avery knew he needed to show that he was being thorough this time. With that in mind, he continued, "But, I only made the suggestion because no one suspected your involvement. Had I known that you knew your nigger buck did the deed, I would not have made the suggestion." He looked at Walker for a quick second. "And I certainly would not have executed six innocent men. None of this really matters now. It is a white woman's word against the word of two niggers. I'm afraid I cannot take the word of two niggers over the word of a white woman. The thing would end my military career."

"What about Christine, Lieutenant?" Walker said. "She's white and she told you the same thing."

"No, sir, she didn't say that at all," Lieutenant Avery said. "She simply repeated what Lauren had told her. Besides, I can't take her seriously when we know her husband was having relations with Mrs. Bouvier, can I? That's clear motive for her to lie on her sister-in-law. No, sir, it's still the word of two niggers against one white woman."

"What about young Beaumont?" Lauren said. "He's white and he's her son. What about his word then? He saw them together tonight." She locked eyes with Cadence. "We walked in while you two were in Aubrey's bedroom naked as a newborn babe, howling like the wind."

"You've got it all wrong again, Lauren. What you saw was me doing whatever I had to do to protect Josette."

"Let's get young Beaumont down here," Lauren said desperately. "He'll tell you what he saw! Guinevere saw it too! She'll tell the truth!"

Lieutenant Avery looked at Walker Tresvant and said, "Sir, I'm in a real fix here. What do you suggest?"

"I suggest we get young Beaumont, Guinevere, and Marie-Elise down here right now. I already heard the boy confess that he'd both seen and heard his mother having relations with Joshua, but, Lieutenant, don't expect the boy to tell on his mother in your presence no matter what. I think it happened just as Joshua and Lauren said, to tell you the truth."

"Really, sir?" Lieutenant Avery asked, shaking his head. "But you're married to a white woman. You have to know perhaps better than I do, sir, that white women are as innocent as the day they were born. It's impossible, sir, I say impossible for this beautiful and delicate creature to seduce this imbecile knowing she could be impregnated by him."

"Yet, she is pregnant with his child, isn't she, Lieutenant?" Walker said. "We heard the words spill out of her own mouth. And don't forget that she never said anything about the baby until Joshua told us. Then suddenly she comes up with a far-fetched tale to gain your sympathy."

"Yes, sir, she is pregnant, no doubt. She's admitted as much. But, it is the child of rape, sir," Lieutenant Avery said.

"Was it rape?" Walker questioned. "If it was, why did the man come to me a year ago, scared to death that one day this was going to happen to him? And why would Lauren, fleeing for her life, come to Château Tresvant, telling us all the same story? And why were young Beaumont and Cadence arguing about this very thing when we came through the front door? Lastly, Lieutenant, why did Lauren think she would be safe coming to Marie-Elise, a white woman?"

Chapter 80

"Wake up!"

Lieutenant Avery quieted himself and thought deeply about the matter for a minute or so, trying to think of a way to save Cadence from sure death, so he could woo her and have her for himself; at least for a while anyway. The night of the murders came to mind, and he remembered something vital that might acquit Cadence. He looked at Walker and said, "In Mrs. Bouvier's defense, Monsieur Tresvant, Lauren no doubt remembers the altercation she had with your wife six months ago the night after Beaumont Bouvier was killed. I certainly do, and I see no reason she wouldn't. It's reasonable then that something happened between Lauren and Cadence and she fled to your home, sir."

Astounded, Walker backhanded Avery and said, "*Lieutenant*, have you taken leave of your senses? Cadence is pregnant! Pregnant, I say! And the father is her slave, who, need I remind you for the third time, came to me complaining a year ago that she was making *him* have relations with her! Wake up!"

"Lieutenant, don't you see what's going on here?" Cadence said calmly, knowing that she had a strong supporter in the young officer who defended her like she had paid him a hefty retainer for doing so. "Walker and his wife stand to gain Bouvier Hill if I die. They stand to gain my thirty percent. It's documented in my late husband's will. They have motive to see me dead, sir. Besides that, Walker wants to merge Tresvant and Bouvier Sugar due to a family vendetta from years ago. The not-so-hidden *real* family secret is that the Bouvier family used to own the Tresvant family. That's why he seduced Marie-Elise and impregnated her, hoping to steal her from Mason Beauregard.

"And I must say his plan worked marvelously," Cadence continued, looking at Walker as she mounted her formidable defense. "But that wasn't good enough for you, was it, Walker? Now you want it all, don't you? You've got Marie-Elise thinking you're the reincarnation of Jesus Christ and can walk on water. You've got her sixty percent because you have her." She looked at Lieutenant Avery again. "Now he wants my thirty percent *and* Bouvier Hill. Walker here wants revenge in the worst possible way. What better way to avenge Alexander Tresvant Bouvier than to have *full* ownership of the land and assets of his grandfather's former slave master?"

Lieutenant Avery looked at Walker and said, "And what do you say to that, sir?"

"I say what you just said. I say my wife is also a white woman and she too is a delicate creature," he said, responding to Lieutenant Avery while glaring at Cadence. "And if Cadence here is as innocent as the day she was born, my wife is a thousand times more innocent. I say I'm still alive and Beaumont Bouvier is dead, sir. Think! What do you think she would say given the circumstances she's in? She cannot tell the truth; as Aubrey said before you killed him, 'her life hangs in the balance.' "

Walker looked at Lieutenant Avery again, calmed himself, and offered his explanation to Cadence's accusation. "As for my family vendetta, all I can say is that I was one of the wealthiest men in New Orleans before I married my wife, and I'm still one of the wealthiest men in New Orleans, but I didn't kill Beaumont Bouvier and his housemen. You and Joshua did. And who benefited from their deaths? Cadence Bouvier, that's who!" He paused for a moment, hoping his words would penetrate the young lieutenant's thick skull. "Now . . . I'm going to go get them all and bring them down here to get the story straight."

Chapter 81

The Sweetest Revenge Imaginable

A few minutes later, Guinevere, young Beaumont, Christine, Marie-Elise, and Walker Tresvant returned to the kitchen. They were all looking at her as if she were Hungarian Countess Elizabeth Bathory, a prolific serial killer who lived nearly a hundred years earlier. According to legend, Bathory, who was infamously branded "Blood Countess," tortured and killed over 600 people and bathed in their blood.

If it were possible, the look in their eyes would have made Cadence's hair stand up. Her thick bust rose and descended rapidly as desperation overwhelmed her. Believing they were going to take her out the back door and shoot her, she said, "Young Beaumont, they're going to kill me, son. They think I let Joshua and I didn't. Don't let them kill me, son . . . please! Tell them the truth, son! Tell them you saw Joshua raping your mother! Tell them you saw me fighting him! If you don't tell them the truth, they're going to kill me! Tell them your mother would never let a nigger!"

"It's too late, Cadence," Marie-Elise said. "Young Beaumont already told me everything the moment we went upstairs. Guinevere says you told her about your relationship with Joshua and that you brought her specifically to Bouvier Hill to give Lauren a hard time." She looked at the Lieutenant. "My husband says you said the word of a white woman carries more weight than that of niggers. Well, I'm a white woman. You tell me, Lieutenant, am I lying?"

"Young Beaumont, don't be afraid, son," Lieutenant Avery began, ignoring Marie-Elise. "Tell me the truth. What were you and your mother arguing about when we came in?"

He looked at his mother and bowed his head.

"Don't be afraid, son," Lieutenant Avery said again. "No harm will come to you. Tell me now truly . . . what did you see and hear in Aubrey's room earlier tonight?"

Young Beaumont looked at Lauren and dropped his eyes to the floor again.

"I hate to be the one to tell you this," Lauren said, knowing she was going to rip the boy's heart out with what she was about to say. "But your father is not your father. Your uncle Tristan is your father! Your uncle is the father of your brothers and sisters too. That means your mother has done this thing over and over and over and over and over again. She killed the man you thought was your father and she'll kill again. Someone has to stop this insanity. If anyone can stop it, you can. Now . . . tell the truth . . . please, before it's too late!"

Young Beaumont was about to say something when Cadence intervened, "Don't listen to her, son! I would never lie to you!"

"It's true," Christine said.

"No, it's all a lie!" Cadence screamed.

"Tristan confessed all last night," Christine said, looking at young Beaumont. "He is indeed your real father. Now, is it true that you walked in when your mother and Joshua were having relations?"

With his head still bowed, young Beaumont nodded and then said, "Yes. It's true."

A sigh of relief saturated the room. It looked like Cadence was finally going to get what was coming to her.

"Oh, God, no!" Cadence screamed. "They're going to kill your mother, son! Don't let them kill me! Don't let them kill me!"

While Avery would never acknowledge it, he knew she was guilty from the beginning. At least he thought she was anyway. He hated to do it, but she had to be detained to let the judge decide what would become of her. She was such a beautiful woman and he wanted her so badly, but there was nothing more he could do. As long as she was willing to fight for her life and niggers were her only accusers, he would fight for her. But there were too many white faces testifying against her now, one of which was her firstborn son. He couldn't continue the farce just so he could have the chance at bedding her and perhaps even marrying her to get control of the Bouvier fortune, and it angered him.

"Sergeant!" Avery shouted angrily.

"Sir!"

"Arrest them both and take them to the garrison where they will both stand trial for the murder of Beaumont Bouvier."

Lauren was thinking, *And Louis and Aubrey and the housemen, you imbecile!*

Cadence Bouvier screamed for her son's help as they dragged her out of the kitchen, down the hall, and out the front door. When Christine saw it, she couldn't contain the glee of seeing her being dragged away for murder. It was the sweetest revenge imaginable.

Chapter 82

Fair Game

All alone now, sitting in her jail cell, how Cadence allowed herself to get involved with Joshua came rushing back to her like the swift flow of the Niagara heading over the falls. It had all started in her dreams; dreams that clung to her and would not leave her alone even when she was fully awake; dreams of Joshua in the stables, working with hot iron. She had wanted him, but could not have him because she was a refined white woman and a lady. Without realizing it, she had begun to consider the psychological conditioning of the American white female in the matter of sexual independence.

Daily reflection led her further down a path that delivered her from sexual tyranny. At some point she began to tell herself that if it was okay for her father and her husband to have sex with niggers, it must be okay for her to have sex with them too—anything else was the pinnacle of hypocrisy. After a while, she abandoned the social norms of the day and wholly embraced her own.

Having been liberated from psychological sexual tyranny, liberation from religious tyranny became axiomatic. The two were not mutually exclusive, but rather, one frequently led to the other. With no further need of God, no further need of his demanding edicts, no further need of his extremely high standards, which she had flung to the wind nearly two decades earlier when her affair with her brother-in-law began, she stopped going to worship service altogether.

Her new ideology crystallized one particular Sunday morning, and instead of going to the house of worship, she went to the house where her horses lived. Instead of grooming one of her prized mares or stallions at the end of the barn farthest from Joshua, she went into a stall a few feet from where he did his work and waited for him.

She watched him as he walked into the barn, expecting to be alone. Their eyes locked and as usual, he looked away. She could tell by the look in his eyes he was surprised to see her there. She continued staring at him, beckoning him with her soft hazel eyes, compelling him to look once more at the woman he dreamed of bedding, but could not. Not if he wanted to stay alive. Not if he didn't have aspirations of becoming the plantation's only eunuch.

He felt the weight of her unceasing probe and looked at her again.

When their eyes locked a second time, when they looked deeper into each other's portals, without saying a word, she told him that he no longer had to dream about her; without saying a word, she told him he could have her any time he wanted—right then, in fact—in the stall she was in. And when she was sure he understood what she was offering him, she dazzled him with her wide toothy grin, pulling him further into her web of sin. She had planned to make him her personal chattel; a sex slave who would do whatever she wanted with the right bait; the bait being the delectably drenched sheath that she believed he had been hungering and thirsting for, but resisting.

She remembered trying to decide how to entice the

young blacksmith without appearing to be a whore. She knew it would be difficult because the young man knew there were strict rules against bedding the master's wife. The dreams of being his amour had become a daily delight that she could no longer control. Besides wanting him, she needed him to do her dirty work and if necessary, die so that she could become the master of Bouvier Hill.

Her method of seduction had indeed been a treacherous one in that it was designed to entice one man into killing another. Her initial weapon of choice was casual conversation. She had learned from Tristan that if you tell a person what they want to hear, what they have already decided was true and good and right for them, the listener could be talked into doing the things they already wanted to do, but for moral reasons, had previously declined. As far as she had been concerned, horses were the key to seducing the virile young man; it was the one thing they had in common; therefore, the deception would begin there.

She remembered maneuvering him into talking about things pertaining to horses and horseshoes, conversation that seemed innocent on the surface, but was in essence designed to force him to talk to her, to get to know her, to relax and be free with her. She had been committed to daily building a budding relationship; a friendship first to put him at ease because they both knew the penalty was castration and death for the slave who had sex with his white mistress. In other words, *he* would be severely penalized for the behavior of his white mistress—*he* being the responsible party. If *she* couldn't control herself, they would kill *him*.

Never mind that everyone on the plantation knew she had already had four children by her husband's brother, yet no such penalty existed for him or her. On the contrary, her secret liaison was a conundrum of sorts. Everyone on the plantation knew of it, talked of it, and even laughed about it, but nobody knew anything *officially*—their very lives hung in the balance.

Sitting in her cell with nothing to do, she remembered the precise moment that the seduction of Joshua Bouvier gained momentum. She had started closing the dress shop early so she could spend more time riding her quarter horses. In truth, her libido was out of control and like opium controlled its captives, her libido controlled her and demanded that she do the very things that nearly two decades earlier were thought of as wicked. Now, however, she saw herself as a liberated, independent woman who had all the privileges that were normally reserved for white males.

She knew that when it came to illicit sexual dalliances, there was an unacknowledged double standard. The standard for men was incredibly low; it was so low that it robbed men of their strength to control themselves and turned them into pathetically weak sex addicts who foolishly measured their prowess by the number of women they entered. Conversely, the standard for women was much higher, and nearly impossible to maintain because the men who sired them often passed on their sexual addictions and then wondered why their wives and daughters were whores.

She had observed that white men could bed whomever and however many women they pleased, but white women could not. She noticed that the same double standard existed amongst the slaves. With few exceptions, black men could bed whomever they chose, but black women could not. (The exception to the "natural law" of promiscuity applied when masters, black and white, often bred the strongest, but broken, black males with the most robust black females to create a stronger, more compliant slave that could be more easily exploited. From this practice arose a certain group of black men and women that exploited each other without thinking twice about what they were doing—and it continues today.)

Worse yet, she knew of her husband's dalliances with black men and that it had been going on for more than twenty years with impunity, and nothing was said or done about it. For those reasons, she started believing that Joshua was fair game like any other slave at Bouvier Hill. As long as she didn't conduct herself like a strumpet, she could live with herself for doing what most of the white men she knew were doing.

Chapter 83

"You know why I'm here, don't you?"

When Joshua realized why Cadence was coming to the stables regularly, he tried to avoid her. Even though he wanted to give her what she wanted, he couldn't. After all, she wasn't the only one who wanted it. He wanted her just as much as she wanted him, if not more. The penalty for bedding her was too severe for a sane man to even consider the possibilities; yet, he was considering them more and more each day, even though he continued to avoid her. However, a strange thing happened. The more he tried to avoid her, the more he thought about her. He decided he needed to get a fresh woman; someone he hadn't already bedded. He would do to her what he wanted to do to Cadence.

There was a beautiful young mulatto female of twenty years at Château Tresvant. Her name was Natalie, and she was Walker Tresvant's slave. While bedding Natalie relieved much of the sexual tension being in Cadence's presence produced, it did not drive away the urge to bed her. In fact, his desire grew more intense with each passing day. Nevertheless, he was determined to avoid Cadence Bouvier and live.

If she were a slave girl like Dorothy Tresvant, Walker's half sister, who was a full-blooded white woman, bedding her wouldn't be a problem. No one would kill or castrate him for bedding a white woman who was a slave. Cadence, on the other hand, was an elite white woman. She represented the need to keep the white race pure because only a white man and a white woman could produce a white offspring. More important, the white woman was the key to the Caucasians' continued existence.

Laws had been specifically enacted to keep free white women from marrying and having sex with black men. However, if the black man was rich, well, that was different—most whites, rich and poor, looked the other way. Cadence, however, did not care about the law or about white elitist thinking. She understood that money trumped the law. All she needed was money and she could do whatever she pleased.

The problem was that she could only get the money she would need to be free from her husband's death. Beaumont was only forty-five years old and he was the picture of health. She was sick of living a lie, sick of the hypocrisy of a marriage that had no basis in truth. She felt like she was a glorified prisoner of Bouvier Hill rather than its mistress.

As a plantation mistress, she didn't have any "real" power. Only the plantation's master had power, and the master was usually a white male. She was getting older and could feel the only power she had, that being her beauty and her voluptuous bust, slipping away. They never had any effect on her husband anyway. If she were ever to acquire power while she was still young enough to enjoy it, her husband had to die so she could inherit all he had.

Joshua Bouvier was the tool she would use to assassinate her husband and get away with it. If he were somehow caught, which was highly unlikely, as the authorities were miles away, no one would believe he was following her orders. She had a fool-proof plan to get Joshua to bed her; a plan that would make it impossible to avoid her advances. Being sexually attracted to him only added to the game of death that only she knew was afoot.

One night she snuck out of the mansion and went to his cabin. She didn't bother knocking. She just opened the door and entered like she owned the place, which she did. Her heart was pounding. Adrenaline flowed. She could tell he was surprised to see her there. She felt his fear oozing through his pores. Knowing he was more afraid than she was gave her the courage to first say and then do what she came there to do. She inhaled his fright and felt a surge of power flowing through her she had never experienced before that moment.

"Joshua," she said firmly, "you know why I'm here, don't you?"

He took a few steps backward, all the while shaking his head and said, "Ma'am, please don't do this."

As he backed up, she moved forward, losing her fear, feeling more and more in control. She said, "I'm not going to hurt you, Joshua. You don't have to be afraid."

"Ma'am, please," he begged, his voice trembling. "Ma'am they gon' kill me fo' sho' if I do this here thing. I'm beggin' ya now . . . please don't make me do it . . . *please.*"

Chapter 84

Seduction's Reversal

When Cadence heard Joshua begging like a helpless child, more power seemed to surge through her. It was addicting. She continued moving forward until Joshua's back was against the cabin wall. The towering hulk of a man, for all of his brawn, for all of his muscle, was left impotent because she owned him. That ownership afforded her the right to do whatever she wanted. He had no say in the matter.

"Now, Joshua, we both know you're going to do whatever I tell you, don't we?"

"No, ma'am," he said, shaking his head.

"Don't be afraid," she said. "I'm not going to let them hurt you."

"I don't wanna die over this here. Please, ma'am, they gon' kill me if I do. Or worse, they'll cut off muh plow."

"Nobody's going to kill you, Joshua, because nobody'll know. I'm not going to tell. Are you?"

He looked at her and frowned. He shook his head rapidly. He wasn't answering her question when he shook his head.

He was begging to be released from what he thought would certainly be his death when it got out.

She reached out to touch his arm, wanting to feel his thick biceps, but he snatched away from her and tried to run out of the cabin. She grabbed his arm, the inside of his forearm, which sent a surging sensation to her private place. He snatched away again and started a quick gallop toward the door.

Angry now, she screamed, "You step one foot out that door and I'll tell my husband you raped me. And when he finds out what you tried to do to me, all your fears will become a horrifying reality."

Joshua stopped in his tracks and turned around. He hadn't fully understood what she had said, but he got the gist of it. He understood that she was going to tell Master Bouvier he had attempted to rape her if he didn't cooperate. Frightened out of his mind, his voice trembled when he repeated, "Ma'am . . . please . . . don't do this here thing."

By then Cadence was so drunk with power that she didn't care what he said or how much sense he made. The fear in his eyes alone sent wave after wave of sexual excitement to her private place, turning it into a thick muggy swamp. Somehow, his repeated refusals had become a stimulating provocateur that she found irresistible. She couldn't stop now if she wanted to. She was going to have him and that was it. Rather than approaching him again, finally feeling like the master of Bouvier Hill, she said, "Get back over here!"

"Ma'am, please."

"Now!"

Reluctantly, the young man of twenty-four years did as he was ordered. She reached out and touched his bare chest with her smallish hands. Another surge of pleasure engulfed her. Wanting the pleasure impulses to continue, she slid her hands up to his shoulders and received the biggest surge of pleasure she had ever known. The heat from the swamp beneath her waist intensified. She closed her eyes so she could enjoy the unrivaled euphoria.

Before long, Cadence was cooing well into the night and continued cooing until the next morning when she heard the rooster crowing. Weak from the all-night activity, she staggered back to Bouvier Manor, climbed the stairs, collapsed onto her bed, and fell fast asleep. By the time she woke up, it was nightfall again. She had missed a day's work at her dress shop, but she didn't care. She snuck back out of the mansion and went back to Joshua's cabin and again stayed there until the rooster crowed. Again she missed work.

A strange thing was happening to her. Each time she visited Joshua, she lost a little more of the power she had over her slave. It was somehow being transferred to him. Six months later, he was telling her what to do, not the other way around. She had become his sex slave. By the time she mentioned murdering Beaumont, he had already thought about it. He wanted to be the new master of Bouvier Hill. He wanted to be like the man whose skin tone was the same as his—Walker Tresvant. He told her he would do it as long as he could kill Louis, too.

Chapter 85

And now for the coup de grace.

Christine was still walking on air when she stepped down from her white carriage and entered her home. Revenge had felt so good that she could not contain the euphoria. Her smile was bright and demanded her husband's attention immediately. She had watched the sister-in-law who had stolen her husband try to worm her way out of the justice that pursued and captured her. Now it was Tristan's turn. He had to answer for deceiving her with a woman who thought so little of him that she had thrown him over and turned to a common slave. She couldn't wait to see his reaction to the news, but she would.

She would wait for as long as she needed to because what she was about to tell him had to be timed perfectly so that the twelve-inch blade she was about to figuratively plunge in his heart would do irreparable damage. She was going to kill him without killing him. She knew the wait wouldn't be very long because Tristan was still awake. The light in the hallway was coming from the library. She assumed he was in there due the lateness of the hour.

"Where have you been?" Tristan called out from the library. "It isn't at all proper for a man's wife to come home at the witching hour."

Still beaming, anticipating his complete and utter destruction, she called out, "Coming, dear."

When she entered the library, he said, "Are you going to answer my question?"

"Oh, I was visiting with your sister," she said, intentionally downplaying why she was there and what happened.

"At Château Tresvant? At this hour?"

"Would you like a bourbon, dear?" Christine said.

"No. Answer my questions."

"Yes, where else would I be visiting Marie-Elise?"

Tristan watched her, trying to see if she was lying to him. "You say you were at my sister's home?"

"Are you sure you wouldn't like a drink, dear?"

"Will you answer my questions?"

"Tristan . . . sweetheart . . . you're going to wake up the dead with all that dreadful shouting," she said as lovingly as she could. "Let me fix you a drink. It will calm your nerves."

"My nerves are perfectly fine," Tristan yelled.

Christine continued smiling and poured him a drink in spite of him saying he didn't want one. She wanted to add to his agitation so that when the time came, he would demand that she tell him why she was at his sister's home. She took the drink over to him.

Fuming now, he slapped the glass out of her hand. It shattered when it hit the floor. "What the hell is wrong with you?" he yelled. "Didn't I tell you I didn't want a drink? And why are you wearing that stupid grin?"

"Am I grinning, dear?" she said, playing with him, watching his anger mount, enjoying it all the while.

Tristan nearly leapt out of his chair and grabbed her by the shoulders. "You weren't at my sister's, were you?"

Still smiling, she said, "Of course I was, dear. Why would I lie about a thing like that?"

"If you were at my sister's, what were you doing there at this hour?"

She had him now.

"We were just sitting around talking, that's all. Oh, and we had some cognac."

"Well, that at least explains the smile."

"Tristan, you're hurting me. Please let me go."

He released her, having no idea how tightly he was squeezing her arms. "You said *we*. Who else was there? Walker?"

"Yes. And Lieutenant Avery."

"Lieutenant Avery? What was he doing there?"

"Believe me, you don't want to know," she said and turned away from him. "Let's call it a night, shall we?"

"Let's not. What are you hiding from me?"

"Hiding from you? I'm not hiding anything from you."

"What was Lieutenant Avery doing there?"

Christine exhaled hard and said, "Well, if you must know, Walker was telling the lieutenant a fantastic tale about who really killed your brother."

"Beaumont?"

"Why, yes, dear. He is your only brother. Or do you have another?"

Tristan paced the floor, wondering if Cadence had done what he thought she had done, but hoping she hadn't. Desperate for answers, quickly, he said, "What was Walker saying? Who killed Beaumont?"

"Come now, Tristan. We both know who did the deed."

"So he told the lieutenant Cadence did it?"

"Yes, but Avery did not believe him."

Relieved, Tristan sighed. "Good."

Christine watched him closely. She knew it was time to start revealing what happened. "But then Lauren came over unannounced and she had an equally fascinating tale to tell."

"Hmpf! What did she have to say?"

"She said the same thing Walker said. She said she heard Cadence confess to the crime the night after the murders."

"Wait a minute. Are you telling me Cadence confessed to Lauren? Why would she ever do that?"

"No, no, no. Lauren says she heard her tell her new lover this after they finished having relations."

She watched him closely, savoring his every reaction.

He whipped around and faced her. "What do you mean, Cadence told her new lover? Who is it?"

"What difference does it make who it is? What's important is that Lauren heard her confess to killing your brother."

"And you believe her?"

"Tristan, please. Why on earth would she lie about a thing like that? She didn't even know Beaumont. She had nothing to gain by lying. As a matter of fact, even saying what she said puts her own life in danger. So you tell me . . . why would she lie on a white woman?" Tristan started pacing the room again. "She wouldn't lie, would she? Lauren knows what we both know. You said as much last night when you told me she wanted you to kill your brother. Don't you remember?"

"Of course I remember."

"Apparently, since you wouldn't do it, she found herself another lover who would and did."

"I don't believe a word of it."

"So she didn't ask you to kill your brother?"

"I don't believe she took another lover. She wouldn't do that."

"Hmpf! I think she could and she did. And so did the lieutenant."

"On the word of two niggers? Avery wouldn't dare!"

"It wasn't the word of two niggers only, Tristan. It was the word of your sister and your son."

"My son?" He thought for a second or two. "You mean young Beaumont?"

Christine nodded.

"What did he say?"

"He said that he and Lauren walked in while she was having relations with her new lover."

"What?!"

"Why would your son lie on his own mother, Tristan? Why?"

He started pacing again, only faster. "You say the boy walked in on them?"

"That's what he says."

Still pacing, he said, "Did he say who it was?"

"Yes."

He stopped pacing and looked at his wife. His eyes were on fire with curiosity. "Who was it?"

"You don't want to know, Tristan. Believe me. It's better not knowing."

He grabbed her by the shoulders again and shook her. Then he yelled, "Who was it, damn you?"

"It was her slave! Joshua!"

He searched her eyes diligently, seeking whatever truth they held. And when he realized she was telling the truth, he let her go, turned around, and doubled over.

Christine's smile came forth again. Seeing his anguish somehow made hers vanish. *And now for the coup de grace.* "And guess what else? She's three months pregnant with his baby." When he fell to his knees, she stood over him and finished the tale. "Lieutenant Avery's men dragged them both out of the house and took them to the garrison. I suspect they'll both die tomorrow morning. Now . . . are you sure you don't want that drink?"

Chapter 86

Clarity

The following morning Cadence and Joshua quietly stood side by side in the courthouse, waiting for the judge to hear their case. Neither had slept the previous night because their consciences would not allow them to. They had sat in two jail cells far away from each other in the basement of the garrison, thinking about what they had done and how they would do things differently if they could make a different choice. While Joshua knew his life would be taken from him, Cadence had no idea she would ever be prosecuted for her crimes. She stood there quietly thinking about her life and how it all had happened to her.

As the reality of a trial that might lead to the death penalty approached, she began to take responsibility for her life and how it turned out. She realized it didn't just happen to her; she had made it happen by making decisions that she *thought* would benefit her. She realized that her life started to fall apart the day she abandoned her core beliefs and embraced Beaumont Bouvier's hand in marriage. She knew he was a sodomite from the very beginning, but needed a beautiful woman from an elite family to cover it up.

She had given much thought to what she was about to do, repeatedly telling herself he was not a sodomite and that he only had feminine ways. She had lied to herself because she coveted his power, his wealth, and his influence. Otherwise, she would not have been able to go through with the ceremony.

In the deepest recesses of her heart, in the place where people hid their secrets, she hoped when the preacher came to the part where he would ask the attending family and friends if they knew of any reason the betrothed couple should not join in holy matrimony, to speak at that time or forever hold their peace, that someone would rescue her from her own nonsense. While Beaumont was an excellent provider and she didn't want for anything, he granted nothing of what she desired most; he granted none of his power, none of his wealth, and none of his influence.

She felt betrayed even though they had made no secret deals, no secret pacts whatsoever, before they donned their white apparel and took their sacred vows in an enormous church jam-packed with closest family and friends. She therefore took it from him, having convinced herself that it was all rightfully and legally hers the moment she said, "I do." But now her deepest desires had her in a court of law, waiting for the judge's decision on whether or not she would be put to death.

She looked at Joshua. He looked the same, but his good looks, his strong muscular arms and chest no longer had the appeal they once had. She had thought about it all night, trying to figure out just what it was that made her think she could ever have a life with him. Much like the previous night, she finally concluded a second time that seeing his muscular physique every day had drawn her away from her Christian ethics and sensibilities just as Tristan's good looks once had.

In short, she had allowed fanciful reveries to not only lead her into two extramarital affairs, but she had allowed the desire to be the master of Bouvier Hill to lead her down a dark path that ended in not one murder, but eight murders. She had seen split-second flashes of Aubrey and the housemen's faces all night long; she had heard them pleading for their lives. Each vision ended with the sound of musket fire and them falling into their graves.

Chapter 87

Truth's Confrontation

Still waiting for the judge to enter the courtroom, Cadence continued an uninterrupted stroll through a series of events that would probably lead to her death. She remembered the surge of elation as it coursed through her mind when she heard Lieutenant Avery commanding his firing squad to make ready, to take aim, and to fire. She remembered the sound of the flintlock muskets as the projectiles exited the barrel and zipped through the air, striking the innocent men *she* had killed. She remembered the contortions their bodies made when the balls of lead penetrated their faces and various other parts of their bodies. She remembered watching them fall back into the graves she had made them dig. And now she realized that she would soon go the same way they went—violently and without mercy.

As the judge entered the courtroom, she remembered the look on young Beaumont's face when he saw her legs on Joshua's shoulders. She remembered the absolute shock that registered. She remembered how embarrassing it was to be caught in the throes of passion by her son, screaming Joshua's name and other vile obscenities while he gave her what her body yearned for. The shame of it removed all traces of hubris and replaced it with humility.

She looked around the courtroom, hoping to see her mother and father and her sisters and brothers, but none of them were there. No friends. No customers. Not even Christine showed up to gloat. The only person she recognized was the face of a woman that she had just learned was her sister—Guinevere Delacroix. Suddenly she remembered that she had lied to her and mistreated her for years, and yet she was the only family member there to support her now that her life was a living hell. And that too brought shame.

Cadence gazed at Guinevere for a few moments and for the first time, she began to see traces of her father: his strong chin, and his wonderful sparkling gray eyes. Although the tignon covered it, she remembered that she also had her father's glorious hair. It occurred to her that Guinevere had known they were sisters all along and had kept that secret for nearly four decades. During those years, Guinevere had been loyal to her and to the Delacroix family, but Cadence had always been jealous of her.

Now Cadence understood to some degree why her father always had affection for her, even though it turned out to be aberrant. She wondered if her mother knew Guinevere was her sister and pretended not to. Of all the people she thought she could count on, the only person who was in the courtroom was the woman she had been jealous of. And that's what broke her. That's when she covered her face and wept loudly. That's when she decided it was time to admit what she had done. That's when she knew she had to try to save Joshua's life. And in so doing, she would remember what it was like to feel again, to be a human being again.

Chapter 88

"Your Honor . . . please . . . allow me to speak."

Judge Harlan Haley was enraged when he learned what really happened out at Bouvier Hill six months earlier. Murder always angered him. He thought it was so unnecessary because the people who committed the act usually did it for frivolous reasons. In certain cases, though, he understood the murderer, particularly if the murder committed was motivated by passionate displeasure. The case before him now, however, did not fall into the passionate displeasure category.

The Bouvier case reminded him of his own misery and infuriated him because a similar thing had happened to him twenty years earlier. The wife of his youth, the woman he loved with everything within him, had run off with a nigger too; a nigger that he owned and trusted, which was why Walker Tresvant used his influence with the mayor to get Haley assigned to the case. Haley nearly went broke trying to find his wife and her nigger lover in hopes of killing them both. He thought that since the Old Testament punished adulterers by stoning them to death, he was justified in killing his wife and her lover if he ever caught them. But his

Keith Lee Johnson

wife, like Cadence Bouvier, had come from money and she had more than enough to escape him forever.

Now was his chance to even the score, even though the two people standing in his courtroom and their case had little resemblance to his own, which was what Walker Tresvant was counting on. It had been twenty years since his wife humiliated him; twenty years since he'd seen her lovely face; twenty years since he'd held her in his arms and made sweet, passionate love to her. And while he wanted nothing more than to get his hands around her fragile throat so he could choke her to death, a part of him still loved her; a part of him still wanted her; a part of him wanted to forgive her and grant her clemency—and he would if he could, only it would be for the white woman standing before him now.

"Cadence Bouvier, you've been charged with murder," Judge Haley said when he took his seat. "How do you plead?"

She lowered her eyes to the floor and said, "Guilty, Your Honor."

"I understand that you are with child," the judge said in a voice full of compassion. "Is that correct?"

"Yes, Your Honor."

Still holding his mallet, Judge Harlan folded his arms and said, "I see, and how far along are you?"

"I've missed three monthly cycles, Your Honor. So I'd have to say three months."

Judge Harlan looked at Joshua, sighed heavily, and shook his head. Then he returned his eyes to Cadence. "And are you saying this nigger is the father?"

"Yes, Your Honor."

"Are you absolutely certain about that?"

Cadence thought for a few seconds, as she remembered the last time she had been with Tristan and said, "I am, Your Honor."

Judge Harlan exhaled hard. "I have reason to believe your brother-in-law, one Tristan Bouvier, fathered all four of your children and could in fact be the father of the child you carry now. Is that right?"

"It's possible but not likely, Your Honor."

Judge Harlan tried to conceal a burgeoning smile. He had been looking for a way to spare her life, and her uncertainty had just given it to him. After all, it was her slave's fault that she fornicated. Not hers. In just a few short minutes, he had dismissed everything she'd done because she was without a doubt led astray by her dark paramour at a time when she was most vulnerable. Were it not for him, she would have continued being the good Christian girl she was reared to be. Without her slave's influence, whatever voodoo spell he cast on her, a white woman from a wealthy and prestigious family never would have gotten herself into such a wicked predicament. He further reasoned that she'd had the dubious misfortune of marrying a sodomite, which so distressed her, it led her to sleeping with her brother-in-law for no other reason than to produce children to carry on the Bouvier name.

"If there is the remotest possibility that the child you're carrying could be a white boy or a white girl," Judge Harlan continued, "I cannot in good conscience sentence you to death until we know for sure whether the child you carry is of the Negroid strain. I will therefore postpone your sentence until you deliver the child in six months. You are hereby ordered to return to Bouvier Hill and resume your duties until then. And, Mrs. Bouvier, for God's sake and the sake of good Christians throughout this great Christian nation of ours, please . . . don't let this happen again. Lastly, if the child you carry turns out to be a nigger, perhaps it will die at birth, in which case I will dismiss all charges against you. After all that's happened at Bouvier Hill, you didn't kill anyone." He unfolded his arms and raised his mallet to strike the gavel.

Cadence said, "May I speak, Your Honor?"

"You may," Judge Harlan said and folded his arms again, still holding the mallet.

"This man"—she looked at Joshua and then back to the judge—"is innocent."

Enraged, Judge Harlan bolted out of his seat. His voice became as loud and voracious as a lion's roar when he yelled, "The hell you say!"

"Your Honor . . . please . . . allow me to speak."

"Speak, but be careful what you say," Harlan said, and returned to his seat. "I have the power to have you executed immediately."

"Thank you, Your Honor. Joshua Bouvier only did as he was ordered. As a matter of fact, he begged me not to make him have relations with me. He told me if he did what I demanded, this day would come and he would be killed for it. I told him that if he didn't do it, I would tell my husband and he would still be killed. Only then did he do as I instructed. So I ask that you let him go."

Judge Harlan raised his left brow and said, "Mrs. Bouvier, are you saying that *you*, not this ignorant *nigger*, initiated this thing?"

"I am, Your Honor."

"And there was no rape and no threat of rape?"

"No, Your Honor. He never threatened me. I threatened him—his very life."

"I see, and are you saying there was no threat whatsoever against your virginal daughter, Josette Bouvier, as you previously asserted?"

"No, Your Honor."

"Hmpf! You must have taken leave of your senses then," Judge Harlan said, shaking his head. He closed his eyes and massaged his temples a few times, remembering the wife of his youth, before saying, "In any case, the nigger knew better. You said so yourself. He should have taken his chances with your husband, *his master*. Since he didn't, I have to believe that on some level, he wanted you and in some way, se-duced you. It's not uncommon. He's no different than the black serpent that seduced the white woman in the paradise called Eden. These nigger bucks somehow have an effect on *our* white women and many . . . I say many . . . cannot help themselves. Therefore, he will die right now! That way, the next nigger will take his chances and tell his master instead of taking pleasure in plundering his master's wife." He slammed the mallet on the gavel and stormed out of the courtroom.

As the soldiers took Joshua out back to shoot him, he looked at Cadence and said, "Ya tried! I sho' thanks ya fo' it! I loves ya, Cadence Bouvier! Do ya hear? I say I loves ya!"

A few minutes later, Cadence heard musket fire, but what clung to her mind was Judge Harlan's reference to the Garden of Eden. She turned around and looked at Guinevere, who was still there. She remembered that Guinevere had asked her many times to read the story and she had refused. She also remembered how badly she had treated her over the years. When Guinevere came over and hugged her, she was so ashamed that she covered her face and wept bitterly.

Chapter 89

Fallen

Later that day, Lieutenant Avery took Cadence back to Bouvier Hill. The long ride back was a quiet one, as the death of Joshua ate at her unceasingly, as did the loss of their reciprocated love. No amount of consolation would quiet her conscience, as the sound of musket fire continued to reverberate in her mind. She could see his face as they dragged him out of the courtroom. He wasn't begging for his life, she remembered. He was forgiving her for what she had done to him because as the end drew near, she had tried to save his life. That, too, ate at her.

As the carriage pulled up to the front door and stopped, she saw Walker Tresvant's carriage. Kimba Tresvant was sitting atop it. Cadence and Lieutenant Avery stepped down and entered the residence. The mansion was still and quiet. Although she had no idea what she was going to say to them, she wondered where her children were.

Marie-Elise Tresvant stepped out of the library and said, "Cadence, could you come in here, please. We have something to say to you."

By "we," Cadence took it for granted she meant Walker was there too. She thought they were there to rub her misery in her face. Walker Tresvant had triumphed. He had gotten the sweetest revenge for Damien Bouvier's treachery, at least for the moment.

"I suppose I should leave," Lieutenant Avery said.

"Yes, you should," Marie-Elise said.

The lieutenant softened his voice and whispered so Marie-Elise couldn't hear his words, saying, "I would very much like to call on you if you're so inclined." He looked in her eyes and saw nothing but contempt in them. It was as if he could read her thoughts.

Without a single word, her eyes told him that she thought he was the lowest of all low men. She knew he thought she was a whore. She was three months pregnant with the baby of the nigger his men had shot to death an hour or so ago, but he still thought she would be willing to open her legs to him that very hour. It didn't matter that she had used him to kill six men. It didn't matter that she and the slave whose baby she was carrying had killed her husband and the man he slept with. It didn't matter that her firstborn son had walked in while she was on her back, folded in half, as it were, with her exquisite legs relaxing on a slave's shoulders while his stiff tool drilled as if there were gold to be had. It didn't matter that she'd had four children by her brother-in-law. It didn't matter that her conscience was in turmoil because of it all. All that mattered to Lieutenant Avery was that in spite of everything she had done, she was still beautiful and for that reason, he wanted to get his piece before her stomach got in the way.

Without another word, Lieutenant Avery turned around and walked out the front door. That's when Cadence realized what she had done to herself. She had lost so much respect for herself, no one, including her firstborn son, had any respect for her. The fact that Lieutenant Avery would even approach her the way he had, told her just how far she had fallen.

Twenty years earlier, before she allowed herself to get involved with Tristan, she thought she was everything that everyone else thought. She thought she was a shining example of virtue, but the last two decades had revealed exactly who and what she was. She was a beautiful creature, no doubt, but inside she was full of murder, adultery, lies, deceit, whoredom, and all sorts of wickedness. For two decades she had denied who she was because it was easy to look at her husband's salacious philandering. His lack of sexual restraint somehow fostered a sense of righteousness on her part, even though she had done worse. And now, the day of reckoning had arrived.

Chapter 90

"Justice, it seems, is incomplete."

When she awoke from her thoughts, Cadence made her way down the corridor and into the library, where Walker Tresvant and Marie-Elise waited for her. Defeated, she walked in, thinking it couldn't get any worse than it already was. She had a nigger's baby in her and by now, all of New Orleans knew about it. To save whatever remaining pride she had, she now had to get rid of the evidence of being the consort of her slave. The judge had basically told her that if she got rid of the child, he would dismiss all charges and set her free. She didn't want to commit yet another murder, but she would. She had four children to think about. Deep down, she was hoping for some miracle; some kind of metamorphosis where the black baby in her would become a white baby, the way a caterpillar becomes a butterfly.

When Marie-Elise was pregnant with Walker's baby while being engaged to Mason Beauregard, Cadence had ridiculed her publicly. The pendulum had swung in her direction and now she was in a worse position. Cadence avoided looking directly at Marie-Elise because she didn't want to see what was behind her eyes. She took a seat at the table they were sitting at and waited for the outpouring of malevolent chastisement she felt she deserved. She sat there for a few moments, waiting for one or both of them to launch a barrage of insults, but neither of them said a word. After a while she raised her head and looked Marie-Elise in her eyes. She saw no hatred, no judgment whatsoever. Surprisingly, she saw compassion only.

"Cadence," Marie-Elise began, "I don't know what you must be going through, but I'm sure it's something close to hellish. My husband and I thought it best, given everything that's happened, that we take the children to Château Tresvant for the foreseeable future."

Cadence lowered her eyes. Tears fell. "You're right, of course. I won't fight you on this. I won't." She looked at Marie-Elise again. "Just let me see them before you take them, okay? That's all I ask. I just want to see them and hug them and let them know I love them. Will you at least let me have that one concession?"

"I'm afraid that won't be possible, not today anyway," Walker said. "We've already taken them. They were inconsolable when young Beaumont told them what happened and who their real father was. We packed their things last night. We thought for sure you would be dead by now."

"Justice, it seems, is incomplete," Marie-Elise added. "The law, however, granted you a reprieve and they are *your* children. We will therefore return them to Bouvier Hill tomorrow, if that's okay with you."

After hearing that, Cadence fell completely apart, nodding her head and sobbing miserably. Marie-Elise, her arch nemesis, the sister of the man she had killed, held her, and rocked her like she had birthed her. They were all members of the same church; they all read the same Bible, and heard the same sermons. How they behaved during difficult times clearly showed the difference between the two women; during difficult times Cadence had abandoned her beliefs, but Marie-Elise clung to hers, lovingly consoling the woman who had killed her brother in cold blood.

"So they know what I've done?" Cadence managed to say.

"Yes," Marie-Elise said.

"Young Beaumont told them everything?"

"Yes, he did," Marie-Elise said. "I'm so sorry for you."

"Where is he? I need to speak with him."

"He left for Cambridge already," Walker said. "He said he didn't know if he would ever return."

When Cadence learned that her favorite son had left without bothering to say good-bye, it ripped her heart out. She couldn't respond so she nodded her head rapidly and continued weeping. She thought the plight of women was so unfair. She thought she hadn't done anything more than any rich man had done, including murder, but because she was a woman, the standard was incredibly high, making her fall from grace a truly harrowing fall indeed.

Chapter 91

"Why did she hate me?"

Now that Cadence was completely vulnerable, Walker decided it was time to get the information he and his wife had come for. "Cadence," he said and looked right into her eyes, "Marie-Elise and I need to ask you something. We've been wondering about it and we've discussed it at length. Actually, the truth is, Marie-Elise approached me, and I thought we should ask you now that the judge has granted you a measure of leniency. I must preface my question by saying that we have our own ideas about this thing I'm going to ask you about." He paused briefly while he and his wife studied her, looking for any sudden change in eye movement that might reveal her true thoughts, any sign of guilt she had not yet confessed. "Tell us truly now. Did you have anything . . . and I mean anything to do with the death of Prince Amir?"

Cadence stopped crying all of a sudden, stunned by the question, wondering where it came from. She looked at Marie-Elise to see if she really agreed with her husband, fiercely holding on to whatever virtues she had left, no matter how insignificant. She had momentarily forgotten that it was quite possible she had something to do with the prince's death. They already knew she had arranged the deaths of eight men. Marie-Elise nodded slightly, letting Cadence know she and her husband were in it together as usual. Her eyes returned to Walker's. She took a deep breath, sighed resolutely, shaking her head all the while before saying, "No, Walker, I didn't. Why? Did someone say I had something to do with it?"

"No one said you did, no," Marie-Elise said before Walker could answer. Even though Cadence would one day have to answer to God for her crimes, Marie-Elise understood that Cadence was still a woman and as such, she understood that women often feel driven to go against norms, both spiritual and societal. While what Cadence had done was far more extreme, she herself had broken the very same societal norms the day she defied her father and married a man of her own choosing; the man she had allowed to impregnate her without the benefit of holy matrimony. More important than that, Cadence was still a mother, and her children would need her and she them to get through this difficult and trying time. "We have reason to believe that someone hired the man who killed him."

Incredulous, Cadence said, "And you think it was me?"

"Well . . . let's just say, it's possible," Walker replied.

"Why would I have him killed, Walker? I wanted her out of here. The sooner she found the man she wanted to marry the sooner she would move out. Killing him only prolonged her stay. Besides, I have no idea how one would find a killer for hire," she said while thinking, *I would think you would know better than me, given your alliance with Madam Nadine.* "Check with some of your other friends in New Orleans; perhaps Basin Street would be the place to start."

Walker's face tightened. His nostrils flared. He knew she was referring to his relationship with Pearl Nimburu. Mentioning Basin Street as the place to check with his friends was the evidence of her wistful sarcasm and he didn't like it. Not in front of his wife. He was somehow able to justify and com-partmentalize his relationship with Pearl. He told himself that both women were necessary. Although his marriage was a move of retribution for Damien Bouvier's treachery two generations ago, he had grown to love Marie-Elise. He trusted and depended on her to rear his children and to teach them good things.

Nevertheless, his relationship with Pearl Nimburu had begun long before he married, and now she was firmly en-sconced in his life. He and Pearl had several children to-gether. He could never leave her, nor did he want to. Pearl accepted his familial obligations long ago; she had vowed to never interfere with it or make unrealistic demands. As far as he was concerned, Cadence had no business making hints about his extracurricular activities, especially since she barely escaped the firing squad herself. Besides, he dutifully did nearly everything his wife asked of him. He rarely said no to his wife's requests, which is how he kept peace in his divided home and justified his extramarital affair.

"Hmm," Marie-Elise uttered.

"What?" Cadence said.

"Lauren told me that Captain Rutgers told her someone had hired the man who shot Prince Amir on the dock," Marie-Elise said. "How would he know that unless he himself had done it? He must have told her that to make her believe you had something to do with his death, when in fact the cap-tain hired the man himself. That makes sense to me anyway."

"Why would he do something like that?" Cadence asked.

"From what Lauren told us last night, the captain is quite fond of her. He taught her how to read and write while they were aboard the *Windward*. She speaks several languages and she's an expert on Shakespeare."

"So she was playing dumb the entire time she was here?" Cadence asked, shaking her head, somewhat amused by the revelation.

"Apparently," Walker said. "The good captain taught her how to behave. Lauren's a very smart girl. She told us it was possible that you had hired someone to kill the prince, but she didn't believe it."

"Why did she think it was me?" Cadence asked.

"Captain Rutgers," Marie-Elise said. "At first she thought you were the guilty party, just like I think he wanted her to think. But last night it occurred to her that all you wanted was for her to move out. That's why you had Guinevere move here. Guinevere was supposed to pester her into leaving. She said her hatred for you clouded her judgment."

Cadence pulled her head back and raised her eyebrows. "Why did she hate me?"

"Because she knew you and Joshua had killed Beaumont and the other men and had gotten away with it," Walker said. "Since Beaumont had left her a sizeable inheritance, she felt the need to stay on here and be a thorn in *your* side, knowing, or at least believing her life was never in danger. Even though you had killed the others, she didn't think you'd kill her because you wouldn't want me and my wife to inherit her ten percent."

Cadence kind of laughed before saying, "Well . . . she was right about that. I would never have harmed her, just as she said. There was no way I was going to let you two get another ten percent of Bouvier Hill."

Marie-Elise looked at her husband and said, "The only question left is: how are you going to handle the Captain Rutgers situation?"

Walker took his wife's hand, looked into her eyes, and said, "If you're right about this thing . . . if Rutgers killed that young man before his time, I swear on Alexander Tresvant's grave . . . he will answer to me now and to whatever God he believes in afterward."

Chapter 92

An Unexpected Arrival

It was nightfall by the time Walker and Marie-Elise left Bouvier Manor. Cadence shut the door behind them and locked it. This was the first time she would ever be alone in the mansion. The day's events left her weary and sleepy. She decided to have a quick bite to eat before going to bed. *I am eating for two.* She wanted something sweet. As she walked into the kitchen, she remembered the pie she had made the day Guinevere had gone into New Orleans. She was a good cook, but she much preferred someone else do the cooking for her.

She cut herself a slice of pie, sat down at the table, and started eating. The pie was delicious and brought a measure of comfort that was missing. Before long, she had finished the piece and cut herself a larger wedge. When she devoured that, she cut herself an even larger third wedge and was now working on that, when she heard knocking. She put another forkful of pie in her mouth and headed for the door.

It had been about twenty minutes or so since the Tresvants had left. She was hoping it was them returning for something they had forgotten because the alternative may have been Lieutenant Avery, who wanted a slice of a very different kind of pie. The pie she had eaten made her feel better and she was prepared to deal with either. If it was Walker and his wife, she would let them in and see what they wanted, but if it was Lieutenant Avery, she would tell him about himself and return to the delicious pie waiting for her on the kitchen table.

She opened the door and was surprised to see neither the Tresvants nor Lieutenant Avery. Tristan Bouvier was standing on her doorstep. In an instant, how she got involved with him surged through her mind, replaying the entire episode in a matter of seconds. Though she had taken a measure of responsibility for her choices the previous night in her cell, anger was threatening to devour her as she remembered every word that led to their smoldering affair.

Chapter 93

The Seduction of a Married Christian Woman

A few days before Cadence decided to begin an affair with her brother-in-law, her husband had insulted her intelligence and her business acumen, which both angered and hurt her immeasurably. Before their first encounter, Tristan Bouvier came into her dress shop with his wife, Christine. Mardi Gras was approaching, and her dress shop was starting to fill with women who needed gowns for the pre-Lenten masked balls they had scheduled. Champagne-colored silks, along with matching folding fans, scarves, and other accoutrements were the rage. The items were selling so quickly she could barely keep them in stock.

Cadence had always been attracted to Tristan and although he had pursued her despite her marriage to his brother, she never seriously considered the possibilities of giving into his wanton desire because she fancied herself to be a woman of impeccable morality. She made allowances for his endless flirtations, seeing them as innocent and almost harmless. That's what she told herself anyway. However, that day was different. She was experiencing a number of different emotions. She was livid with her husband for his demoralizing commentary. She was also feeling stupid for the same reason. Both emotions engendered an emotional frenzy, which produced incredible vulnerability.

Tristan sensed something was wrong with Cadence. When he asked her about her deflated visage, she turned away from him, preferring to suffer in silence, rather than allow him to see how deeply injured she truly was. He looked deep into her eyes, and in them he saw that her moral defenses were down. He sensed that she was susceptible to emotional persuasion, and he pounced on her.

Much like the serpent in the Garden of Eden, he, too, subtly led her down the road of temptation by telling her what she wanted to hear; that being that everything wrong in her life began and ended with her husband. She was a woman, so the problem had to be him. Never mind that she chose to wed a known homosexual, believing him to be someone she could easily control.

Using the conversational buzz of excited women shopping as cover, Tristan had said, "Ever since our father died, Beaumont's been trying to run everybody's life, including yours, Cadence."

"He sure has, and I hate him for it!" she said, agreeing wholeheartedly, barely allowing him to finish speaking.

Smiling within, yet presenting a façade that offered sincere sympathy, he went on, "I don't blame you for hating him. It's his fault you're unhappy. As your husband, he's responsible for providing you shelter, clothing, food, sex, and children. As far as I'm concerned, that makes him equally responsibility for your unhappiness. It would serve him right if you took a lover."

She frowned and took a few steps backward. "Oh, I could never do that, Tristan. Never. It's sin. I would never break any of the Ten Commandments. Ever."

Frowning now, giving the appearance of righteous indignation, he said, "I understand what you're saying. I do . . .

but . . . is it still wrong if your husband is a Molly? A flaming sodomite? And to bed the men in the house he shares with you is unconscionable! You've been a dutiful wife, but *Jesus Christ*, how long are you supposed to put up with such behavior? How long?"

Cadence didn't respond. She looked at the floor for about ten seconds, considering the truth Tristan pointed out. She cut her eyes to the left for a quick moment, checking to see if Christine or any of her customers were paying attention to them. No one was. She then looked into Tristan's eyes again, wanting and needing to hear more of his thoughts, which mirrored her own.

At that precise moment, Tristan realized that in spite of her spiritual musing, she was closing her eyes to her own morality, her own adulterous yearnings, and was now focusing on her husband's, as if his somehow justified hers. He realized that was the only way she could justify sexual surrender to any man that wasn't her lawful husband. He understood that a married woman with a desire to be faithful couldn't just open her legs to a man. Being an experienced serpent, he knew that if he was to get between them, he had to pry her legs open with words and time as his only tools.

Words set the stage for sex, but time pried open the stage door. He knew all he had to do was say what she wanted to hear, something delicious, something for her to ponder, yet nothing decadent, and time would do the rest. The passage of time would be his ally in that it would give her time to think about his words, to dwell on his words, and then her imagination would turn the key and unlock the stage door. But there needed to be a delicate balance. He could not allow too much to pass; otherwise, she would realize she was falling, and stop her descent.

He looked deeper into her eyes and saw her desire to hear more. She had already made up her mind to surrender; she just needed more reason to, he deduced. Just as it was important for her to justify adultery, it was also important to her that he know she was not a whore, giving herself to any man that wanted to slide inside her to boost his inflated ego.

Confidently, he said, "Listen, if it isn't wrong for Beaumont to have several lovers at his disposal, all of whom are men, all of them *niggers*, it cannot be wrong for you to take one white lover who would love you tenderly and exclusively."

When her eyes agreed with him, when he saw her nodding, approving, he really poured it on.

Chapter 94

"What about Christine?"

Tristan continued talking, feeling as if he were only inches away from taking her in the back office and ripping her dress down the middle so he could see the large melons on her chest, so he could see the eyes on them staring back at him, beckoning him to give them the much-needed attention they wanted and needed. The idea of doing this to her was a daily fantasy that motivated the pursuit. "You know, Cadence, I would never treat a woman with your intellect . . . your incomparable elegance . . . and your exquisite beauty that way. My dear brother must be the biggest *fool* that ever lived. And if he isn't . . . surely he comes pretty close. Why, the Molly doesn't realize that instead of shunning you for being ambitious, he should be taking full advantage of your talents and desires to be all that a wife could and should be. Any *real* man wouldn't be afraid of having a wife that was a full partner with power to veto any decision that wasn't in *her* best interests."

When he saw her giving him her undivided attention, nodding, giving him permission to continue the adulterous conversation, he said, "If you were *my* wife, I would not only listen to you and your ideas of how to run any business *I* owned, but *I* would cling to whatever wisdom you had to offer. I would take your advice on everything as if God himself had spoken to me through you."

That was exactly what Cadence wanted and needed to hear. His final words helped her cross the line of morality and enter the world of immorality. The strange thing was that she had no idea she had crossed the line until much, much later.

Worse yet, all of these things were said while his wife, Christine, was less than thirty feet away. She was oblivious to what was taking place right under her nose as she perused the many dresses and accessories the shop offered. She had no reservations about her husband's fidelity. She believed Tristan could walk on water. There wasn't a man alive that was as faithful as he was. That's how good he was at deceiving her.

Tristan, sensing that he now had the freedom to say exactly what he was feeling, then said, "Cadence, I need to tell you the truth."

Desperate to hear more of his thoughts, almost pleading, she said, "What truth, Tristan?"

He looked at Christine and then looked at the floor before saying, "My marriage is a complete and utter sham, Cadence. I'm totally and hopelessly miserable. I wish to *God* that I could turn back the hands of time and pursue you. I now know that if I had,"—he paused for effect and then continued—"I couldn't say that it would be perfect, but, I think we would both be happier than we are right now."

Still smarting from Beaumont's stinging words concerning her business acumen, Tristan's words were like iced water sliding down her dehydrated throat on a blistering day. They were a welcomed haven from the growing dryness and lack of passion in her marriage. She looked at Christine for a few seconds and then searched the floor. Her conscience stung a bit because she was on the verge of giving her brother-in-law the thing that her husband could do without. She looked at her sister-in-law again. For a quick second, they locked eyes and smiled at each other. She then looked into Tristan's eyes and said, "What about Christine?"

Chapter 95

"I hate them both!"

Tristan realized Cadence was closer now than ever to surrendering. He stole a quick peek at her considerable breasts before looking at his wife. The desire to both see and handle them drove him on, pushed him to push her into a relationship she had sincerely tried to avoid. He stared at his wife for a few long seconds. As if she could sense him looking at her, Christine looked at her husband and smiled. Then she continued shopping, still looking for just the right dress for the upcoming church picnic. When Christine looked away, his face twisted into an angry scowl, like she was not only the worst wife on the planet, but the worst person that ever lived. Still looking at his wife, he said, "The truth?"

Desperately wanting him to give her what she needed to alleviate the accompanying guilt of committing adultery, she said, "Yes, the truth."

He locked eyes with Cadence for a long minute and then lowered his to the floor. "The truth is she couldn't hold a candle to you." He looked at Cadence again, needing to see what effect his words had on her. When he saw that she was still receptive, and still desired to hear more, even after verbally pummeling his wife, he continued the seduction, pleading like a beggar who hadn't eaten in weeks. "The truth is . . . not only are you a goddess to be worshipped . . . you're a good woman, and my brother doesn't deserve you. The truth is I hate her." He looked at Christine. "And I hate my brother. I hate them both! The truth is I hate them because they keep me from you. I hate them because as long as they live, I will be in excruciating torment, wanting you more than anything, being near you, but unable to possess you; to make you mine; to set you free so you can be who you want to be. And so we're both slaves of the law until death. And I will go on hating them until I breathe my last breath."

That was all she needed to hear. As far as she was concerned, adultery was fine and could be justified as long as the husband or the wife breaking their vows to God had a wife or a husband they hated. Adultery was fine and should be tolerated as long as there was genuine love between those committing it; or at the very least some sort of affection for the person she was committing it with.

Tristan returned to the dress shop early in the morning three days later, allowing time to work on her mind, so that she would give him permission to work on her body. He knew what time Cadence arrived. This was it. This was the day he was going to have the woman of his dreams. He waited at the back door, hoping she would come into the office first. She did.

When she saw him, she was startled at first, but glad he was there. She had thought of nothing but him and them being together for three days. She offered him a warm smile, opened the door, and said, "Tristan, what on earth are you doing here?"

"I had to see you, Cadence," he said as he walked into the shop. He paced back and forth like he was a nervous wreck. "I can't go on like this." He stopped pacing and faced her. Looking into her eyes, he said, "I love you, Cadence! I do!

I've been in love with you for years and I can't pretend anymore. I refuse to."

"We can't just break our vows, Tristan. We've made commitments."

"Then let's not break them," he said. "Kiss me just once, and I'll leave and never bother you again."

"Just once," she said with no real conviction.

"Just once," he said, almost begging.

"You promise?"

"I promise."

"Okay, but only one time and then you'll leave, right?"

"I swear to God."

Slowly they moved forward, turning their heads to avoid bumping noses. When their lips touched, an indescribable surge of pleasure coursed through them, pulling them further and further in, until their hands began to explore. When they pulled away, they were both breathing heavy, and could tell neither wanted it to stop there.

Cadence said, "Tristan, if we don't stop now, God will strike us down for what we're doing."

"I know," Tristan said. "But just once more . . . please, Cadence . . . I beg of you."

They kissed again and it was more powerful than the first. Again they pulled away. Again they wanted to continue and they did. But when they pulled away the third time, Tristan ripped her dressed down the middle, just as he had envisioned. Her breasts bounced a few times, which stimulated him. They embraced in an even deeper kiss, and then there was no stopping.

"Oh, God," Cadence said, no longer having the power or the will to stop herself as she heard her white undergarments ripping. "Please don't kill me for this."

Before long, Tristan was regularly visiting Cadence without Christine. The back office of the dress shop became their highly combustible love nest. While they tried to be careful, passion overrode sound judgment and soon, Tristan was there nearly every day, whisking her away for a few stolen moments of passionate kissing, tender fondling, and eventually, quick, but fever-pitched lovemaking.

Cadence had felt like a whore for doing such wicked things, but the sensations Tristan gave her were like nothing she had ever felt. Even though she knew it was not only wrong, but a sin against her God, the excitement of it all overpowered her spiritual sensibilities.

A few weeks later, she experienced her first bout with morning sickness. She realized she had Tristan's first of four children in her uterus. She went to Beaumont's bedroom that very night and demanded fulfillment. Eight months later, she gave birth to a boy child that Beaumont named Junior. Whenever she missed her menstrual cycle, she demanded sex from Beaumont to conceal their separate acts of adultery—her own, Beaumont's, and Tristan's.

Chapter 96

"Yes, I love him!"

The momentary reverie ended abruptly when Tristan barged in, pushing her out of his way with his shoulder. His heart was still bruised from the battering he took when his wife told him the truth about the woman he had loved with all his heart, with all his soul, with all his mind, and with all his strength. Cadence was a goddess to be worshipped, and worship her he did. Now, though, his love was gone. It had been replaced with disdain, dislike, and disrespect.

"What do you want, Tristan?" Cadence demanded, as she stumbled a few steps to the right.

"I've came to pay my little strumpet a final visit," he said. "I heard the judge was quite lenient with you because you have a child in your belly. But a *nigger*, Cadence? It would have been bad enough if it were a white man of means, but a dumb *nigger*? How could you lay down with a nigger, let alone let yourself get pregnant by him? How?"

She could smell the bourbon on his breath. Still holding the door open, Cadence said, "Tristan, you're drunk. Please leave before I say something we'll both regret."

"Before you say something we'll both regret? I think

you've already done that." He paused for a second. "Oh, I know. Let's ask my dear brother, Beaumont. Is he here? Oh, that's right, you and Joshua killed him! That must have been some conversation. Tell me, dear . . . do you regret the delicate words you used to first seduce him and then convince him to do what you could not persuade me to do?"

"Get out, Tristan! I don't ever want to see you again!"

"Don't worry . . . you won't see me again," he said. "If you're not careful, you won't ever see anybody again. Now . . . close the door."

"Gladly! As soon as you're on the other side of it!"

Tristan walked over to the door, pushed her aside with one hand, and closed the door with the other. "Let's have a talk, shall we, my dear?"

"I have nothing to say to you, Tristan! Please leave this instant!"

"Oh, you're going to talk to me," he said. "You're going to talk to me if it's the last thing you do." He grabbed her by the arm and dragged her down the hall and into the library. "Undress!"

Bewildered by his arrogance, she said, "Are you serious, Tristan?"

"Very! I've always wanted to take you in here," he said, and started undressing. "And by God, I will! You can enjoy it or don't, but I'm going to have you tonight!"

"Have you lost your mind?" Cadence yelled. "Or is it just your memory? I told you in this very room that I don't love you anymore. I told you it was time we ended everything between you and me. I told you the day we met Lauren in here. Now please . . . get it through your thick head! You've ruined my life, my marriage, and my family."

"I ruined *your* life? I ruined *your* marriage? *I* did that Cadence? Me?"

"Yes! I was doing just fine with Beaumont until you came along and ruined everything we shared together."

Tristan stared into her eyes for a few seconds, attempting to determine if she was seriously expecting him to buy into what she had just offered him. She needed to justify herself, he knew. But he wasn't going to allow her to. She was just as guilty as he was; in fact, more guilty, because she was the architect of eight murders. The judge may have let her off the hook, but he wasn't going to.

"Do you really expect me to believe that you were happy before I came along and rescued you from your misery with my brother? Life was so good with him before I came along, huh? Is that what you're saying?"

"Yes, that's exactly what I'm saying."

"Let me get this straight. You're saying that you and my dear brother, the Molly that he was, were having marvelous relations, sexual and otherwise, before I stole your heart?"

"Yes!"

"If that's true, my dear, if you were so happy with Beaumont *and* his homosexuality, what do your adulterous actions say about you?" He paused briefly to let his words do the damage intended and then continued. "I'll tell you what your actions say about you. They say that your spirituality is not only a joke now, it was a joke then! Long before I came along! The proof of this is the fact that you have committed eight murders, Cadence! Eight of them! And not one of them was in self-defense! Not one! I was nothing more than an excuse to be the lewd whore that you already were! You were a whore in your mind long before I seduced you! Long before!

"And now that you know who and what you are, you still have the audacity to blame me for giving you what you wanted long before I came along! For further proof of this, consider your current condition! You have a slave's pickaninny in your belly, Cadence! A slave's! That fact ought to wake you up to who you really are! You think you're the Virgin Mary when in fact your actions, past and present, represent another Mary—Mary Magdalene, who had seven demons in her! I fear that Christ himself will have to cast seven demons out of you as well!"

Tristan's words were like a harpoon that had been launched a mile away, picked up speed as it sailed through the air, and then plunged deep into her heart. While she had taken responsibility for her actions, Cadence had never given any thought to this new truth. This particular truth exposed her for who she really was on the inside. She was beautiful to behold, sure, but on the inside, she was a complete mess—death incarnate.

She was ugly and barren inside, and now she could finally see the truth she had been denying since the day Tristan and Christine entered the dress shop she formerly owned. It was true that Tristan had a hand in leading her to the road of perdition, but once there, she freely walked to the final destination of murder without any guidance or assistance from him. As a matter of fact, he had tried to talk her out of it, which was why she broke off the relationship. Besides, he could never lead her anywhere she didn't want to go.

Pacing the library floor now, a new reality was settling in and threatening to wash over her like a two hundred foot tidal wave on final approach. Tears welled and slid down her cheeks. But when she heard him laughing from his belly, the tears disappeared. Blinding, all-consuming rage filled her heart. She turned around and looked at him. He was doubled over, still laughing, with no sign of stopping any time soon.

Finally he stopped laughing and said, "So . . . did you love that nigger they killed today? The one you used to kill my brother, the husband you *now* say you were happy with before I came along and ruined it all. Tell me, dear, how long do you think it would have been before you killed the nigger as well?"

Cadence quieted herself for a second or two and thought.

She wanted to destroy him, and the best way to do that would be to agree with him. Since he thought she loved Joshua, she would give him what he wanted and in so doing, stab him in the heart. "Yes, I love him! He's the best lover I ever had! Is that what you wanted to hear?"

Chapter 97

"You're the strumpet! You're the strumpet!"

When Tristan heard Cadence say Joshua, a common ignorant nigger, was a better lover than he was, his laughter disappeared suddenly and the back of his hand found its way to the right side of her cheek. Her head snapped back and to the left, but she was unmoved by it. A red bruise surfaced; her cheekbone swelled. When she realized that she wasn't the least bit hurt by the blow, and that he had been drinking what smelled like a lot of bourbon, she backhanded him. He staggered to the left a little. When she saw that her blow had more effect than his, she thought she could win if he wanted to tussle.

Seeing that he was still a little off balance, she took a couple steps forward and kicked him in the groin—hard. His face twisted, his eyes bulged, he made a circle with his lips, and a long groan came forth before he doubled over. She then grabbed a hunk of his hair, pulled his head down, and kneed him in the nose. Blood splattered all over his face. Dark, thick drops splashed on the floor. When she saw his blood, she knew she could win. Besides, he deserved it. She had told him to leave. He refused and then threatened to rape her. She kicked him in the groin again and then kneed him in the nose again as hard as she could.

After the day she'd had, it felt good to take out her frustrations on Tristan because he had started it all. She therefore thought it appropriate that he feel the sting of her anguish. Because of him, she lost her moral compass and ended up bedding her slave. Because of him, she had lost it all. She had lost her self-respect. She had lost her children. And after she had Joshua's baby in another six months, she would then lose her very life. She was enjoying the damage she had inflicted. Instead of finishing him while he was dazed and disoriented, she starting talking to him.

"Who's the little strumpet now?" She drew back and let a haymaker connect to his chin. The blow sounded off. Smack!

Tristan stumbled backward and as he tried to balance himself, he staggered more and fell through the library's glass and wood paned door. Small cuts were on his face and hands. When the sound of hearty laughter rang in his ears, he struggled to get back up. He waited for a few seconds, trying to get his equilibrium back. Her laughter had made him angry and gave him incredible focus, but his body wasn't ready to cooperate with his mind. He took a few staggering steps forward with every intention of beating her to death—literally.

"Come on, Tristan," Cadence taunted. "You were never that much of a man when I was bedding you. And you certainly aren't much of a man now!" She laughed again. "I'm going to beat the hell out of you. And then I'm going to put you on the horse you rode over here on and send you back to Christine where you belong."

Tristan was still a little disoriented when he drew back to hit her. She waited on the blow and at the last second ducked out of the way. Tristan lost his balance again and she took full advantage. While he was trying to regain control, she balled up her smallish fist and hit him right in the eye.

Smack! He fell up against the table. Smack! Smack! She hit him with a left-right combination. He was dazed again, and struggled mightily to regain his balance. Cadence doubled over laughing hysterically.

She walked over to him, grabbed him by his lapels, and said, "You all right, sweetie?"

Then she kneed him in the groin again. Tristan's face twisted. The air in his lungs left him in a hurry and he groaned in agony. She then lifted up his head by his hair and hit him flush on the chin. Smack! Dazed but furious, Tristan swung wildly. She ducked again and hit him in the stomach, knocking the rest of his wind out of him.

While he gasped for air, she grabbed him by his lapel again, pulled him close, and said, "You thought you were going to take it, huh? Well, I'm not going to let you." She spun him around, drew back, and let him have another heavy blow. Smack!

The blow sent him spiraling out of control across the room. He fell in the doorway. She decided to destroy his ego with her words. Cadence calmly walked over to him, looked down and said, "I swear to God I don't know why I ever let you talk me into sleeping with you. Beaumont, the Molly that he was, was a much better lover than you." Then she slammed the door against his head repeatedly until he stopped moving.

She then pulled down her underwear, positioned herself over his face and peed. The yellowish fluid splashed down on his face, went into his open mouth, and down his nose. He started choking and coughed without restraint. When she finished, she pulled up her underwear, stooped down again, and whispered in his ear. "You know what, Tristan? They can only kill me one time. So you know what I'm going to do? I'm going to kill you. Walker Tresvant had it right. I've had other people kill for me, but you, I'm going to kill myself. Wait right here. I'll be right back."

She kicked him in the face and then walked down the hall and entered the kitchen. She opened her cutlery drawer and pulled out a big knife. She was just about to go back to the library when she saw her pie. She sat down and started eating. For reasons she didn't understand, the pie tasted even better now. By the time she got to the last bite, a thoroughly bloodied and battered Tristan staggered into the kitchen and fell up against the door opening. He still hadn't regained his balance fully, but he had murder in his eyes.

When she saw how much damage she had done, she laughed again and said, "You just don't know when to quit, do you?" She put the last bite of pie in her mouth, stood up, and said, "Okay, come on. And you know what . . . to show you there's no hard feelings . . . I'm going to give you the first shot again. After that, I'm going to take this knife and cut your plow off. After that, I'm going to cut your heart out."

Tristan, still off balance, staggered over to her and drew back to hit her with everything he had. He just wanted to get one blow off. One heavy blow would change everything, he told himself. Then he was going to slam the door on her head repeatedly. Afterward, he would return the favor of peeing in her face and watch her choke like he had.

Cadence, full of arrogance having beaten him the first round, just looked at him, believing she could take whatever he threw at her. Big mistake! She saw the punch coming, but hubris told her it wasn't going to hurt. Hubris told her, "It won't even move you." Crunch! Her jaw was broken in two places. The knife she was holding flew up into the air and clanged when it landed. She crumpled to the floor without trying to brace her fall. He got on top of her and using both fists, punched her repeatedly in the face. Smack! Smack! Smack! Smack! Smack! Smack! Smack! Smack!

He delivered vicious blows until her face was more of a bloody mess than his. With every blow, he repeated, "You're the strumpet! You're the strumpet!" Smack! Smack! Smack! He punched her until he was exhausted. Then, having completely subdued her, he ripped off every stitch of clothing she was wearing and had his way with her on the kitchen floor several times.

As he raped her, Cadence never moved. She was perfectly still, like she was a corpse—but not. Although she was powerless to stop what was happening to her, she was fully conscious. While Tristan was thrusting himself inside of her, while he enjoyed plundering her, she got the feeling they were being watched. She cut her eyes to the open window. Christine was watching and listening to it all. And she was laughing hysterically. When their eyes locked, Christine smiled and waved. That's when Cadence knew that Christine had set up this whole scene so she could watch the fireworks between her and Tristan and thus be a witness of her ultimate revenge.

Christine had followed Tristan over to Bouvier Hill. She watched and listened from a library window, laughing uproariously as the two former lovers verbally insulted each other. What she saw belonged on stage. It was comical. Then when the fisticuffs began, it became even funnier to see her husband being pummeled by Cadence. When they moved to the kitchen, she went with them and watched Tristan return the favor by beating Cadence senseless. But when her husband stripped off her clothes, she knew what was about to happen. She didn't care what they did to each other. When she had seen enough, she left them to each other's mercy.

Chapter 98

"It's good to know that chivalry isn't dead."

Lauren and Rokk Baptiste entered Bouvier Manor. About an hour and a half had passed since Tristan and Cadence's altercation began. "Mrs. Bouvier," Lauren called out, "I don't want any trouble. I just came to pick up my trunk. That's all. If you let me get my things in peace, I won't ever bother you again."

They heard some commotion in the kitchen and went to investigate. As they passed the library, they saw the broken door. Pee was on the floor. Glass was everywhere. They walked a little further down the hall and looked into the kitchen. A puddle of pee was on the floor near Cadence's head, and in her hair. Tristan was repeatedly stabbing Cadence's stomach with a huge knife. She was obviously dead, but he kept right on stabbing her, repeating, "You'll never have that nigger's baby!" Stab! "Never!" Stab! "Do you hear me?" Stab! "Never!" Stab!

Lauren screamed in horror. As much as she had seen, nothing topped seeing a naked white woman, who appeared to have been raped, being repeatedly stabbed by her former lover. Tristan was now holding one of her large breasts in one hand, while the other hand had a large bloody knife in it. When his hand started moving forward, like he was about to hack off her breast, Lauren nearly fainted. What she found more terrifying was that he was wearing a smile, which indicated he was going to enjoy the surgery he was about to perform.

Tristan heard screaming and stopped his forward motion. He wiped the drying blood on his face with his sleeve to see who was watching his horror show. "Lauren," he sang. "Oh, look, Cadence. It's the bane of our existence . . . little Miss Lauren Renee Bouvier herself." He saw the big black man with her and said, "And who do we have here? A wild card in the deck, I suppose." He pulled out a flintlock pistol and pointed it at Lauren with every intention of making her as dead as Cadence was. Rokk stepped in front of her. Tristan smiled and said, "It's good to know that chivalry isn't dead." He laughed heartily, put the gun to his own head, and pulled the trigger. Pow! His dead body slumped over Cadence's.

Chapter 99

Unexpected Revelation

It had been six months since Tristan killed Cadence and then took his own life. It was a tragedy to be sure, but Cadence had sown the seeds of violence, and those same seeds grew up and did to her as she had done to others. It was all so senseless, so very unnecessary, Lauren thought as she waited on the docks for Captain Rutgers, who had recently returned to New Orleans.

Rutgers paid her a surprise visit at her shop earlier that day when he delivered more perfume from the House of Creed. She had told him she wanted to speak with him in private over dinner that night. To keep him disarmed and relaxed, she added that it would be good to talk like they once had aboard the *Windward* in his quarters. Being fond of her, he agreed and had no suspicions of why she wanted to speak with him.

While she waited for Rutgers, she thought about Rokk Baptiste, who she had grown very close to. They needed each other now that the prince was no longer in either of their lives. Rokk had been willing to save her life without thought for his own when Tristan pointed a pistol at her. She admired him for that. Rokk took her to work every morning in her carriage. They talked endlessly about Amir and all the things Rokk learned from him. When she realized that brawling was the thing he loved above all else, she asked Lieutenant Avery to setup a few bouts for him at the garrison.

On Saturday nights they would go to the garrison and Rokk would brawl with the soldiers. The officers and the regular soldiers were betting on the bouts; bets that Lauren covered. There were some tough fighters in the garrison, but none could defeat Rokk. After a while, brawling become so popular that they moved the matches to Congo Square, where Rokk took on all challengers. Rokk was so talented that Lauren had to start giving odds. She finally had to tell him to take a few more punches and make it look good before winning. They had a marvelous time together and made a lot of money in the process.

One night after an impressive win, Rokk asked Lauren to be his wife. At first she thought it was too soon. The prince had only been dead for three months when he proposed. She thought that if they had married, she would mourn him at least a year before considering another. That was the appropriate thing to do. However, she was in New Orleans. She had learned from experience that life was cheap there. And even though she had survived every obstacle in her path, she was still mortal, and death was always lurking, waiting to take the life that wasn't prepared. She told Rokk that she would think about it.

A week later, Walker and Marie-Elise gave them a huge wedding at Château Tresvant. The whole Tresvant family was there, including granduncles, Simeon and Christopher, grandaunt, Kayla, who was fathered by Damien Bouvier, his fully white half sister, Dorothy, and even Jude, the overseer who had beaten Kimba into submission. Walker gave away the bride and Marie-Elise was the maid of honor. Now Lauren was three months pregnant, having conceived the first time she had sex with her husband.

She was happy and finally able to let her guard down, but she never forgot the conversation she'd had with Walker and Marie-Elise the night Tristan killed Cadence. They had told her that Cadence had told them she had nothing to do with the prince's murder. Even though she had defended Captain Rutgers, she couldn't think of one other person who would have wanted the prince dead. No one else benefited. The three of them reasoned that Rutgers had fallen in love with her on the journey to the Americas. She naïvely rejected the notion at first. The idea of Rutgers being in love with her never crossed her mind. She thought he was just trying to make up for what he had done to her and the prince.

Chapter 100

"How could you do it, Joseph?"

Captain Rutgers's disembarkation was very similar to Amir's. When they saw Lauren, both men smiled as they descended the gangplank. The difference between the two men was that Amir and Lauren embraced and kissed before a man shot and killed Amir. Rutgers then killed the man he hired and put on the performance of a lifetime when he grabbed his brother's leg and said he had forgiven him, all in an effort to curry favor with Lauren. Rutgers had even allowed the prince to live in his quarters. He had eaten with him day after day, and had convinced the prince to forgive him, knowing that an assassin's bullet was waiting for him shortly after the *Windward* docked—that's what Lauren and the Tresvants believed anyway.

Rutgers had to kill the assassin because he had improvised. All he had to do was shoot the prince and run off. But he decided to get creative by saying that Helen Torvell was his sister. Rutgers knew that at some point, Lauren might start questioning what had happened when she was no longer in shock. She might even find out that Helen Torvell didn't have any brothers. And if she found that out, she might start asking more questions that would lead to him. It might occur to her that there were a lot of blacks coming off the *Windward*. Why kill the one who was not wearing chains? Why not go straight to the men and women who were already shackled? Lauren was smart, Rutgers knew. She would have asked those troubling questions eventually, Rutgers had deduced. After all, he was the one who helped facilitate her Shakespearean education, and that alone would eventually lead her to asking a myriad of questions.

The affair that his wife had with his brother, coupled with the expediency of slavery, so twisted Rutgers's mind that he saw virtually nothing wrong with what he had done. He had done it all for love. And of course love is a great reason to kill someone—that's what he told himself anyway. He loved Lauren nearly as much as he had loved Tracy, his former wife. Amir's return had threatened his desire to make her fall head over heels in love with him.

"Hi, Lauren," Rutgers said as he approached her. "I finally did it."

"Did what?" she said reflexively.

Full of jubilance, he said, "I finally bought a place in the Quarter. I'm going to open a brandy and wines shop. I'm going to serve the best liquors in the world in the best city of the world!"

Lauren locked eyes with him and stared. She didn't say a word. She just kept staring, not even batting an eyelash.

When she didn't congratulate him, when she didn't say anything, Rutgers became nervous and was unable to maintain eye contact. He began to wonder if she had figured it out. Offering a phony smile, he said, "What's wrong, Lauren? Is something bothering you?"

Still staring at him, she said, "How could you do it, Joseph?"

Rutgers's heart raced, pumping hard and fast. He said, "Do what?"

"How could you kill the prince, Joseph? How could you do it?"

Without conviction, Rutgers said, "What are you talking about? I didn't kill the prince. I thought we agreed that Cadence did it."

Chapter 101

"Excuse me, good sir, are you the captain of the *Windward?*"

Lauren's eyes were still glued to Rutgers's eyes. Slowly, she started shaking her head, unable to discern just how morally bankrupt he really was. She wasn't certain that he had killed the prince, but she believed wholeheartedly that he did. It was just a matter of getting him to confess. The thing that really shocked her was that he was much better at play acting than she was. "All this time you knew that you had planned to murder Amir, yet you were able to pretend like you were looking forward to our reunion. You even cried to make your version of Shakespeare's Iago seem authentic." Her heart seemed to break more with each word she spoke. Her voice was trembling when she said, "You knew that I loved him. You knew that I sacrificed all for him. You knew that I would die for him. And yet you took him from me. Why?"

When he saw her tears, when he heard the pain in her vacillating voice, he said, "What can I say? No answer I give will be sufficient for what I took from you."

As the tears flowed, she said, "Try me, Joseph. Explain to me why you would do what *you* of all people did." She folded her arms, desperately needing to be held. A moment later, her tear ducts stopped begging for the freedom they were yearning for and took it. "Help me make sense of it all."

Rutgers's love for her was so strong that he could feel what she was feeling. When he saw the anguish behind the tears, when he saw her holding onto herself for comfort, he realized just how much damage he had done, and he wept too— real tears. "I never thought I'd love again after what Jonah and Tracy did to me. I really didn't. At first you were just a commodity like the rest of the slaves I bought or captured. In the beginning you were worth more to me, but only monetarily. But you had to go and save my life. And that changed everything."

He reached out to touch her and she snatched away.

Desperate for answers, she said, "How, Joseph? How did my saving your life change everything?"

"We got to know each other. I became your teacher and we grew close. At least I grew close to you. As I watched you absorb everything, as I heard you articulate ideas, as I read your thoughts through the papers you wrote, I fell completely in love with you. There was nothing I could do about it. I thought that if I separated you from the prince, you would forget about him, but you didn't. I specifically picked a master for you that I knew wouldn't touch you; one who wouldn't recklessly and callously plunder you. I thought Beaumont Bouvier was a friend and fit the bill perfectly."

Still crying, she said, "Did he know what you were doing?"

"No. He was just doing a friend a favor. How could I know he would be dead just three days later? I couldn't know that! I couldn't! And I certainly couldn't know he would emancipate you and make you a wealthy woman in the process. Damn him! I *thought* that he would live! I *thought* you would eventually get over the loss of the prince! I *thought* that you, having no equals other than me, would then give me the chance to be the man in your life.

"But you still loved the prince. You had to hire a lawyer

and find the prince." He was shaking his head. "With all the turmoil on the island, there was no way he should have been able to find one man, but he did. I didn't think he'd find him, but there was always a chance. So I found a man deeply indebted to me to do the deed. But then I made another mistake. I thought there was no way you'd be interested in Rokk Baptiste. The man is beneath you and yet you"—he looked at her stomach—"are pregnant with his child. I wanted to kill him too, but I thought you'd soon tire of him and then you'd come to me."

Just then, Solo Nimburu came out of the shadows and walked up to them. He looked at Lauren for a fleeting second, waiting for her to change her mind. She didn't. He looked at Rutgers and said, "Excuse me, good sir, are you the captain of the *Windward*?"

"Why, yes, I am. What can I do for you?"

"You can die!"

Pow!

And poof, Solo Nimburu disappeared into the dark night without another word.

Lauren then stooped down and looked into Rutgers's eyes. She could tell he was confused as his blood poured out of him. He was dying. "Look into my eyes, Joseph." She watched his eyes focus on hers. With a voice full of compassion, she said, "The prince's death had to be avenged. You had to answer for what you did to the prince and what you did to me."

Joseph kind of smiled and said, "Touché, Ibo Atikah Mustafa. I taught you well. That's what I paid my assassin to do. Too bad mine couldn't follow orders like yours did. When you think of me, remember that I did it all for love. I loved you, Lauren Renee Bouvier. I . . . love . . ."

She continued looking into his eyes, waiting until he breathed his last. When his eyes lost their focus, she left him there on the dock, and returned to her carriage where Rokk was waiting to drive her back to Bouvier Hill.

Chapter 102

The Sweetest Hangover

In the near distance, Walker Tresvant and Pearl Nimburu watched it all with eager anticipation. When they were reasonably certain Rutgers was the guilty party, they met with Lauren and planned his murder. They considered going to Lieutenant Avery or the commandant of the garrison, but they didn't believe justice would be delivered. After all, a white man had killed a black man, and blacks were only three-fifths of a human being. The authorities would have seen it the same as a man killing an animal. They therefore took justice into their own hands.

Lauren's one and only stipulation was that the assassination had to happen the same way Rutgers had planned Amir's death. It had to be equally cold and equally calculated, which was why Lauren agreed to have dinner with Rutgers. She needed him to relax, just as Amir was relaxed and thinking he was going to reunite with the woman he loved.

Walker had come to love Lauren like everyone else. After all, he had played the role of her father by giving her away at her wedding. Besides, what Damien Bouvier had done to Jennifer, his grandmother, still bothered him. Damien had taken sexual liberties with Jennifer on her wedding night when she was still a virgin. He continued having relations with her regularly—even though he had promised it would be one time only—and eventually impregnated her. Making sure Lauren got justice was almost the same as getting justice for Alexander Tresvant; the man who was responsible for his education and the millions of dollars he enjoyed. Now that the deed was done, he and Pearl went back to Madam Nadine's House of Infinite Pleasure.

Leading him by the hand, she took him to her bedroom and undressed and bathed him. She then led him to her bed and softly kissed him all over. She had paid a small fortune to learn a secret form of acupuncture that was over five hundred years old on her latest trip to the Orient. She had been practicing the art on Walker nearly every day since she returned six months ago. He couldn't get enough and neither could she. Using six golden needles, she strategically placed each one in a special sequence that gave Walker an erection that would remain until she removed the needles. Then she made sweet, passionate love to him for as long as he wanted her to.

Chapter 103

Like Mother Like Daughter

Six months later, Lauren gave birth to a beautiful baby girl. Rokk named her Antoinette Jacqueline Gabrielle Baptiste. From the time Lauren realized she was pregnant, she daily placed her hand on her belly and told the unborn child her life story. The night Antoinette was born, Lauren relayed the story again, and continued telling her the story every day until she was a teenager.

When Antoinette was a little girl and could understand the story, her eyes would fill with wonder. But by the time she became an adolescent, she grew weary of the stories and wondered why her mother made her continue to listen to them even though she could probably tell the stories in a more interesting way. What Antoinette couldn't know, being so young, was that she would tell her daughter, Josephine Baptiste, the stories so that Ibo Atikah Mustafa and Prince Amir Bashir Jibril would live forever in their hearts and never be forgotten.

Shortly after Antoinette's birth, Rokk met a British man who had seen him brawl in Congo Square. He had brought a couple of black brawlers with him from England. They were very good fighters, but the Brit had never seen anything like Rokk. His speed, timing, and balance put him in a class all by himself. He told Rokk that they could make lots of money together, and they set sail for England, where brawling was popular. Rokk promised Lauren he would return, and had every intention to, but the distance, the lack of communication, and the lonely nights proved to be too much to overcome.

Because he was a fighter and he was becoming famous and wealthy, women flocked to him in droves. He thought of his obligation to his wife and Amir, his mentor, but having so many willing English women available, he eventually succumbed to the need for female companionship. Before leaving the Isle of Santo Domingo, he had developed an insatiable desire for women that he thought marriage would cure. Being with Lauren in New Orleans made him think he had conquered the temptation to roam.

A few years after he left, Lauren received a letter from an English woman telling her that Rokk Baptiste had been killed for stealing another man's wife. The news was upsetting, but far from devastating. It had been years since she had seen him, and the feelings she had developed for him immediately after the prince's death had subsided. Learning of his death was more of a relief than something that caused her more grief. She still had Antoinette, and that was more than enough for her.

Ten years had passed by the time young Beaumont returned to New Orleans and became the master of Bouvier Hill. He was twenty-six years old, and had found the love of his life, Brigitte Bouvier. His half sister was exactly where Lauren said she'd be. She was in the convent she had been sent to in Italy. They were married and had three children. In spite of everything that had happened, he still had affection for Lauren. She was the one person who had first shown him the truth and then told him the ultimate truth. Initially, he had hated her, but over the years, he turned away from it. He realized it wasn't Lauren's fault that his mother and father were who they were.

Lauren lived in Bouvier Mansion for the ten years that young Beaumont was gone. She raised Josette, who became a beautiful and desirable young woman. Walker and Marie-Elise were planning to raise her with the other children, but Josette wanted to stay with Lauren, and they approved. Guinevere, who opened an eatery in the Quarter and lived in the Tremé, approved too. Lauren would have lived out her remaining years at Bouvier Hill, but when young Beaumont returned, she could tell he still had eyes for her, and she knew it would be a problem if she stayed. The last thing she wanted to do was cause problems in his marriage. She eventually purchased land of her own and had a home built on it in the Tremé, where well-to-do kept women lived with their mixed offspring. The Bouvier estate paid for everything according to Beaumont's last will and testament.

The years passed quickly, and young Antoinette was growing up rapidly. She was ten years old and gorgeous already. Black men and white men often stopped in her mother's dress shop, pretending to look for items for the wives, but they were really there because they wanted to see Antoinette, who again, was just ten years old, but quickly blossoming. By the time she was sixteen, she had become exactly what her mother had been at that age: a drop-dead beauty with a mind of her own that was filled with conceit. And she had her mother's eyes.

A strange thing happened. In spite of the years of separation, in spite of the distance between New Orleans and Africa, Lauren Renee Bouvier had become Jamilah, her mother. Now that Antoinette was sixteen, Lauren thought it was appropriate that she marry, raise a family, so that the stories would continue. New Orleans was still a violent city and she feared that she or her daughter could be killed at any time for any reason. And if that happened, there would be no one left to remember what happened to her and Amir.

Of the many suitors that literally begged for Antoinette's hand in marriage, she approved of only one—the firstborn son of Walker Tresvant. He was twenty years her senior. Years later, Antoinette gave birth to a baby girl, who she named Josephine Baptiste.

<u>Questions</u>

1) What are your thoughts on race in America?

2) Can you list five positive interactions you've had with another race?

3) Can you list five negative interactions you've had with another race?

4) Which was easier to answer? Question 2 or 3? Why?

5) Prior to reading this series, did you know there were blacks that owned black and white slaves?

6) Prior to reading this novel, had you ever heard of the terms *quasi-free Negroes* or *gens de couleur*?

7) Lauren wished she could have changed her mind after her dream turned into a horrific nightmare. Do you think she should have obeyed her father's wishes and gone along with the arranged marriage? Why or why not?

8) What's your opinion on arranged marriages? Why do you feel as you do?

9) Why do you think the author killed off Amir? Was it shock value, or are there other possibilities? If so, list them.

10) What are your personal thoughts on Walker and Pearl's relationship?

11) Why do you think Tristan and Cadence turned on each other?

12) When Cadence sold Joshua out, how did that make you feel?

13) How did you feel when Lauren embraced Josette and wept?

14) Considering all the actions of all the characters in this novel, is all fair in love and war?

15) Why did Guinevere, after buying her freedom, continue to think and act like a slave?